The

Portuguese

Affair

MORE BY THIS AUTHOR

The Anniversary
The Travellers
A Running Tide
The Testament of Mariam
Flood
The Secret World of Christoval Alvarez
The Enterprise of England

Praise for Ann Swinfen's Novels

'an absorbing and intricate tapestry of family history and private memories ... warm, generous, healing and hopeful'
VICTORIA GLENDINNING

'I very much admired the pace of the story. The changes of place and time and the echoes and repetitions – things lost and found, and meetings and partings'
PENELOPE FITZGERALD

'I enjoyed this serious, scrupulous novel ... a novel of character ... [and] a suspense story in which present and past mysteries are gradually explained'
JESSICA MANN, *Sunday Telegraph*

'The author ... has written a powerful new tale of passion and heartbreak ... What a marvellous storyteller Ann Swinfen is – she has a wonderful ear for dialogue and she brings her characters vividly to life.'
Publishing News

'Her writing ...[paints] an amazingly detailed and vibrant picture of flesh and blood human beings, not only the symbols many of them have become...but real and believable and understandable.'
HELEN BROWN, *Courier and Advertiser*

'She writes with passion and the book, her fourth, is shot through with brilliant description and scholarship...[it] is a timely reminder of the harsh realities, and the daily humiliations, of the Roman occupation of First Century Israel. You can almost smell the dust and blood.'
PETER RHODES, *Express and Star*

The

Portuguese

Affair

Ann Swinfen

Shakenoak Press

Cover images
Coat-of-arms of the Portuguese royal dynasty of Aviz
Contemporary drawing of the English army on the march

Cover design by JD Smith www.jdsmith-design.co.uk

For

David

Chapter One

London, December, 1588

For two years I had believed myself safe from Robert Poley, that scheming viper of a double agent. As long as he remained a prisoner in the Tower, the secret of my identity was safe, a secret which could cost me my life. He had played an ambivalent part in bringing the Babington plotters to justice and I was still unsure where his loyalty lay, if indeed he had any. Had he been a sympathiser as the conspirators had believed, almost to the end? Or had he been truly working as an agent for my sometime employer, Sir Francis Walsingham? Perhaps even Sir Francis himself was unsure. Whatever he believed, he had ensured that Poley was securely locked away in the Tower when the plot was uncovered, but unlike the other conspirators, Poley was not executed by that most brutal of methods – hung, drawn and quartered. Instead he had remained for more than two years a prisoner, yet a prisoner (so it was said) who lived like a lord. And had murdered a fellow prisoner, the Bishop of Armagh, with a gift of poisoned cheese.

The source of his riches was one of the many mysteries which surrounded Poley. A man of obscure birth, dubious employment and cautious patrons, he yet commanded considerable wealth. When I had first encountered him he was a prisoner in the Marshalsea, yet there, too, he lavished his money on rich food, receiving his mistress at fine dinners in his room, while refusing to see his wife and daughter.

We were sitting, Simon Hetherington and I, beside a generous fire in a tavern on Bankside, south of the river and not far from the Rose, where Simon had just given his first performance in a man's part, having at last been able to turn his back on the women's roles he had played with such success as a boy. It was a double celebration, being also Simon's nineteenth birthday, and several of his fellow players had joined us – Guy Bingham (musician and comic), Christopher Haigh (young romantic) and Richard Burbage (heroic), second son of James Burbage, head of Simon's company. It was not Burbage's company which had been playing at the Rose. Simon had been on loan to Philip Henslowe, who was short of players, three having died in the late summer of the sweating sickness.

'It was no great part,' Simon said, modestly but truthfully, 'but at last I have shed my petticoats and wigs.'

Christopher raised his glass. 'I never saw a halberd carried with such a flourish. We shall have you back with us and speaking at least six lines before we know it.'

Simon flushed, but took the teasing in good part. He turned to Richard.

'And is there any word yet from your father?'

'He hopes to join us here,' Richard said. 'He had a meeting with Lord Strange this afternoon.'

Burbage's company had been, for many years, Leicester's Men, but the Earl of Leicester had died in September. It was now nearly Christmas. They had been allowed to carry on performing until the end of their planned season, but could no longer continue without a patron. Despite the growing importance and popularity of the playhouses, in the eyes of the law of England a company of players without a noble patron would be classed as vagabonds and could be imprisoned. They could even lose an ear or a nose, a fate no player dared contemplate. Burbage's men would have ceased performing anyway as winter closed in, for audiences would not come to the open-air playhouses in bitter weather, but if the company were not to drift apart Burbage must secure a new patron soon. He had received an encouraging reply from Lord Strange to his request for a meeting, and the present company, who had come to cheer Simon in his small part, could ill conceal their anxiety beneath all the banter.

2

'Simon Hetherington!' A big man, built like an ox, had approached our table. His dark hair sprang from his head like coils of wire, surrounding a bald circle, a secular tonsure, while more dark bristles sprouted from his ears and nostrils. There was something familiar about him, but I could not place him.

'Arthur!' I was not sure Simon was quite pleased to see the man. He was not hostile, but rather embarrassed. He turned to us.

'Arthur is the gatekeeper at the Marshalsea. I used to lodge with his sister. How is Goodwife Lucy?'

'Hearty as ever,' said the man, hooking a stool with his foot and drawing it up to our table. He sat down and drank deeply from his jar of beer, then wiped his mouth on the back of his hand. I remembered now where I had seen him.

The other players looked faintly amused that the man should join us, but they were a motley, tolerant lot. The gatekeeper looked round at us all, then pointed at me with a finger like a well-filled sausage.

'And I know you,' he said. 'You're the physician's boy Simon fetched that time to the prisoner Robert Poley, who thought himself poisoned.'

'Aye,' I said dryly. 'Poisoned himself with eating bad oysters. I remember.'

The man shook his head. 'Never had a prisoner like him. Entertaining his mistress, that slut Joan Yeomans, like any lord. Playing at cards or dice with the other sad papists and cheating them of the little they had before they went into exile or to the fire.' He glanced round the table and nodded sagely. 'Mark my words. Never have dealings with Poley. He will beguile you either of your wife or your life.'

Having delivered himself of this pronouncement, he buried his nose again in his beer and drained it.

'No danger of that,' Simon said, smiling lazily and tilting his stool back. He was still glowing in the aftermath of his performance, a state of mind I recognised. 'He's locked away from all decent men in the Tower.'

The doorkeeper waved his empty mug at the potboy and grinned. 'That he is not. I see you are behind with the news. Robert Poley was released from the Tower yesterday evening. He'll be about his devious business in London by now.'

I felt bile rise in my throat as Simon shot a glance at me. He knew I feared Poley, though he did not know the reason. My jaws were locked together and beneath the table I felt my leg jerk convulsively.

'So,' said Guy, 'the men in authority, they've decided Poley bore no guilt in the plotting two years ago.' He sipped his beer thoughtfully, and looked at me. 'I wonder.'

'I've heard the fellow was employed by Walsingham to spy on Babington,' said Christopher. 'He certainly used to work for Leicester. I've seen him with the Earl, God rest his soul. And later with Walsingham's cousin Thomas.'

'And wasn't he in Sidney's household, when he and his lady lived in Walsingham's house in Seething Lane?' Richard Burbage turned to me.

The players all knew that I had worked in the past as a code-breaker for Sir Francis Walsingham. Such a thing was impossible to keep from them, for players are as eager for gossip as bees for nectar. They were not aware of my other activities within Sir Francis's secret service. Simon knew or guessed a little, but nothing dangerous. Any time now Richard and the others would be probing me for what I knew of Poley. This was not the place to speak of it, this public drinking house, where the very ale jacks have ears. And the man Arthur had already caught their eyes fixed speculatively on me.

At that moment the door was flung open and a blast of snow and icy air blew James Burbage in and across the room to us. The fire swooped and flung a cloud of smoke into the room. Men cursed. Someone kicked the door shut.

'Snow!' Someone else exclaimed.

'Just managed your performance in time,' Christopher said to Simon. 'With this snow starting up there'll be nothing more doing in the playhouses now till spring.'

Burbage was roaring at the potboy to bring more beer for everyone, and a dish of collops and onions. He swept his arms over us all, including the doorkeeper.

'Fill your bellies, lads!' He was wearing a magnificent cloak usually reserved for stage kings. He must have borrowed it from the costume baskets.

4

'Good news, then?' Guy asked. The lines of worry I had noticed round his eyes had vanished.

The potboy arrived, ladling out mugs of beer as if he were dealing cards. One of the maids came with a copper pan from which a stomach-teasing steam rose, another maid brought a stack of pewter plates.

Burbage was still on his feet, flourishing his beer like a trumpet.

'I give you, gentlemen, the Lord Strange's Men, signed, sealed and delivered. To continue to perform at the Theatre. And,' he paused for effect, 'to perform at Lord Strange's house in the Strand, this day sennight.'

They raised a cheer. It meant a secure future for them. In their joy at this auspicious news, they had forgotten that other news, of little account to them, that Robert Poley was free again to walk the world and work his devious, self-serving schemes.

But I had not forgotten.

Ferdinando Stanley, Lord Strange, was heir to the Earl of Derby, but on his mother's side he ranked even more highly, very highly indeed, for he was descended from King Henry's sister Mary, who was grandmother of Lord Strange's mother. In his last will, setting out the future for England, King Henry had named Lord Strange's mother – his great-niece – as next in line to the throne, should all his three children die childless, of whom our present Queen Elizabeth was the last. As this now seemed more and more likely, given the Queen's age and unmarried state, it meant that Lord Strange was second in line to the throne. In securing him as patron, James Burbage was biting his thumb at the Queen's Men, who, in the past, had stolen a number of the best players from Leicester's Men, including Richard Tarlton. This had all occurred before ever I had come to know the players, but I was well aware that it still rankled.

It seemed that Lord Strange already had a company called Lord Strange's Men, but they were nothing but acrobats and jugglers, simple performers for after-dinner amusement, possessing their own skills, certainly, but more fit for Bartholomew's Fair and a far cry from the sort of plays Burbage's company had begun to perform. When I asked a tentative question about this, the next time I saw the players, Guy answered with enthusiasm.

'Ah, but you see, Kit, my lord is a great lover of poetry and a patron of poets. He has been wanting his own company of dramatic players, so was eager to welcome Burbage's proposal.'

'And that is why you are rehearsing here?' For despite the bitter December weather, and half an inch of snow on the very boards of the stage, the company had gathered at the Theatre. They were muffled to the eyebrows in cloaks and scarves, but were determined to rehearse where there was space enough to move and declaim.

'Aye. We are to perform *The Spanish Tragedy* at my lord's house on Thursday. There is no time to prepare anything new, but we shall give of our best.'

'Who is to play Bel Imperia?' It was a woman's role Simon had played in the past with great gusto, but no longer.

Guy shrugged. 'It will have to be Edward Titheridge. He has not Simon's fire in the great female parts, but he will do well enough.'

I remembered Simon training young Edward in how to walk like a woman and suppressed a smile.

'Have you brought the pastilles?' Guy said.

'Aye. And a honey tincture as well.' Some of the players were suffering from sore throats and feared for their voices before this all-important performance. 'You were better not rehearsing in this cold air.'

'We are nearly done.'

Indeed they made an end soon after, for the snow had begun to fall once more and even the most dedicated player could not perform in such conditions. We parted hastily, the players home to their lodgings and I back through Bishopsgate and across the city. By the time I reached Newgate, the snowfall had become a regular blizzard and the hot chestnut seller who had his place there was packing away his gear, for there were but a handful of people left on the streets. I bought my usual farthing's worth, with another for the Newgate prisoners crowded behind the grill, where they were allowed to beg for food from the passersby. There seemed to be fewer faces than usual in the dark chamber sunk below ground level behind the grill. It must be bitterly cold beside the open grill and they could not hope for many people on the streets, fewer still inclined to be charitable. On second thoughts I thrust my own paper cone of chestnuts through after the first. There would be a meal waiting for me at home, while these poor creatures had little to hope for, unless they had money to send out for food. They must live on whatever scraps might be given them. I pulled the hood of my cloak over the woollen cap I was wearing instead of my physician's bonnet and hurried on to Duck Lane, through snow that danced like dervishes, blurring the lines of streets and buildings until all seemed the insubstantial landscape of a dream.

It proved the onset of a bad winter. After all the rejoicing of the summer and autumn, following our defeat of Spain's Armada, a kind of lethargy seemed to have settled on England. All the desperate frenetic energy which had driven our resistance to the enemy had sapped our strength and we were exhausted. In the aftermath of the war, far more men had died of disease than the hundred or so killed in battle, as typhus and the bloody flux had swept through the ranks of soldiers and sailors. Those who had survived and managed to struggle home, begging their way, were paid late and grudgingly. It was not a situation to lift the spirits of the nation. Added to this, the Spanish attack and the subsequent outbreaks of disease had occurred at harvest time, so that labour was scarce in the countryside and the crops gathered in fell short of what was needed to feed the people, especially in a great city like London, which could not feed itself.

The inevitable outcome was that our wards at St Bartholomew's Hospital were overflowing, not only with the usual winter ailments but with the destitute poor, lingering just this side of starvation. My code-breaking services were not needed, it seemed, by Thomas Phelippes in his office at Walsingham's house in Seething Lane, for which I was mostly grateful, but it meant that I knew no more than any other citizen about affairs of state. In my more honest moments, I admitted to myself that I missed being part of that knowledgeable coterie, aware of all the beating secrets at the heart of the nation. Besides, I needed to know what Poley was up to.

One day in February I left the hospital early on an errand for my father. Our friend and fellow Portuguese exile, Dr Nuñez, usually obtained his medicines from an apothecary near his home in Tower Ward, but with all the sickness in the city, even amongst his noble patients, some supplies were running short, so he had sent a message to my father, hoping he might be able to spare some medicines from the hospital stores. We had our own apothecaries, including my friend Peter Lambert, who made up the package for Dr Nuñez.

'I can deliver it for you, Kit,' Peter said.

'Nay,' I said. 'I thank you, but you have been working since dawn and should have a rest before supper. I've finished with my patients for today.'

It was not altogether unselfish of me, for I had a plan of my own in mind. I stopped briefly at our house in Duck Lane, where I pocketed a couple of rather withered late apples, and set off across the city. There had been no fresh snow for three or four days, but it was still lying deep in the streets. The traffic of men and horses had hammered it down in the centre of the roadways so that it was as slippery as solid ice, stained with horse droppings which lay on the surface or were encased within a frozen cage, like unsavoury flies in amber. I kept to the edges of the streets where the snow was less densely packed, but even here it was slippery, except in front of the better houses or shops, where servants or apprentices had been set to clear a space.

Despite the cold, I was quite warmed from my brisk walking by the time I reached the Nuñez house, where Beatriz Nuñez insisted on inviting me in for hot ale and a sweet bun. When I could leave with politeness I made my way quickly around the corner to the stableyard of Walsingham's house in Seething Lane, where – as I had hoped – I ran into the stable lad Harry.

'Come to see Hector, have you, Master Alvarez?' he asked, when he saw that I had turned, not to the backstairs which led up to Thomas Phelippes's office and my old desk, but to the stable where I knew I would find my favourite amongst Walsingham's horses.

'Aye.' I grinned at him. 'There's no hiding anything from you, Harry. How is Hector?'

'Missing you, I daresay.' He returned the smile, knowing full well how I felt about the ugly piebald who had served me well on several missions for Walsingham.

Harry lifted the bolt for me on the tightly closed stable door, for the horses needed protection in this bleak weather, and followed me in as I went to Hector's stall. He perched himself on a saddle stand, ready to gossip, as I had hoped he would. It would save me tackling Phelippes. As I caressed Hector's neck and scratched him between the ears, Harry gave me all the latest news of Seething Lane – how the lads had been given a day off to go skating over in the frozen Kent marshes, how the washerwoman had given birth to twins and miraculously both had lived.

'Moll says it's because she's so strong, from heaving pails of water and lye, and great buck-baskets full of wet linen,' he said. 'Her babies were bound to be strong.'

'Boys or girls?' I said, holding one of the apples on my palm so Hector could lift it softly with his velvet lips.

'One of each. She's called the boy Francis in honour of Sir Francis and called the girl Bess after the Queen.'

He chattered on while I gave Hector the second apple and he blew affectionate juice into my ear.

'And what of all the backstairs coming and going?' I said casually. The stable lads never missed anything.

'The usual. That Kit Marlowe was about here last week, him you don't like.'

I gave him a startled look. I hadn't realised the lads had even noticed that. He gave me a cheeky grin.

'Oh, never fear. I'll say nothing to Master Phelippes or Sir Francis.'

'I'd rather you did not. It is a private matter, nothing to do with Seething Lane. Marlowe has insulted me more than once.'

'Arrogant bastard,' Harry said dispassionately.

I saw that I would need to ask him outright if I was to get the information I wanted.

'Have you seen anything of that fellow who was in the Tower?' I said, making my voice as casual as I could and keeping my back to him. 'Poley, was he called? I wonder if he'd dare show his face around here again.'

'Oh, him.' Harry spat into the straw. 'Aye, he was here, two-three weeks ago. Master Phelippes has sent him off to the Low Countries with despatches. He can't do much harm there.'

It seemed Harry shared my doubts of Poley, but it would be wiser to probe no further. Our talk turned to other matters, and when Harry went off to his supper, I bade Hector an affectionate farewell and left, dropping the bolt on the door as I went.

Soon after the defeat of the Spanish fleet, a remark made by the Lord Admiral Howard had been discussed everywhere amongst our community. He had said that now was the time to invade Portugal and defeat the Spanish. All the older men amongst our Marrano people seemed carried away on a wave of expectation and excitement. At last the chance had come to return to their homeland, to restore Dom Antonio to the throne – Dom Antonio of the royal house of Aviz, claimant to the lost crown. We would drive the Inquisition, together with the Spanish, out of our country. Then Portugal, that great nation, once a power in the world, with colonies to east and west, with ships trading on every sea, and above all with tolerance of the Jewish faith, would rise again; the Golden Age of a century before would be restored.

Part of their argument was based on the ancient Anglo-Portuguese Alliance, ratified two hundred years ago when John of Gaunt's daughter married the king of Portugal, but dating back more than two hundred years before that. The alliance of perpetual friendship had begun when England helped Portugal to drive out the Moors, but it had been strengthened in the days when Portugal was the greater power, home of seafarers who explored all the world, discovering new lands. Back in those times, England was the lesser nation. Now the situation was reversed again and Portugal cried out for help from her ancient ally. And with such aid, Portugal would once again become great, free of her Spanish overlords. So they argued.

These were the old men's dreams. We who were younger did not share them. Anne Lopez and I discussed it one day towards the end of winter when I was visiting them.

'I am glad, Kit,' she said violently, '*glad* that my proposed marriage to the banker of Lyons has been abandoned. I want to stay in London. My father talks of nothing but returning to

Portugal in glory, as Dom Antonio's chief adviser and courtier, but my mother is English and so am I. The Queen is going to pay for my brother Anthony to attend Winchester College. What interest have we in Portugal? It is nothing to me or my brothers and sisters.'

I nodded. 'I have no wish to go back,' I said. 'My memories are too bitter.'

I did not tell her of unfinished business there, which filled me sometimes with hope, and sometimes with despair. And, always, there was the shadow of remembered terror.

'Yet our fathers think differently,' I said. 'Even my father, after all he suffered, dreams these dreams of a free Portugal.'

Anne's mother Sara, too, shared her worries with me.

'Ruy is drawn more and more into Dom Antonio's affairs, Kit. He has poured every penny we possess into this expedition they are planning. Dom Antonio has pledged him fifty thousand crowns and five percent of the proceeds from the West African franchise when Portugal is freed, but what if the expedition fails? We will lose everything. Somehow they have even persuaded the Queen to invest five thousand pounds, but the greatest burden is being borne by Ruy and Hector Nuñez and my father and the others.'

'Drake is a partner in the venture, is he not?' I said. 'And Sir John Norreys. The greatest sea captain and the greatest professional soldier.'

'Drake,' said Sara bitterly, 'is a pirate. Everyone knows that whatever other men gamble and lose, Drake always manages to fill his pockets – nay, his very barns – with gold and precious stones. If there is profit to be made, Drake will find a way, and the freeing of Portugal will not be the first thing on his mind.'

Yes, Sara was bitter, but she had good cause. Ruy was prepared to throw away everything in this venture, destroying her peace of mind and risking her future in her homeland of England. She had never even trodden the soil of Portugal, for her father, Dunstan Añez, had come to London long ago. Like her brothers and sisters she had been born here and thought of herself as English.

I was also growing worried about my father. Ever since our long weeks caring for the sick and wounded after the Armada, I had watched him becoming older and more frail before my very eyes. Of late he had turned forgetful, setting down a tincture half made and wandering off to some other task, and then to another. More and more often in the hospital I had to conceal some business he had left unfinished and finish it myself before anyone noticed. I was terrified lest he should lose his position. If he did, would I retain mine? How would we live?

It was when he began to call me 'Felipe' that my heart clenched with alarm. For some time now I had suspected that he had forgotten that I was his daughter Caterina, and truly believed I was a son. Now his confusion grew as I seemed to become, in his mind, my long-lost brother somehow come back to him. There was no one I could confide in but Sara, and she had worries enough of her own. I kept my fears to myself, but the more I tried to seal them up in my heart, the more they grew like some monstrous cancer, eating me up from within.

One evening very early in that spring of 1589, I returned late from the hospital to find Dr Lopez seated with my father in our small parlour, with a jug of malmsey and glasses on the table, and their heads together. The glasses must be a gift – a bribe? – for we normally drank from pewter. They stopped speaking when I entered, like guilty boys cheating over their lessons. What could be afoot? I discovered soon enough.

'Good evening to you, Kit,' said Dr Lopez, with a little too much geniality.

'Shalom.' I helped myself to a glass of malmsey and sat down opposite them. 'Have I interrupted a private conference?'

'Not at all, not at all!' said my father. His eyes were bright and he looked more like his old self than I had seen him for days.

'The plans for the Portuguese venture are nearly complete,' he said. 'Drake will command the fleet, aboard his ship *Revenge*, while Dom Antonio and our Portuguese party will sail in his ship, the *Victory*. Altogether we will have a hundred and fifty ships, and an army of thirty thousand to land at Lisbon.'

'And when we land,' said Dr Lopez excitedly, 'the oppressed people of our homeland will rise up and join us, proclaim Dom Antonio as king, and slaughter the Spaniards to a man.'

And proclaim you, I thought, the Lord Burghley of Portugal. I saw coronets glittering in his eyes, and ermine robes, and country estates, and wealth beyond measure. A fine pinnacle indeed for a man who had come as a penniless refugee to London, and once filled my father's humble role as physician to the city's destitute and homeless.

'Father,' I said, thinking it best to have it out in the open, 'Father, you do not intend to join this expedition yourself, I hope? For you are hardly strong enough for such an undertaking.'

'I am younger than Hector Nuñez,' he said petulantly.

'If your father is not well enough,' said Dr Lopez smoothly, 'you may come in his stead, Kit.'

'I have no wish to return to Portugal.'

I tried to keep the fear out of my voice, and found that I was clutching my glass too tightly. The bitter cold of the prison. The stench. The screams. My throat is raw with the screams. Lest I snap the stem, I forced myself to ease my grip on the glass.

'Ah, but you might wish to follow the success of your father's investment,' said Lopez.

I felt my heart tighten in my chest till I could scarcely breathe.

'Father? Surely you have not invested in the venture? We have little enough put aside.'

My father looked shifty, but Dr Lopez said smoothly, 'Your father has kindly invested a thousand pounds, Kit, so you see, the success of our venture is of some interest to you after all.'

My hand flew to my mouth and I gasped in shock. The wine slopped over the rim of the glass and the stain of it spread over my knees. My father had handed over every shilling and groat we owned to this adventurer. Money painfully put aside over seven years, while we lived so shabbily and worked so hard. We had debts which must be paid – to apothecaries for supplies of herbs and other materials, to the butcher and fishmonger, to the alewife. I could scarcely hold back my tears, and when Lopez had left, I could restrain them no longer.

'How could you, Father? You have gambled our future on this venture. What if it fails?'

Suddenly he looked frail and confused. 'But Ruy has promised us all great profits from the voyage, and we could go

13

home again, Felipe. I will return to my university once the Inquisition is driven out. We will live in our old house again; it's so much better than this hovel, and your mother will have her garden that she loves so much!'

I felt chilled to the very bone. Felipe! *He thinks I am my dead brother. And Mama . . . Our old garden. Oh, Papa, I am losing you.* I could not berate him any more, but took his hand and stroked it, and said that perhaps all would be well in the end.

After this my father's health grew worse, both in body and mind. He took it as agreed that I would sail with Drake and the others in his place, and do my part in freeing Portugal. I felt another trap closing about me. Portugal! The very name terrified me. I began to have nightmares again, the same dreams which had haunted me when we had first come to England. I was back in the prison of the Inquisition and could hear my mother screaming, but I could not reach her. The scars the scourges had raised on my back began to burn again with pain. I did not know whether this was a true physical pain, or some trick of my frightened mind, but it felt real enough. And I feared to leave my father. Some days he was brisk and eager, discussing plans for the expedition, then the cloud would descend over his mind and he would forget what he had just said, repeating it again and again, or wandering off into the streets until I fetched him home. Yet when I suggested that I should not go but stay with him, he grew angry and distressed. What should I do? Deep in my mind, a voice whispered that there was something I could do in Portugal, that my conscience would never be clear until I made the attempt. But I was mortally afraid.

Chapter Two

One morning I woke early, still shaking from the horrors of the dark hours, but with the sudden gleam of an idea. I was still troubled by thoughts of what I might be able to do in Portugal that would ease both my father's mind and my own evil memories. Although it was mostly dread that held me back, I knew that I could only join the expedition as one of those, like Ruy Lopez and Hector Nuñez, who went to keep a sharp eye on their investments, all of them aware that Drake would need watching, else he would turn the venture into yet another of his piratical raids. I would be regarded as a gentleman adventurer, not committed to any part in the fighting.

I might also be welcome for my medical skills. Like all naval expeditions, the ships would carry their own surgeons, but they were a class of unskilled butchers, whose main purpose was to hack off injured limbs too fearfully smashed to preserve. They probably killed more men than they saved. As a physician I was better qualified to help the men, both afloat and ashore, with the many illnesses that sailors and soldiers are heir to. However, as a physician I would have little freedom to carry out the plan I was tentatively forming in my mind. I would need a reason to leave the expedition at some point and venture into the interior of Portugal on my own. I decided I must call on Walsingham.

Never before had I gone willingly to offer my services to Sir Francis. Originally, when I was but sixteen, I had been coerced into his service as a code-breaker and translator by the contrivance of Robert Poley, who had discovered my sex. For a woman to disguise herself as a man was regarded as heresy, and the punishment, as for any form of heresy, was burning at the

15

stake. Threatened with exposure by Poley, I had entered Walsingham's service in fear and resentment, yet gradually, working under the chief of his agents, Thomas Phelippes, I had found I enjoyed the challenge of breaking new and seemingly impossible codes. They were the most intriguing and exciting of puzzles, and yet they were not mere trivial entertainment. My work with Phelippes was aimed at the protection of the nation and the Queen against our many enemies, principally Spain, France and the Papacy.

When Phelippes trained me in forgery, I was less happy, but many of the 'projections', as he and Walsingham called them, required slipping false reports and misleading information in amongst the enemies' own intercepted papers, and I proved to have a useful skill here as well. When Walsingham had despatched me on other missions, first in England and later in the Low Countries, I had survived and had some small successes – more through accident and luck than through skill on my part. A few times my own clumsiness had nearly cost me dear.

One skill which they had arranged for me to be taught – swordsmanship – I had chosen to improve for my own satisfaction. Since returning from Amsterdam I had spent more time with Master Scannard at the Tower, who had undertaken my original training at Walsingham's bidding. Although I would never be a master at the skill, nor wish to be, yet I hoped I would no longer fall over the sword Walsingham had provided for me. I did not carry it in London, preferring the simple dagger my father had given me, but if I was going on the Portuguese expedition, I would wear it. Scannard, a man scanty of words and even scantier of praise, conceded that I had made some progress.

To go now to Walsingham and willingly offer to serve him was contrary to everything I had felt before, but it seemed the only way to accomplish what I had in mind to try. He had agreed to see me, and I presented myself in good time at Seething Lane, to be shown into Sir Francis's office by his chief secretary, Francis Mylles.

'We have not seen you since last autumn, Kit,' Mylles said. 'You are well?'

'Aye, never better. And you?'

We exchanged the usual pleasantries.

'Sir Francis will be here shortly,' Mylles said. 'If you would not mind waiting?'

As if I should take offence at waiting for the Queen's Principal Secretary, her most senior advisor after Lord Burghley.

Mylles offered me wine, but I refused, wanting to keep a clear head. Indeed he was gone only a few minutes when Sir Francis appeared, apologising. He looked, as he so often did, tired and ill but resolutely indomitable. I never knew a man so determined to defeat his physical weakness by strength of mind.

'Kit, my dear boy, it is very good to see you! Has Mylles not offered you wine?'

Before I could object, he was pressing a glass into my hand. As always, it was of the very best quality. He had his sources. However, I took only small sips.

'The Portuguese expedition, Sir Francis.'

'Ah.' He gave me a knowing smile. 'You are to sail with it, of course.'

It was no surprise to me that he knew. He always seemed to know my affairs before I did.

'Possibly. Probably. If I can get leave from St Bartholomew's. My father–,' I paused. 'My father has invested in it.'

'And you are not happy about that.'

I suppose my feelings were writ large on my face.

'Nay, I am not, but it is done now.'

'The Queen has invested twenty thousand pounds.'

So the Queen had been persuaded to increase her stake in the venture.

'The Queen has rather more means than my father and I!' I should not have said it, but the words were out before I could stop them.

He did not rebuke me, but I apologised quickly.

'You are concerned, of course,' he said. 'And you will go with the expedition to ensure that all is well.'

'There is little I can do, surely, to ensure that, but my father wishes me to go. Otherwise he would try to go himself, but he is not strong enough. I have no wish to return to Portugal.'

I swallowed hard and Sir Francis nodded. He knew a little of my history, but by no means the most dangerous part.

'However, I do not want to be merely a passenger.' I cleared my throat. 'It would seem a fruitless waste of time. I thought I could perhaps serve you in some way, if there is any mission you want undertaken in Portugal? I know you have agents there already, so perhaps there is no need.'

My voice trailed away. My whole purpose in coming here suddenly seemed foolish. Yet Sir Francis looked at me thoughtfully, not at all dismissive of my suggestion.

'I see.' He got up and drew down a rolled-up sheet of heavy paper from a shelf and laid it out on his desk, weighing it down with books and an ink-pot and his little Roman statue.

'You have probably not yet been told the detailed plans for the expedition, am I right? Yet I know I can trust your discretion. Look here at the map.'

I joined him at the desk. The map covered the area from the southern end of the Bay of Biscay to the Pillars of Hercules, showing the whole of Spain and Portugal, with all the major towns, cities and ports clearly marked, and the courses of the principal rivers. My heart jumped at the sight of the word 'Coimbra'. My old home, where my father had been a professor of medicine at the university.

'The Queen wishes the expedition to undertake three main tasks,' Sir Francis explained, 'all intended to weaken the power of Spain both in Iberia and abroad. The first I am sure you know: to install Dom Antonio on the throne of Portugal and drive the Spanish from the country.'

I nodded. I had though that was the sole purpose.

'Secondly, our fleet will destroy as much as possible of the remaining Spanish fleet. The merchant ships armed for war last year in the invading fleet were mostly destroyed, either by our navy or by storms in the Atlantic. Many of the largest warships, however, managed to return to Spain, though the majority were damaged and unfit for war without extensive repairs. Most of the repairs are being carried out here.'

He tapped his finger on Santander, on the southern shore of the Bay of Biscay.

'More of the ships, some needing minor repairs, are here.'

He pointed to Coruña, out near Cape Finisterre.

'The route of the expedition, therefore, will be to cross the Bay of Biscay and invest Santander, where the fleet under repair will be fired.'

'Like the ships in Cadiz,' I said, 'two years ago.'

'Aye.' He smiled grimly. 'When Drake singed the King of Spain's beard, as the common folk like to say.'

'If they are being repaired, they will be immobilised,' I ventured.

'Exactly. It should not be a difficult task. Our fleet will then proceed to Coruña and repeat the attack on the ships there.'

He had shifted the map slightly so that one edge slid from under the books. It rolled shut with a snap, so I unrolled it again and held it down with my palm.

'Next, the ships will sail down the coast of Portugal to Lisbon,' he said, tracing the route with the tip of his finger, 'where, so Dom Antonio has assured us, the citizens of Portugal will rise up in his support and join our own army to seize Lisbon and evict the Spanish.'

'Sir Francis–' I hesitated.

'Aye, what is it, Kit?'

'When Drake attacked Cadiz, I remember asking why he did not attack Lisbon, and you said it was because sailing up the Tejo to Lisbon would be like walking into an ambush.'

'Aye, quite right. But that was Drake on a raiding expedition. This time it is different, with the next King of Portugal on board.'

'Forgive me,' I said. 'Perhaps I am being stupid, but will the people of Portugal know that?'

'His standard will be flown throughout the fleet. In addition, once the raids on the northern Spanish ports have been carried out, we will ensure that news is passed secretly to the Dom's supporters.'

Sir Francis could probably do this. I believed he could do almost anything once he set his mind to it. Privately, I thought that the attacks on the fleet would be warning enough to the Spanish that Lisbon might be our destination. Would they not take the opportunity to strengthen their defences?

'You said there were three goals for the expedition.' I looked down at the map, trying to think what else might be meant. Surely not a voyage round into the Mediterranean and an attack on Spain's eastern ports?

'The third goal, after Lisbon has been taken and the Dom crowned, is to sail south and west, to seize the Azores from the Spanish, establishing a permanent English base there, in order to hamper Spanish trade with her colonies in the New World. You can see how the three parts fit together, to weaken Spain's world power. Destroy her Atlantic fleet. Drive her out of Portugal and thus rob her of the excellent Portuguese harbours. And finally, take control of the route to the New World. The Azores are of vital importance as a staging post for ships making the Atlantic crossing, a final stop for water and provisions.'

He rolled up the map and restored it to the shelf.

'There is an additional goal, if the timing proves favourable. To capture the returning Spanish treasure fleet.'

Drake would be glad of that. I did not speak aloud, but I saw from the gleam in Walsingham's eye that he was thinking the same thing.

He motioned me back to my chair and poured us both more wine.

'Now you understand the route and purposes of the expedition, Kit.' He sipped his wine. 'There is indeed a mission you could undertake for me. In fact there are two.'

I held my breath. What would he say? Could I even undertake what he had in mind?

'You can pass for Spanish, can you not?'

I nodded. 'I grew up speaking Spanish as well as Portuguese.'

'I thought so. I know you have worked as a translator in that language. We have an agent in Coruña, Titus Allanby. In the most recent despatch we received from him, he said he feared that his identity might have been compromised. He did not say how. He needs to leave the town, but fears to make a move as he believes he is being watched. He is privy to too many secrets for us to risk his being taken and tortured by the Spanish. In our reply, we instructed him to send no more despatches and to behave like an innocent citizen. He has good Spanish and is working as a tailor.'

'You want me to contact him, when we reach Coruña?'

'I want you to do more than that. I want you to bring him out. And if you cannot, you will have to kill him.'

My head shot up and I gasped.

'Oh, do not worry. I do not think it will come to that.' He gave a bleak smile. 'If it looks as though the Spanish authorities will take him, he is a brave enough man to take his own life, rather than fall into the hands of their torturers.'

I gripped my hands together until I heard the joints of my fingers crack. I had volunteered for this. I would simply have to ensure that this man Titus made it back to the ships with me. I knew I could not kill a man, an ally.

'You said there were two things you wished me to do?'

'Aye. The other is easier. When Lisbon is taken – if it is taken – there is a man of ours in prison there. Even from prison he has been able to send us valuable intelligence.'

'Hunter?' I said.

'You remember. Aye, Hunter. I want you to make sure he is found and brought safely out of prison. He can return with the expedition.'

'If we take Lisbon.'

'Indeed. I do not have quite the same confidence as Dom Antonio in the readiness of the Portuguese to rise up on his behalf. His birth, unfortunately, was illegitimate. There is another, legitimate, claimant to the Portuguese throne, Catherine Duchess of Braganza. At one time a man had always a better claim to a throne than a woman, even if his birth were questionable. Now our own great Queen has shown that a woman can be a mighty monarch. The Portuguese leaders, should they decide to rebel against their foreign overlords, might well prefer a woman with a more legitimate claim. The final decision could well lie with the Portuguese *Cortes-Gerais*, whether or not to support Dom Antonio.'

'I knew of the Duchess of Braganza,' I said thoughtfully, 'but did not know she might make a claim.' So much for Ruy Lopez's dreams, I thought, and for my father's life savings.

'I do not know that she will, but it is a factor to bear in mind. Now.' He rose briskly and took out the keys to his strongbox. 'We must provide you with coin of the realm.'

When he had unlocked his strongbox, Walsingham gazed for a moment out of the window. He had always been careworn, but in the stronger light I saw now that his skin had the yellowish grey tinge of those consumed by some inward malady. His eyelids drooped heavily with lack of sleep and the whites of his eyes were reddened. I saw him, perhaps for the first time, as a man like other men, and not as a figure of power, the spymaster moving the pieces on the chessboard of his secret world. A sick man, anxious, vigilant, exhausted by his burden of care, worn out, body and soul, before his time. Had he been my patient, I would have said: *Forget the Court and all your schemes; go home to Barn Elms and enjoy your garden this summer, for it may be your last.*

Before I left with my instructions and my well-filled purse, he took me by the shoulders and studied my face as if he too were seeing me for the first time.

'You came to us originally, Kit, because Thomas Harriot recommended you to Robert Poley for your talent with codes. And I fear that during these last years I have used you simply as a tool come conveniently to my hand. But lately I have learned more of your history and the sufferings you have endured.'

I lowered my eyes, fearing somehow that this shrewd man, fixing me with his sharp glance, might suddenly discover the truth about me.

'You have worked well,' he said, 'and I hope that you find some peace or fulfilment in this journey to Portugal.' He sighed, then added so softly I barely heard him. 'Though I fear it is ill-conceived. When you return – if you return – I will always be glad to employ you.'

I looked up at that, and opened my mouth to speak, but he forestalled me with a smile.

'I know, I know! Your work as a physician is of far greater importance to you. But our work is similar, yours and mine. You care for men's bodies. I care for the body politic.'

I was astonished that he should rank me so highly and murmured some kind of incoherent thanks. I left soon after, without seeing anything of Thomas Phelippes or Arthur Gregory, the seal-forger. My purse was weighed down with Sir Francis's heavy bag of Spanish and Portuguese coins, and tucked into the breast of my doublet was a plan of the town of Coruña. If I felt cold at the thought of what I must do there, I had no one but myself to blame.

On my way down to Seething Lane past the disapproving portraits that lined the hallway and thence by the backstairs I came suddenly face-to-face with Poley. I stopped with a gasp. I had believed him still to be in the Low Countries. It was a shock, the way he could suddenly appear out of the blue, like the devil in a masquerade. Would I never be rid of him? Since he had been released from the Tower, doubtless he was once again busy about the darker side of Walsingham's affairs. He would have had no scruples about killing the agent Titus Allanby. Indeed, he might have found it less inconvenient than trying to smuggle him out of Coruña.

'So-ho!' he cried, seizing me by both arms, so that I could not move. 'It is our fine young gallant. Well met, Christoval Alvarez.'

'I have no business with you, Robert Poley.' I spoke coldly, keeping the fear out of my voice.

'But I might have business with you.' He stroked my cheek and I twisted away. 'I'm off to Denmark. I could do with a fine young *lad* to run errands and share my bed.'

'I too am away on Sir Francis's business,' I said, jerking myself free. 'So you will need to find some other lad to suit your purposes.'

I pushed past him and ran headlong down the stairs and into the street.

On the final Sabbath before our departure I made my way to the Nuñez house to attend a service to bless the mission and pray for success. I went alone, for my father was weak and tired, and had taken to his bed. As I swayed to the hypnotic rhythm of the prayers, I wondered how many of those around me were saying their farewells, intending never to return if the attack on the Spanish garrison in Lisbon were successful. Sara's father Dunstan Añez was there. He had invested heavily in the expedition, but would not be going to Portugal, for the Queen could not spare him from his duties as her Purveyor of Groceries and Spices. Dom Antonio, standing between Hector Nuñez and

23

Roderigo Lopez, had come from Eton to attend the synagogue, though in Eton he was a regular Christian church-goer. The three of them were in a state of exaltation which turned me cold with apprehension. During the years since the Inquisition had come for us, I had grown fatalistic. Hopes too high, expectations of glory and triumph, seemed to me to invite a crushing blow from the hand of fate. I suppose my inherited Jewish pessimism had been further shaped by my own life and my education in the classics – a man who indulges in 'ὕβρις must expect to incur νέμεσις.

I had been lax in attending our hidden Jewish services in recent years. Like the others in our Marrano community I was also a baptised Christian, and my mother's father was a great Christian nobleman. As I had grown older I had become more confused about my faith, not less. Like every citizen of England I was obliged to attend church every Sunday, or else pay a fine as a recusant. The Christian services of Elizabeth's largely tolerant church had become comfortingly familiar to me. Even suspected Catholics who compromised and attended the Protestant services would not be examined too closely, provided they kept their Catholic masses private and did not aid the missions of militant priests sent over from France. Even William Byrd, our most eminent composer, was widely known to be a Catholic, but he was tolerated. On the whole, I found the English church accorded much with my own beliefs.

Yet the services in our makeshift synagogue – the central hall of the Nuñez house – brought back memories of my childhood, before the Spanish came. Perhaps this expedition would help me to understand whether I was Portuguese Jew or English Christian. I had seen Anne Lopez climb the stairs to the women's gallery with her mother. They would be here at Ruy's urging, but from conversations I had had with her over recent months, I knew that she too was troubled by divided loyalties. For her the magnet of England was even stronger, since like her mother she had been born here. But for her father, she would hardly have counted as a Stranger any longer.

I joined in the prayers and responses as dutifully as ever, but I felt a stranger here myself, and my thoughts took me elsewhere, to my work and friends here in London and the unforeseeable prospects which lay ahead.

The night before we were to sail from London to Plymouth, on the first stage of our voyage, Simon appeared at our door, having somehow got word that I was leaving, though I had been careful to suggest to the players, whenever I saw them, that the likelihood of my joining the expedition was remote. I was half glad and half sorry to see him. I had come to value the friends I had made in these last few years, so his good wishes and prayers meant much to me, but I have never liked saying farewell. As for my most intimate feelings for Simon, I could hardly admit them even to myself.

I brought him into our inner parlour, where my father was dozing beside a small fire. It was a warm day outside, the spring weather having brought early and unreliable sunshine, but he had begun to feel the cold more often, so I had lit a fire to comfort him. I motioned Simon to a stool while I tucked a blanket around my father's knees, then I poured us each a tankard of small ale.

'So,' he said, wiping his mouth on the back of his hand, 'you are off on this expedition against the Spanish in Portugal.'

I nodded. I did not ask where he had heard this. Actors are such very demons for gossip.

'But why should you go? What has it to do with you? I thought you were done with that past of yours.'

'Sometimes the past will not let you go,' I said, watching the bubbles which formed on my ale as I swirled it round and round. 'Besides . . .' I hesitated. I was reluctant to admit my father's folly. 'Besides, my father has put money into the expedition. I am going to keep a watchful eye on his investment.'

'Ah, so it is to be a raiding expedition. The treasures Spain has looted from the Americas!'

'No doubt that is part of it, since Drake is to command the fleet,' I conceded, without needing to reveal my knowledge of the plans Walsingham had shared with me. 'But for my father and his friends, the principal purpose is to drive the Spaniards out of Portugal and restore Dom Antonio to the throne.'

'Will he make a good king?'

I could tell by the expression on his face that he had heard something of Dom Antonio. I could say little in the defence of such a man. Indeed, the nearer the time drew to when we were to leave, the more absurd did it seem to commit so much money and so many men to put him on the throne. Would he benefit Portugal? I doubted it. But even Dom Antonio was better than the occupation of a hated foreign power and the imposition of the Inquisition on a previously more tolerant nation.

'Perhaps not a great king,' I said, as diplomatically as I could, 'but we Portuguese are his people and he will rule as a Portuguese king amongst his own subjects. The Spaniards treat us little better than they do the savages of the New World. We exist merely to do their bidding and enrich them. If we resist, we are killed.'

'Then why should you go back? Will you not be in danger?'

I made much of drinking my ale and thought of the missions Walsingham had set me, and of my own private plans. I could not answer that. I set down my ale and poked at the fire, which did not need it.

He gave me a troubled look and leaned forward to take both my hands in his.

'Have a care, Kit. Your friends have need of you.' There was something different about the way he looked at me, as though he were trying to peer into my very soul.

I felt a foolish tightening of my throat and hoped he would not notice the tears blurring my eyes. He must not find me out. He must not. It would be too dangerous by far. I must not weep or I should give myself away.

'I shall not be fighting,' I said. I drew my hands gently from his and got up to fetch more ale, my back to him. 'I go merely to see Dom Antonio crowned, to watch over my father's investment, and to lend my medical skills if they are needed.'

'Say rather: *When* they are needed.' He drew a deep breath. 'I can see that your role as a physician will be valuable to them. But remember, if your ships are fired on, as surely they will be, cannon fire makes no distinction between soldiers and gentlemen observers who come merely to see a puppet king crowned. And there will be fighting ashore as well. Will you stay aboard ship? I doubt it, for I know you. Nay, you will be in the thick of it, tending the wounded, and, like cannon at sea, cannon and crossbow and musket on land will make no distinction between soldier and physician.'

'I will promise you to set up my hospital tent well out of range of the guns.' I spoke as lightly as I could. Burdened with my other knowledge, I had carefully pushed thoughts of the fighting to the back of my mind. 'Come, Simon, you should be cheering me on my way with good wishes for our success. And besides,' I said, as the import of his words struck me, 'why do you call Dom Antonio a puppet king?'

'Oh, now, Kit, you cannot tell me that he will be anything else? When English money and English ships and English lives have put him on the throne? When the Queen herself bears a quarter of the expense?'

'She wants to follow up the success of the Armada by crushing Spanish power.'

'I am sure she does. But once she has put that weak and vain man on the throne, she will not sit back gracefully and allow him free rein. You may count on it, she will expect to be paid back every penny tenfold in taxes and trade concessions. King Antonio will be tied hand and foot to Her Majesty.'

I could say nothing to this. I knew a little about some of the conditions attached to the expedition. I did not expect Simon to have guessed so much and deduced more. Yet he was clever and well-informed. He too attended the discussions of politics and world affairs, as I did, held by Raleigh at Durham House. I should not have been surprised.

I turned the conversation then and we talked generally of how he and the other players were faring under their new patron, and whether the good weather would last so that they could begin performing at the Theatre in a week or two's time. And whether this year the harvests would be better, and hunger less amongst the poor.

'What of your patients at St Bartholomew's?' Simon said. 'Surely you will be away for months. Are you not troubled for them?'

'Numbers are much less, now that the winter is past,' I said. 'The deputy superintendent has arranged for a retired physician to come in two days a week. They will manage without me. It will be a swift expedition, a few weeks. I shall soon be back.'

He still looked troubled, and I found my heart beating uncomfortably fast. Did Simon indeed care whether I went or stayed? But I was afraid to confront the thought. I was never sure what he felt about me, and would not stop to examine what I felt about him. Instead I turned our conversation again to what he and his fellow actors were planning for the coming weeks. At first he seemed reluctant to leave the matter of the Portuguese expedition, but at last he began to talk of a new play and a new boy actor he was training to undertake women's roles. We shared a cold pie Joan had left in the hanging meat safe, and I hoped I had successfully put an end to his disquieting questions.

However, before he went, he threw a comradely arm around my shoulders and gave me a rough hug. I felt my heart jump in my breast and knew he would not have done such a thing, had he known I was a girl. My boy's disguise had been for so long my sanctuary, where I had felt safe and at ease. In this role, this actor's part, I could share Simon's companionship, sit with him virtually alone of an evening while my father slept, with a freedom that the truth would have destroyed in a moment. And yet, and yet, my sanctuary was beginning to feel like a prison.

'Take care of yourself, Kit, in the company of those pirates and lunatics! And come safe home again.'

At that moment I very nearly broke down and gave away my secret.

Chapter Three

Next morning, very early, I took leave of my father. He gave me his blessing, his eyes shining with hope at the prospect of all this expedition might gain for us. If it had done nothing else, the Counter Armada, as it was beginning to be called, had restored to him something of his old strength of body and mind. His movements were vigorous and in the last few weeks there had been no signs of those wandering wits which had so frightened me in recent months. My dog Rikki, accidentally acquired last year in the Low Countries, sensed that something was wrong and howled mournfully as I closed the door on them.

The previous evening I had packed my knapsack with two changes of light-weight clothes, recalling as I did so the thick garments I had taken with me on my first mission for Sir Francis to the Low Countries in the winter of 1587. Then I had been warned of the bitter cold. Now I was returning to a country I knew well, where the heat of summer would have overtaken us before the expedition returned, and I hardly had clothes thin enough for the weather we would encounter on shore. Aboard ship there would be some hope of a cooling breeze, but even the lightest of my English clothes would be hard to bear in the full heat of a Portuguese summer. The cool cotton fabrics we had known there, a legacy of Arab days, were unknown in London, where the thinnest materials were the silks and fine linens, too costly for me to afford.

As well as clothes I packed a pair of summer shoes that I wore normally at the hospital, my physician's gown, and two books. One was the volume of Sidney's poetry which Simon had given me for my seventeenth birthday. I was never sure how he had managed to obtain it, for it had been privately printed and circulated simply amongst the circle of Sidney's friends. There was talk of a public edition being printed, but nothing had come of it yet. The other book had been given me the previous Sunday by the rector of St Bartholomew's church, the Reverend David Dee. It was a small, rather badly printed copy of the four gospels, produced in Geneva. He was not himself a Genevan, deploring their extreme Protestantism, but they were very active in producing inexpensive books of piety.

'I am sure you will have many tedious and idle hours at sea, Kit,' he said, with a slightly repressive smile. 'This may help to pass them. You have told me that you wish to read the Bible for yourself, and this is the most important part, the life and works of Our Lord. It may also be a consolation for you, in the difficult times which lie ahead, for I fear there will be fighting.'

'Aye, Father,' I said. 'I fear there will.'

The Reverend Dee was a somewhat difficult man. My father, amongst those of higher rank in the parish, respected him for his learning and certainly his sermons were models of well-argued prose, straight from the Oxford Schools. However, he had one over-riding passion, and those afflicted by this particular passion are rarely loved by their neighbours. He was a builder. I was not privy to the details of his vision, but I knew – for he often dwelt on it in his sermons – that he fervently deplored the destruction of so much of the ancient and beautiful priory of St Bartholomew's and dreamt of restoring it. After so many of the monastic buildings had been pulled down in the time of King Henry, a huddle of cottages had been built on the glebe land, mainly from the broken stone and timber of the priory buildings. They were an unlovely collection, but they provided housing in the parish for a number of families. The Reverend Dee wanted to eject the tenants, pull down the cottages and replace them with an extension to the church and other parochial buildings. As a result, he was regularly at loggerheads with the tenants, who had countered by laying charges of lewd behaviour against him.

I believed none of it, for he was an upright man, even if obsessed and prepared to drive a carriage and four through other people's lives in pursuit of his dreams. The dispute, if taken to the law courts, could drag on for years. He had never been other than courteous to my father and myself, so I thanked him for his gift, wondering the while whether he had any idea of the extent of danger and fighting which lay ahead of me. Privately, I felt that Sidney's poetry might bring me more consolation than these dense, almost indecipherable pages, but it was kindly meant of him.

In addition to my knapsack, I carried my satchel of medicines. This was crammed as full as it would hold, until the seams strained and I could barely buckle it shut. I retained the special compartment at the bottom, which the leatherworker Jake Winterly had made for me, and into this I placed my most precious items – ground pearls and unicorn horn, calabar beans against poisoning, and the rarest of our herbs. The rest of the satchel was filled with every sort of wound salve, febrifuge herbs, extract of poppy, vomitives, senna, and binding tinctures against the flux. I took few instruments, just a scalpel, a probe, tweezers large and small, needles and thread for stitching wounds. Dr Nuñez and I had consulted over the medical supplies which should be carried by the fleet. Our own ship would be better provided than the rest, with the two of us and Dr Ruy Lopez on board. We advised the captains of the other ships, but they had their own naval surgeons and whether they would listen to us was doubtful. We were regarded as civilians, with no experience in warfare, at sea or on land. The fact that I had cared for the wounded soldiers who had survived the siege of Sluys counted for little, as did my brief encounter with a naval battle the previous summer.

It was a beautiful morning when I left home, soft with the pearly light of early spring, and the whole of London was aflutter with courting and nesting birds. In muddy corners primroses raised faces as shiny as butter and in a patch of waste ground, where a house had collapsed and not been rebuilt, there was a patch of bluebells as gloriously bright amongst the rubble as the southern skies we would soon be seeing. There was a tightness in my chest, part fear, part – I suppose – excitement, for although I was apprehensive, there was something gallant and defiant in this whole undertaking. We might have won the great sea battle in the previous year, but we all knew in our hearts that we had come near to defeat, confronted by that fleet, the largest the world had ever seen. Had the great wind not come to our aid, scattering the Spanish ships and preventing the rendezvous with their army in the Low Countries, we must surely have been defeated and would now be living under the iron heel of the Spanish conqueror.

I shivered, despite the bright morning. It had come very close, that defeat. And now we were to sail south to Spain, into the mouth of the lion, and attempt to turn the tables on them, by destroying their fleet, landing on soil they held, defeating their army. Could we possibly achieve such a victory, unless God were once again on our side? We would have a fleet of nearly a hundred and fifty ships and an army of thirty thousand soldiers, but the Spaniards had but to hold fast where they had fortified towns and harbours. Moreover, of these ships of ours, eighty were pinnaces or Dutch *vlieboten*, small and manoeuvrable, but carrying limited fire-power. There were only six war galleons. The rest were armed merchantmen, built for trade rather than warfare. And our soldiers would mostly be untrained recruits, with just a small leavening of experienced troops drawn from our forces who had been supporting the Dutch rebels in the Low Countries. If the two armies should ever meet in pitched battle on land, there was little doubt what the outcome would be, in the face of Spain's professional army. Ours was the greater task and could not be accomplished unless the people of Portugal – my own people, I reminded myself – rose up in support of the invasion and fought side by side with us.

When I reached the Legal Quays near the Tower, there was a great bustle and shouting. Only the smallest part of the fleet was here, for most was in harbour at Plymouth, or on the way there. Nevertheless the cranes on the dockside were hard at work loading provisions and weapons on to the ships moored here, or on to the supply boats ferrying goods out to the largest ships anchored off shore. The cranesmen were stripped to the waist and sweating profusely. Sailors crowded the decks of the ships, catching hold of the awkward bundles which spun dizzily at the ends of the cranes' hawsers and guiding them down through the hatches into the holds below deck.

I scanned the ships, searching for the *Victory*, the ship which had been allocated to the Portuguese party. Amongst this busy throng I could not see her, but then caught sight of Dr

32

Hector Nuñez, standing on the quayside, a little behind Ruy Lopez, who was attending obsequiously on Dom Antonio. All three were splendidly dressed, as were the men in the Dom's livery, marshalling what appeared to be an immense amount of personal baggage. I might be one of this Portuguese party, but I could hardly compare with all this sartorial splendour, despite the fact that I was wearing my best doublet, a shirt topped with a small but elegant ruff, and a pair of woollen stocking finer than any I had ever possessed before, a parting gift from Sara Lopez. I would keep my distance.

Skulking half hidden behind a massive barrel which, from the smell, contained stock fish, I thought I would watch where they went and follow at a distance. However, Dr Nuñez, glancing round, spotted me and motioned me to join them. Reluctantly, I did so.

Dr Nuñez clasped both my hands in his. He was glowing with excitement. 'Well, Kit, so we are on our way at last! I never believed this day would come. Soon we will walk again on the soil of our motherland.'

I tried to smile. At the same time, I wondered. For had not Dr Nuñez and his wife left Portugal to come to London long before Spain had invaded? They had chosen to leave, to make their home in England. They were not enforced exiles like my father and me, driven out by the terror of the Inquisition. I could not quite understand his enthusiasm. Instead, I turned to practical matters.

'Which is our ship?' I asked. 'I can see none called the *Victory*.'

'There.' He pointed to one of the galleons anchored off shore, too large to tie up beside the quay. 'We are just waiting for a boat to take us on board.'

She was certainly a fine ship, I had to admit. Of course I should I have realised that the ship which would convey the new king to his kingdom would be one of the finest in the fleet. He could not be expected to travel in one of the merchantmen, however comfortable. One consolation, I supposed, was that she carried a full complement of forty-two guns.

The first boat took off Dom Antonio, Ruy Lopez and some of what I imagined must be their most precious possessions. I went in the second with Hector Nuñez and more of the luggage, carrying my own knapsack and satchel myself. It needed a third and fourth boat to convey the remaining servants and bundles. The Thames was at the slack of the tide, so that it was easy enough to climb the sturdy ladder lowered for us, not like a frightening experience I had had when joining Dr Nuñez's ship the *Santa Maria* off the coast of Portugal when I was twelve. That was past, I told myself firmly, jumping down on to the deck. I would not let myself think of the past, but only of the future, of the three missions I must accomplish, two for Walsingham and one for myself.

It was some time before we sailed. While the older members of our Portuguese party were being received graciously by the captain and his senior officers, I kept out of the way and found a place by the railings of the poop deck where I could watch all the activity of the loading. Most of the *Victory* must have been loaded already, but there were still goods coming aboard, besides the Dom's possessions. The ship had its own crane for lifting goods from the supply boats inboard. When I grew tired of watching that, I strolled about the decks, making myself familiar with the layout of the ship which would be my home for all the weeks ahead. Apart from that first journey from Portugal I had never been on such a large ship, for those which had taken me twice to the Low Countries were pinnaces, as small by comparison as a terrier beside the mythical oliphants that are said to inhabit the inner lands of Africa, or like a herring beside a whale.

The size of the ship reminded me of that first ship I had travelled in, although that had been a merchantman, not a ship of war, and despite my determination to banish all thoughts of that voyage seven years ago, I knew a moment of panic. We would be travelling back over those same waters, in a ship not so very different. I tried to concentrate on immediate and urgent problems. I needed to know where I would sleep. Here I could not offer to sleep with the horses, as I had done when Nicholas Berden and I had travelled together on Walsingham's business. Would I be expected to sleep with the crew? It would be impossible, and still conceal my sex. To share a cabin with the distinguished members of our party, or with the ship's officers would be just as dangerous.

I investigated the ship from bow to stern as unobtrusively as possible, keeping out of the way of the sailors, and at last found what I was looking for. There was a corner on the foredeck, behind a massive water cask and between two huge coils of thick rope, where I reckoned I could bed down unseen, if I could make my way here without being forestalled. It would be uncomfortable, but not cold, even while we were in English coastal waters, and it would be far better and safer than sleeping hugger-mugger in a hammock amongst the crew. I stowed my knapsack here, but kept my satchel on my shoulder.

That was one problem solved, I hoped, but as the last of the supply boats drew away and the swirling river waters showed that the tide was turning to the ebb, I felt a terrible lurch of fear in my stomach. It caught me so suddenly that it stopped my breath. A single topsail was hoisted on the mainmast. The anchor chain rattled up as six of the crew trudged round the capstan with a rhythmic chant to help their efforts. The great anchor rose, dripping weed and Thames mud. The signals from officers to crew on this huge ship were conveyed by whistles or trumpets, unlike the friendly shouts I had known on the pinnaces. I saw a ship's boy climbing the main mast, nimble as a monkey, with something gripped in his teeth. The mainsail and the lateen sail on the mizzen mast were hoisted, but not yet the rest of the canvas, for the ship would need to manoeuvre slowly down river until we were clear of London's water traffic. All around us, other ships in the fleet were making ready to sail down the Thames on the ebb tide, bound for Plymouth.

The boy had reached the masthead and seemed to be busy up there, then I saw what he was about. As he shinnied down again, the wind caught the standard fixed there, and it broke out fully in view: Dom Antonio's standard, bearing the coat of arms of the Portuguese royal dynasty, the Aviz. There could be no going back now. The sight of that flag, the increasing speed of the ship, the diminishing view of the Tower and the Bridge behind us was like the stuff of nightmares, as though some hidden, malevolent force were sucking me back the way I had come, making a mockery of my escape from Portugal.

Plymouth, where we were to take on supplies and recruits to the expedition's army, was the first place I had seen in my new country, all those years ago. Now it would be the last place we would see in England. My life seemed to be rolling in reverse. Although it had been the scheme of those three influential men in my life – Dr Nuñez, Dr Lopez and my father – that I should take my father's place on the expedition, yet I also clung to my own reasons for returning to Portugal, despite these moments of panic. I could not tell whether my half-formed plans would even be possible. I had said nothing of them to anyone, not even my father, not even Walsingham, who might have been able to help me.

More signals were sounded on the whistles and more canvas was broken out, until we were under a full complement of sail. I had loved the sleek lines and beauty of the two pinnaces, *Silver Swan* and *Good Venture*, but there is no denying that a great galleon – however huge and seemingly top-heavy compared with the smaller ships – is a magnificent sight. The modern race-built English galleons look more elegant and graceful than the heavier Spanish galleons I had seen at sea last year. Even as I was, sick with nerves and apprehension, I could appreciate the splendour of the *Victory*. Around and behind us the rest of the fleet filled me with a grudging pride. We were a fine sight, even this small part of the fleet. The only time I had seen an English fleet before had been amidst the confusion of battle. Now we sailed bravely in formation down the spreading waters of the Thames, flags and pennants flying, the polished wood of the hulls gleaming, the new canvas of the sails a warm cream, every scrap of brass reflecting the spring sunshine. The shores on either side of the river, even when we reached the lower, muddy reaches, were lined with people on both the Kent and Essex banks, waving and cheering us on our way. I wondered whether any of the players I knew had come to see us off from London. I had not thought to look, and now it was too late. We were past Greenwich and moving with tide and wind down towards the estuary and the open sea.

The journey itself as far as Plymouth was uneventful. The weather was calm, but with enough of a breeze to take us out into the German Sea and around the easternmost nose of Kent. As we stood out into mid Channel, I remembered what both Captain Thoms and Captain Faulconer had told me last year about the dangers of the Goodwin Sands. For a vessel of this size, the danger must be all the greater, for she needed deeper water than the pinnaces and even had they grounded they could probably have rowed away, provided they were quick about it. Or they could have lowered a skiff, so it could tow them off, always supposing it was daylight and the tide was not ebbing fast.

A vast ship like the *Victory* could take neither of these measures to extricate herself from the shoals, so I was relieved to see that our helmsman was steering a wide course over towards the French coast. We were not far from Gravelines, where I had been caught up in the battle aboard the *Good Venture* last year. It was hard to imagine it now, the explosions and smoke, the glare of the burning fire ships, the screams of injured men, and the air choking with dust and the reek of gunpowder. Now there was nothing to be seen but our well-ordered fleet and a few fishing boats closer to land on the calm waters.

Dr Nuñez came to stand beside me, where I was leaning on the starboard rail, looking toward Kent.

'Will that be Dover?' he asked, pointing to where we could now make out the castle high on its promontory. I realised that, although his ships traded regularly throughout the known world, he had probably never travelled this way except on his original voyage to England.

'Aye,' I said. 'That's the castle up there, and, down below, the harbour I sailed from when I went to Amsterdam. They light a signal fire on the old Roman lighthouse after dark, as a guide to ships.'

'We'll see that, no doubt,' he said. 'We are to put in to the harbour for the night. Some of the ships are to embark a contingent of soldiers from the garrison.'

'Are they?' I wondered whether Andrew Joplyn would be amongst them. 'Their commander will not be pleased. He does not care for anyone to interfere with his running of the Dover garrison.'

'Ah, of course, you met him.'

'Aye. A pompous, rude man. We should be thankful he is not part of this expedition.'

He laughed. 'I think Sir John Norreys would soon lick him into shape.'

We stood in silence as the *Victory* furled some of her canvas and turned slowly to make her way into the harbour. Flights of gulls shrieked from the nearby cliffs, skimming over the sea around us and plucking fish effortlessly from the water. I could see untidy nests being built on the ledges of the cliff face, which was streaked with their droppings, a dirty cream against the gleaming white of the limestone.

'The birds will be nesting in Portugal too,' Dr Nuñez said dreamily. 'When I was a boy, we used to go to spend the hot weather in our summer home on a headland overlooking the sea, to escape the heat of Lisbon. It is one of my earliest memories, travelling there in a coach with my mother and brothers and sisters, with my father riding beside us. We used to listen for the cry of the gulls and try to be the first to catch sight of the sea. Later, when I was older, I rode with my father, so I always saw the sea first, having a better view.'

I thought, *This is why he is here. It has nothing to do with driving out the Spanish and putting Dom Antonio on the throne. He is in search of his lost childhood.*

I turned away. Perhaps that was partly why I was here as well.

We spent the night at anchor in Dover harbour. The leaders of our party went ashore to attend a banquet given by the mayor and councillors of the town. Although Dr Nuñez tried to persuade me to accompany them, I had no wish for a long evening of eating and drinking too much and listening to too many worthy speeches. As dusk fell, after taking supper with the junior officers, I made my way to my corner behind the water barrel. No one paid any particular attention to me. I was no part of the working crew, nor was I one of the distinguished passengers, the leaders of the gentlemen adventurers. Grateful for the anonymity given me by my ambivalent position amongst the people aboard the *Victory*, I did my best to bed down on deck. Earlier I had managed to filch a couple of blankets from one of the hammocks below decks, but I could not pretend I was going to be comfortable. Sleeping on straw with the horses on the *Silver Swan* had been luxury compared with this. By the time we reached Portugal I should be black and blue all over.

It was well past dark when I heard the shore party returning, well wined and dined by the sound of them, Dom Antonio's voice overriding them all, strident and assertive. I had had little chance to observe him so far, but what I had seen did not impress me with a sense of his royalty and dignity. He seemed inflated and boastful, full of pride at the moment, yet I sensed he would become querulous and ill-tempered if matters should fail to go his way.

My bed proved uncomfortable but private, as I managed to keep out of sight of the crew while they went about their duties. I felt secure, though I hoped the weather would remain fine. That first night I slept in fitful snatches. We remained at anchor in Dover harbour; the night was still and full of stars. Without even a thin palliasse or a layer of straw beneath me, every position I took hurt my shoulders, my hips or my back. Before dawn I was sitting propped up against the barrel, wondering how I could make my hidden bed more comfortable.

After we had broken our fast, we watched a troop of soldiers marched down from the castle to the harbour, then ferried out to two of the other galleons, not our own ship. I counted just twenty men. Either Dover could spare no more or else Sir Anthony Torrington, the commander of the garrison, had beaten Sir John Norreys down to this paltry number. Apart from the experienced soldiers due to be sent over from the Low Countries to meet us in Plymouth, these were the only trained soldiers we would be carrying. I screwed up my eyes, trying to make out whether Andrew Joplyn was amongst them. If he was, I did not see him.

Once the soldiers from Dover were aboard, we weighed anchor and with the rest of the fleet made our way out of the harbour and into the English Channel. In the early summer the Channel was calm, and we proceeded along the south coast of England with a moderate following wind. Before last year's battle we would have feared attack from Spanish ships plying back and forth along these waters to the lands they occupied in the Low Countries, but the Spanish navy was still at home, licking its wounds. Not even the French were to be seen, apart from a few fishing boats, busy about their own affairs close to their own coast. We dropped anchor in Plymouth harbour three days after leaving Dover without any incident to trouble us. Here, as off Gravelines, it was hard to imagine the bloody conflict which had taken place over these waters so few months earlier, when ears were deafened with the thunder of artillery and nostrils choked with the bitter stench of gunpowder. If all went according to plan, we would experience our own share of naval artillery in Portugal, but the plan was for a quick campaign, catching the Spanish forces in Portugal unawares, with capitulation and peace negotiations to follow.

'These houses must have witnessed the battle,' I said to Dr Nuñez as we leaned on the rail, looked over at the peaceful activity in the harbour.

'Perhaps, but probably not. They would have seen the fleet depart, but I think the fighting in this part of the Channel was further off. The people of Plymouth should be glad we are taking the fight across the seas,' he said. 'They came very near finding Spanish soldiers marching up their streets.'

'I wonder how many of those Spanish soldiers found their way home again.'

'Not many. All through the final months of last year despatches arrived from my agents handling the Spanish and Portuguese trade. Broken ships trailing in, manned by skeleton crews. Their losses were terrible.'

I did not answer, torn two ways. Part of me was fiercely glad that so many of the invaders had died, yet I could not forget what I had seen at Gravelines, men slaughtered on deck or drowning in the unforgiving sea.

The plan set forth in London before we departed was that we would remain in Plymouth no more than a week or so. We had brought some of the new 'army' with us from London; others had been gathered at Plymouth from all parts of the country, drawn by the prospects of looting which Dom Antonio had been forced to concede to the Queen in order to gain her support for the invasion. They were not to loot just in Spain, for – as I was to learn much later – once the soldiers had seized Lisbon, they were to be allowed to loot the city, as payment for their services.

Thereafter the Dom had pledged such vast sums to Elizabeth that he would sit a beggar on his throne. Portugal was to become a province of England, her precious trade in the hands of English merchants, her castles manned by English garrisons. When I had heard this, I could not understand how the old men like Lopez and Nuñez and Dunstan Añez could consent to such terms. How could Portugal be free, loaded with such chains? But perhaps, like me, they were too entangled to escape the inexorable current of fate which was carrying us all onwards.

This 'army' which had been mustered was as vile, dirty, vicious, and ungovernable a rout of men as you have ever seen – beggars and thieves, wastrels and men fresh out of prison. When we reached Plymouth, those recruits we had on board scrambled ashore (they had puked all the way down the Channel) and joined their fellows who had been gathering here on land. This landward group had already discovered the warehouses where the provisions for the voyage were stored. Now more than doubled in their numbers, this army of gallant men set to, besieged the warehouses and took them in a matter of hours.

Over the next days, while we awaited the arrival of a trained contingent of soldiers who were to join us from the Low Countries, all the provisions – meat, drink, flour, salted fish, ship's biscuit, dried fruit and vegetables – found their way down the gullets of these starving wretches. When they had devoured our substance, like a biblical plague of locusts, they descended upon the taverns and inns of Plymouth and the surrounding villages. Boasting that they were the Queen's army and must be fed, they told the frightened innkeepers to send their bills to London, where they would be paid by the Privy Council or the Queen herself. When the inns ran out of food, they broke into houses and ransacked them. The terrified people of Plymouth cowered behind bolted doors and prayed for the arrival of the ships from the Netherlands, hoping to see the last of us. When a Flemish boat put into port, our gallant men stripped it of its entire cargo of dried herrings, after beating the crew half to death.

At last, to our great relief, the professional soldiers arrived from the Low Countries, long after they were due, and with their help Sir John Norreys rounded up such of the rioting men as could be found (some had grown tired of waiting and gone home). Once they were herded, most unwillingly, on board, we were able finally to set sail. I was still living aboard the *Victory*, with the rest of the Portuguese party, where I had remained all the time we were in harbour, scarcely setting foot on shore. We were relieved at last to be on our way, for we were already three weeks past our planned departure date. Yet once out of harbour and in the Channel our ships were met by head winds and could make no way against them. They blew us straight back into Plymouth Sound.

And back at Plymouth, anchored in the harbour, we found there was more bad news. It was Dr Nuñez who told me the story. I think he had grown a little tired of the company of Ruy Lopez and the Dom, sitting in state in their fine suite of cabins, for I often found him on deck like me.

The Queen's favourite, the wayward Earl of Essex, had been forbidden to come on the Portuguese venture. This was common knowledge before we left London.

'However,' said Dr Nuñez, 'the Earl of Essex has disobeyed Her Majesty and fled London. It seems he was traced to Falmouth, and there he took ship on the *Swiftsure*, which had been ready provisioned and armed and waiting for him. He made his escape from Falmouth, with winds more favourable than those we encountered.'

'Her Majesty will be furious,' I said. 'And so soon after the death of the Earl of Leicester, she will not want his stepson to run into danger.'

'Nay. But he is headstrong and accustomed to getting his own way. Drake and Norreys have received instructions from Her Majesty to send Essex directly back to London, but he has slipped past everyone, not only the men she sent after him but our own expedition, what with his more favourable winds. He set sail while we were kicking our heels, waiting for the troops from the Low Countries.'

For another twelve days we continued to kick our heels at Plymouth, with the provisions and the water dwindling away, until only a few days' supply was left. And then, at last, the head wind abated, and under a threatening storm sky, which was as ill-omened as all that had gone before, Drake's aptly named *Revenge* led us out to sea, and the *Victory* followed. Despite all the oaths I had sworn to myself, I was returning to Portugal, but nothing could drive away the memories of my final weeks there. As the fleet passed down the Channel and Plymouth Sound disappeared behind us, fear rose like vomit in my throat.

Chapter Four

Coimbra, Portugal, 1582

The darkness closed over me and I was blind. I groped for my mother's hand and found it, as cold and clammy as my own. Somewhere, someone was whimpering. I could not tell if it was my mother or myself, or someone else in the blackness which stretched out ahead, where we huddled by the iron-bound door which had slammed behind us. My mother put her arms around me and we clung together, not daring yet to speak, straining for any sound which might penetrate from beyond that door.

'Where are we?' I whispered at last.

'In the prison of the Inquisition.'

'But where is Father?'

'They will have confined him in a separate cell, so we cannot confer together about how we should answer their questions.'

'Questions?'

'You must be brave, Caterina. Your father and I have always known this might happen. Ever since the Spanish came two years ago, and the Cardinal-Archduke Albrecht was made both governor of Portugal and Inquisitor General. He is most zealous against New Christians.'

'What shall we do? Oh, what shall we do?' I wailed.

She held me tighter and put her lips to my ear. 'Hush, Caterina. We will not choose martyrdom. We will swear our undying faith to the Pope and the Catholic Church. We will admit some small transgressions, that we donned clean linen on Friday evenings and forbore to eat pork, but we shall say that these were

44

simply old customs in our families, and we do not know the reasons for them.'

'But, Mama . . . '

'Listen to me, Caterina.' She took hold of my shoulders and shook me. 'I do not know if they will put you to the question, but you must know what to say. You know that you are a baptised Christian.'

'Yes, of course.'

'We regularly attend the church of San Piero, do we not?'

'Well . . .'

'Caterina!'

'Yes, Mama. We *do* attend church every Sunday, and make confession, and take communion. I took my first communion last Easter.'

'As you did.'

'Yes.'

She relaxed a little.

'Good.'

I looked about me, for I found that my eyes had grown a little accustomed to the dark, and a ghost of grey light, no more than a strip half an inch wide, filtered under the door. The cell was about fifteen feet square, with a deep litter of dirty straw and rubbish on the floor and a heap of old rags in the far corner.

'Come as close to the light as you can.' My mother was fumbling in the purse she wore under her outer skirt, which the Inquisition's men had not noticed in their haste to drag us from home and through the night-time streets.

'It's so cold,' I said, rubbing my arms, for I was barefoot and wearing nothing but my night shift. 'How can it be so cold in the summer?'

'We're deep underground here,' she said absently. She had found what she was looking for and now seized a handful of my hair.

'What are you doing?' I tried to pull away.

'I'm going to cut off your hair.'

'My hair!' I clutched my head with both hands and tried to pull away from her.

'Keep still, Caterina. You are flat-chested still. In that shift you could be a boy, but for your hair. I'm going to cut it off.'

'Why, why?' I tried to push her away and she gave my hair a jerk.

'Caterina, as a girl you are in far more danger here than a boy would be. Your hair will grow back.'

I stood still at last as she began to hack at my hair with the tiny pair of scissors she carried with her. I kept silent then, but I could not stop the silent tears rolling down my face as she threw handfuls of my hair into the litter on the floor and stirred it in with the toe of her shoe.

'That's the best I can do,' she said. 'Take off your earrings and put them in here.' she held out her purse and I dropped into it the small gold pendants I had put back in my ears after I had taken off the heavy pearls I had worn at dinner last night. My mother took off her own earrings, still her jewelled ones, and added them to the purse.

'We must find somewhere to hide this,' she said, 'for we may need to bribe the guards.'

She felt her way across the floor to the far corner, groping along the wall as she went, trying to find some hollow or loose stone where she could conceal the purse. As she trod on the pile of rags there was a sudden shriek and a curse, and she jumped back, her hand to her heart.

'Leave me be,' a whining voice came from within the rags. 'Let me sleep, let me sleep.'

I crept up behind my mother and peered down. As far as I could make out, an old woman, her thin wisps of hair the colour of curdled milk, was curled up there, her arms clutched protectively around her head.

'I'm sorry, Senhora,' said my mother. 'I did not see you in the dark.'

'Jaime will come soon,' said the woman in a voice as flat and dull as the stones of the prison. She nodded her head, up and down, jerky as a marionette. 'Yes, Jaime will come. Then I will cook his dinner and we will go to my sister. He said we would go to my sister.' She gave a strange shrill laugh and strained up towards my mother. 'Have you brought Jaime? He has been gone so long, so long.'

Then she started muttering to herself and rocking there on the floor, clutching a bundle of clothes to her. We stepped back to the door.

'Poor creature,' said my mother. 'Her wits are wandering. I think they must have taken Jaime away for ever. Come over here, Caterina, away from the draught. We'll gather some of this straw together and sit on it.'

'It's horrible,' I said, 'filthy. We can't sit on that.'

'It is better than cold stone,' she said brusquely. 'If you have nothing worse to suffer than dirty straw, God will truly have spared you.'

Reluctantly I did as I was bid. The straw was infested with lice and fleas which were soon crawling over my shuddering flesh, but my earlier tiredness suddenly rolled over me again as I sat there amongst the stinking straw. I found myself lying with my head in my mother's lap, and slept.

I suppose it was morning, or some time the next day, when they brought us a bowl of slops, some stale bread, and a jug of muddy water. The old woman seemed not to want anything, but my mother persuaded her to take a little. Her name, she said, was Francesca, and she did not know how long she had been in the prison. It was certainly months, perhaps even years. Her talk rambled still, but she did not seem as crazed as she had in the night. She had been brought here with her son, who was thirteen, accused of Judaizing, and put to the question. They had taken Jaime away and she was still waiting for him to return. They had stripped him first, and it was his clothes she kept always beside her. I saw my mother take note of this, and I realised what she was thinking, for I was shivering in my thin shift. I did not want to wear a dead boy's clothes, which had mouldered here perhaps for years, but I was very cold.

They left us alone for several days. I could not be sure, but it must have been nearly a week. By then my mother had broached the subject of the clothes to Francesca, who became frantic and refused.

'But Jaime can have them again when he returns,' my mother pleaded. 'You see how cold my son is. Look, I will give you this gold earring for the use of them until then.' She held up one of my gold tear-drops.

Francesca laughed wildly. 'What use is gold to me? Keep your gold.'

She would not part with the clothes, for which I was partly grateful and partly regretful.

When next a guard brought our food, I heard my mother whispering to him, and the following day he brought cheese and figs and new bread and wind-dried ham and a small flask of wine. I saw my mother hand him one of my earrings, and I started forward, my stomach groaning in expectation of the food, but my mother batted my hand away.

'Now, Francesca,' she said winningly. 'You see all this good food? It shall all be yours, in exchange for the loan of Jaime's clothes to my son here.'

Francesca fought with herself and her hunger for an hour at least before at last she agreed, handing over the rancid, sweat-stained garments, and huddled in the corner, muttering over the food. Curling my lip with distaste, I pulled on a pair of breeches the colour of horse dung and a grey tunic whose frayed sleeves hung down past my hands. At least my own shift protected me from contact with them about my body. Our long confinement in the dark cell had caused my eyes to adjust to the scant light, and I could see that I might be able to pass for a boy.

'We must choose a name for you,' said my mother, 'and use it even when we are alone. Something pious and Christian.'

'Christoval,' I said. It was the first boy's name that came into my head.

'Christoval Alvarez.' She tried it on her tongue. 'Yes, that will do very well.'

I looked enviously to the dark corner where Francesca was mumbling over the food. She did not appear to be eating it. Instead she had made it into a pile and was crooning to herself.

It became obvious in the next few days that she was keeping the food for Jaime. I tried to steal a little of it before it grew mouldy in the damp which clung to the stone walls of the cell, but my mother caught me and made me put it back.

'The food is not yours,' she said. 'If Senhora Francesca chooses not to eat it, that does not mean it is yours to steal.'

I complained bitterly, for I was hungry and could not bear to see the food rotting away, but my mother would not relent.

It is strange how need will drive a creature. I would swear that the gap under the door was no more than half an inch, but before the week was out the rats had smelled the food and found their way somehow into the cell. Whenever she was awake, Francesca mounted guard over the food, though the rats became bold in their hunger and bit her. When at last she fell asleep they ran about the cell, squeaking for joy over their booty, or fighting each other viciously over a fragment of ham. I sat pressed against the wall, my knees drawn up and my arms about them in an attempt to make myself as small as possible so they would not come near me. Before three days had passed, the rats had devoured every crumb, but I still wore Jaime's clothes, which clung to me with the dead boy's smell.

Chapter Five

English Fleet, 1589

For two days, out in mid Channel, our ships had fought against cross-winds that blew us first back east, up towards Dover, then down, out past Cornwall, as if determined to blast us all the way to Virginia. By the time we had finally reached the tip of Cornwall and then the Atlantic, the fleet was scattered over several miles of sea, unable to keep together, the driving rain and mist so thick the *Victory* might have been alone on the deserted ocean. Our rag-tail army spent the time hanging over the side of the ship, emptying into the sea the little they had been given to eat. I felt queasy myself, as much from the sight of them as from the motion of the ship, but I managed to keep on my feet and attend to the occasional patient, although my nights were wretched, huddled in my corner between the water cask and the ropes, under a piece of patched sail I had found and draped over the top of my hideaway to provide some protection against the rain. Dr Lopez – and even, to my disappointment, Dr Nuñez – had metamorphosed into Portuguese aristocrats, and were too busy discussing affairs of state with Dom Antonio to exercise their medical skills. Besides, tending the men kept my mind off what lay ahead.

I had other more immediate concerns. Living with my father but otherwise keeping myself at a distance from others, even those in Phelippes's office, I had not found it difficult to hide my sex. I was still slender and flat-chested, I was still young enough to be beardless, even had I been a young man, and the thick padded doublet I wore, sometimes further covered by my physician's gown, helped to disguise my shape. When I had travelled abroad with Nicholas Berden to the Low Countries, we sometimes shared a room, but slept in what we wore by day, all but our boots. However, in the close proximity of the ship, it was far more difficult to conceal my personal and private needs, so during those first days at sea I hardly slept, snatching brief moments of rest sitting in my partially sheltered corner of the deck. I began to grow frightened at what would happen to me if it should be discovered that I was a girl. I had known this before ever we set out, but I had pushed this particular difficulty to the back of my mind. Now it confronted me every day. Would it be possible even for my father's friends to protect me, if my deceit became known? They might turn against me, horrified that they had been tricked all these years.

On the fourth day out from Plymouth, the rain eased off, the wind swung round to a steady north-east, and the scattered fleet started to draw together. We sailed on, rounding the Brest peninsula, the westernmost tip of Brittany, and began to head south across the Bay of Biscay, keeping well offshore, so that we should not be spied from the French coast and word sent to warn Spain. As the sun came out, the whole ship began to steam, as canvas, ropes and planks dried in the heat. The sailors were kept on the run, adjusting the set of the sails and the tensions on the rigging as the ship started to recover from the strains of the previous days. All of us on board responded to the passing of the storm and the return of the sun. After so much wet misery, the outlook began to seem more hopeful.

Although we wanted to avoid encountering any French ships, clearly our leaders were also reluctant to veer too far west into the wider Atlantic, so as we sailed south I was able to watch the French coast in the distance. My eyes had always been sharp, so from time to time I could make out a cluster of cottages in a village, or a small group of fishing boats. The rocky coast of Brittany held dangers, clearly marked by huge waves that crashed on to the shore, sending fountains of spume as high in the air as the tower of St Paul's. Further south the coast looked more tranquil, with here and there a small harbour.

One of the sailors explained why we were keeping out from the coast. The *Victory* was furthest inshore of the fleet, most of which stood more to the west of us.

'An't no danger of attack along here,' he said. 'The froggies are so busy cutting each other's throats, they won't bother us. Protestant against Catholic. Fighting for the crown, I heard.'

I nodded. 'So I've heard too.' I would not admit how many despatches on the subject I had decoded. 'So why keep away?'

'Captains don't want the froggies passing word to Spain that we're coming.'

'The French and the Spanish are not the best of friends,' I objected.

'Aye, but Philip of Spain will have spies along the coast.' He was shrewder than I realised.

'Then surely we should move still further out. If we can see their villages, they must be able to see that.' I jerked my chin up, indicating Dom Antonio's banner at our masthead, with its golden castles on a crimson border and its five blue shields forming a central cross. It was as large as a wall covering.

'Not our job to point that out,' he said.

For the whole of the fifth day we made steady progress southwards, but the wind was not the most favourable. Although strong enough to fill the sails, it kept veering round from the northeast to the north and then to the northwest, which would tend to push us in toward the coast of France, and also toward the shallower waters where the southeast corner of the Bay lay. The whistles of the officers were forever sending the sailors to trim the sails to keep the ship on course. That night we had to heave to, until daylight should show us our best route.

By the sixth day we could make out the line of Cape Finisterre dimly on the horizon, the westernmost tip of Spain. Beyond, not many miles further south, the coast of Portugal began.

I recalled the map Walsingham had shown me, when he had explained the three goals of the expedition. Our first, to destroy Spain's Atlantic fleet, would mean attacking Santander, where the damaged ships from last year's Armada fleet were being repaired and refitted. As we sailed further south that morning Dr Nuñez came to stand beside me on the forecastle, where I leaned on the rail, watching the lands of Iberia draw perceptibly nearer.

'I saw you sleeping on deck this morning, Kit. Have you not been given any accommodation?'

I avoided his glance. 'I was told I could have a hammock on the gundeck. But–' I hesitated, 'I did not like the idea.'

With an angry snort he said, 'That is no place for one of the ship's physicians. I will see whether I can find you somewhere more suitable.' He looked at me sideways, a curiously knowing look.

I gave him a grateful smile. 'Thank you.'

'Don't worry. We'll find somewhere.' He turned to look again towards the loom of the coast. 'Not long now, till you see your homeland again.'

'Nay.' I kept to myself that I did not feel the affection for the place that lit up his eyes and made him stride about the deck like a much younger man. Portugal. Not my homeland. Never that. A place of nightmare. My stomach churned and I clenched my fists to hide the shaking of my hands.

'Are we not heading too far to the west?' I said, anxious to change the subject. 'I thought we were ordered to attack the Spanish fleet where it is being repaired at Santander.' I gestured towards the port bow, roughly in the direction where I thought, from my sight of Walsingham's map, that Santander must lie. 'Should we not be aiming more in that direction?'

He looked somewhat startled. 'I did not know you were privy to that plan.'

'Sir Francis told me. First to Santander, then to Coruña, firing as many of the Spanish ships as possible, to cripple their Atlantic navy. Then on southward to besiege Lisbon. Though I would have thought,' I added, 'that it would have been wiser to attack Lisbon first, to retain some element of surprise, even if the Spaniards spot our fleet as we sail down the coast.'

'Perhaps. Though there would also be some merit in putting the Spanish fleet out of action first,' he said, 'so that Lisbon would require a land battle alone and not a naval one. It is for our military and naval leaders to make these decisions.'

'A land battle with our amateur army?' I laughed. 'Besides, the ships under repair at Santander and Coruña are not seaworthy. They could not engage us at sea. But,' I said, sticking to my point, 'we do not seem to be making for Santander.'

'There is a problem,' he said.

I looked at him enquiringly.

'Two problems, in fact. First, you must have noticed the strong on-shore wind. Drake is worried that we might become embayed in Biscay and vulnerable to attack either by the French or the Spanish. Trapped, with no way out. He has decided that it will be safer to bypass Santander and make directly for Coruña. Part of the Spanish fleet is there, so we should be able to inflict considerable damage.'

'Though surely not as much as we could have done if we had attacked Santander as well,' I said. 'I suppose we must defer to Drake's judgement in naval matters.'

Though I recalled how Drake had sailed off on a private plundering action in the middle of the Armada battle. How much was he to be trusted?

'You said there were two problems,' I reminded him.

'You recall how that riffraff consumed our stores in Plymouth?'

'Dr Nuñez,' I said, 'I don't suppose any of us will ever forget those disgraceful scenes.'

'It has left us very short of provisions. The money invested in the venture by the joint stock company was all spent in providing those original stores and the small amount of arms we carry. Drake and Norreys were unable to purchase more to replace what was lost.'

'You mean we are going to run out of *food*?' I was incredulous, that these men, with all their experience of mounting armed expeditions and voyages of exploration, could prove so inept in the most fundamental of preparations.

'Food and drink. You see all these flags they are running up on the yardarms?' He pointed over our heads, where lines of brightly coloured flags flapped against the heavy canvas of the sails. I had no idea of their purpose.

'They are signalling from ship to ship,' he said, 'trying to decide what best to do. On some of the ships the men are rioting

54

already, for lack of food. Our captain says we will have consumed all our own food by this evening. The ale will be finished by tomorrow. We cannot reach Lisbon in our present state.'

'But . . .' I stared at him. 'We cannot turn back. It would take as long to sail back to England as to sail on to Lisbon.' For a moment I had hoped the whole wild scheme would be abandoned, until I saw this flaw.

He nodded, and motioned me to follow him.

'Come. You might as well listen to the discussion, though I do not think anything either of us can say will have any influence on the decision.'

When we reached the main deck, Sir John Norreys, Ruy Lopez, Dom Antonio and the captain of our ship were huddled together. Captain Oliver held a chart in his hand. He looked up as we approached.

'Directly to Coruña, then?' he said, addressing Sir John.

Norreys, who had joined us by pinnace from his own ship, the *Nonpareil*, nodded his agreement. 'We must reprovision. The harbour is large enough to accommodate the fleet, and the garrison will be taken by surprise. From reports we received before leaving England, Spain has been stockpiling provisions there. We will attack and seize enough stores to take us on to Lisbon, as well as eliminating as many of the Spanish warships as possible. We will also take the town.'

Those reports about stockpiling provisions, I thought, were probably sent to Walsingham by Titus Allanby, the man I must try, somehow, to rescue from Coruña. How, I could not imagine.

'But . . .' I said, emboldened by this alarming turn of events to speak out amongst such high company, 'but won't that give warning to the Spaniards? If we made a swift attack on the ships, as was intended, then sailed quickly on our way, there would be little time for word to reach the Spanish military command and allow them to marshal their forces. If we stay longer, not just to load with provisions but to attack and take possession of the town, won't they realise this is no mere raiding expedition, but we are heading for Portugal?'

Even as I spoke, I was torn two ways. For the main purpose of our mission to succeed, we needed to make the greatest

55

possible speed to Lisbon. Yet if I were to find Titus Allanby, a delay at Coruña would help.

Norreys shrugged. 'The men must be fed. Otherwise we will have a full-scale mutiny on our hands.'

'But we do not need to make an attack on the town with a view to taking it.'

He gave me a quelling look and turned to Captain Oliver.

'Run up the signal,' he said. 'We make for Coruña as swiftly as possible.'

I was silenced. From the very start the plans for the expedition had begun to fall apart. First the wholesale looting of the provisions in Plymouth by the new recruits, then the delayed arrival of the troops from the Low Countries and the contrary winds which had kept us held up for days at Plymouth, then the storm in the Channel, then the abandonment of the raid on the main part of the Spanish fleet at Santander, and now, instead of a swift attack on the ships at Coruña and an equally swift departure, we would be delayed here, not only seizing and loading provisions but attacking the town. For what purpose? What was the strategy? Who could guess how long we would be held up there? Our goal was in southern Portugal, not northern Spain.

A few hours later at dusk, we sailed into Coruña harbour, Drake joyfully in the lead, with his personal standard flying at the masthead of his flagship, the *Revenge*. We learned the next morning from the embittered and frightened inhabitants of Coruña that the Spanish garrison had been so terrified by the sight of the standard belonging to the man they called *El Dracque* – the Dragon – that they had fled at once to the walled citadel in the upper town, abandoning the port, the lower town, and the citizens to their fate. However, our first and most urgent objective was to find where the stores of food and drink were held. Our seasick and rebellious soldiers were wonderfully cheered at the sight of land and the prospect of booty. When half of them were put ashore to hunt out provisions and load them on to the ships' boats to restock the fleet, the remainder begged to join their comrades.

While the men were being ferried ashore in the pinnaces and skiffs of the fleet, I stood on deck beside Captain Oliver, looking out over the water. To starboard and some distance away I could see a massive *castillo*, guarding the western side of the harbour.

'Why is Sir Francis not attacking that fortress?' I asked. It seemed the one place that threatened us.

'Ah,' he said. 'The new fortress. The Spanish began building that island fortress two years ago, when King Philip was preparing his Armada to attack England. After mustering the following year, it was from here, the harbour at Coruña, that the Armada fleet set out.'

'So it was built to protect this harbour,' I said. 'I can understand why. It's the most important port on the northwest coast of Spain. So why are they not using it to defend the harbour now? They have not fired a single shot at us since we arrived.'

'Great stone-built fortresses do not arise overnight. Even now it's incomplete.'

He studied it and gave a nod of approval. 'It's well placed. It lies on a small island just off that peninsula on which the town is built. From land it can only be reached by a narrow causeway, easy to defend. Do you see? Originally a small chapel to St Anthony stood on the island, so the fortress is known as the Castillo de San Antón.'

'Our ships could attack it from the harbour, couldn't they?'

'Aye, they could. Have you noticed the strength of the fortifications on this side?'

From here I could see that the huge stone walls on the seaward side of the new fortress rose from the sheer rocky sides of the island, which looked impregnable.

'The unfinished fortress is of no real importance to us at present,' he said, 'since we've been told that the Spanish garrison has abandoned it in favour of the citadel formed by the walled upper town. They believe they can hold out in safety there, while the inhabitants of the lower town suffer our attack undefended. Our ships' guns could indeed attack the fortress from the harbour, but, as you can see, the strongest fortifications, already complete, are on the seaward side, since it's from this direction that they would expect attack.'

'So we will ignore it?'

'There is no point in wasting gunpowder and shot in taking it. There seems to be only a token garrison left there, if any.'

Later I heard that one small detachment of our soldiers had been deployed near the town end of the causeway, the most vulnerable part of the fortress. Here the walls were only partially complete, for the builders had not envisaged attack from the town. The lower courses were already laid in stone, but above this nothing yet protected the landward side of the fortress but roughly constructed wooden ramparts. If our soldiers had possessed siege guns, they would have made short work of taking possession of the *castillo*, but, as the captain had said, it was not worth the wasted ammunition. If any men of the garrison had been left there, they did not show their faces.

Even so, Drake and Norreys seemed bent on capturing Coruña itself, though the seizure and occupation of any Spanish town was no part of the expedition's orders from the Queen. Our goal was Portugal. Taking possession of a Spanish town could serve no purpose and would cost us dear. I could not imagine how our leaders could have any hope of taking the citadel and doubted their wisdom in lingering here at all. Why did we not sail on, immediately, for Lisbon?

In the meantime, the most urgent task was to reprovision the fleet. On the Portuguese ship we could only watch what happened once the men went ashore. This was no part of Dom Antonio's campaign of triumphant return to his kingdom. And we did watch. We watched, helpless, as our band of villains ran amok in Coruña. Instead of obeying orders and loading the boats with barrels of beef and fish and casks of wine and fresh water, that filthy rout of masterless men went berserk in the town. There were provisions a-plenty to be found, for it seemed the Spaniards had indeed been laying in supplies for a fresh Armada against England. Before an hour was out our gallant soldiers had smashed and murdered and burned their way to the wine and were reeling in drunken splendour through the streets, looting shops and churches, raping and cutting throats as they went. From the heights of the citadel the garrison fired down on them, but our men made no attempt to counter-attack. Some of them fell, wounded or dead, rolling in the gutters amongst the spilt wine and the piles of salted sardines. Their fellows let them lie, too intent on their own drinking and looting to care what happened to the wounded and dead.

We watched in horror from the rail of the *Victory*, but there was nothing we could do. Dr Nuñez sat on a water cask with his head in his hands, groaning and muttering to himself. Dom Antonio strode angrily from one end of the ship to the other, his drawn sword in his hand, slapping it from time to time against his thigh, while Dr Lopez trotted behind him, with soothing, meaningless words. He had donned a bejewelled breastplate, an ornamental thing of little military value, but with it he still wore his square physician's cap of purple velvet. Nothing could more clearly have spelled out our helplessness, our absurdity. This was an affair of Drake's, not ours, just one more episode in his long personal war of attrition with Spain.

Sir John Norreys seemed helpless, for he had lost control of our untrained mob of men, his experienced soldiers far too few to marshal them into any kind of order. Drake, meanwhile, was sending fire parties in amongst the ships in the harbour, most of which were careened or laid alongside the quays under repair. Within a few hours smoke was drifting across the water toward us from those ships his sailors had managed to set on fire.

I tried speaking to Captain Oliver, who had retired to his cabin, as if to mark his wish to have no part in what was happening on shore.

'Do you have any idea of how long we will be here, Captain?' I asked. 'If ever it is possible to get the men and the supplies back on board the ships?'

He gave me a bleak look. 'I was concerned from the start that we were encumbered with this rabble. I would send my own crew ashore to secure provisions, but I dare not risk their lives amongst those drunken louts. We will never be able to reprovision until they drink themselves into a stupor and we can send reliable men to load up what we need.' He grimaced. 'That may take several days.'

'But surely now Sir John will give up his plan of seizing the town,' I said.

'He has sent no signal to that effect.'

'But these men are incapable–'

'Aye, they are certainly incapable, but he has the experienced troops from the Low Countries.'

'Only about eighteen hundred men,' I said. 'Enough to take possession of the undefended lower town, I suppose, but not the walled citadel, the old town up on the hill. We have no artillery.'

'We have not,' he agreed, 'and the ships' guns have not the range to reach so far. The garrison up there does have cannon. They have been firing down on our men.'

'I have seen it. So what must we do?'

'Await the first opportunity to reprovision, then hope we can persuade Sir John to abandon this unnecessary diversion of capturing the citadel of Coruña. Sir Francis is likely to want to do what damage he can, to both ships and town, but I doubt he will want to be held up here by a long siege.'

'He would prefer to be at sea, hunting for the Spanish treasure ships.' I smiled. Drake's intentions were always easy to foresee.

He returned my smile, somewhat ruefully. 'Aye, he would.'

Speaking to Oliver was a wasted effort. The captain himself was no better informed than I was. I returned to the foredeck and joined the other watchers there.

There was nothing for it, then, but to wait on events and hope that Sir John would change his mind or that Drake would persuade him to leave Coruña as soon as the fleet was reprovisioned. An early departure would benefit the whole expedition. As for Walsingham's mission, in all this chaos, I could not see how I could make my way ashore and go in search of his agent Titus Allanby. I had been given very little information to guide me, apart from the fact that he was working as a tailor. I could see that it was a profession which might offer opportunities for gathering information.

Like most of the agents in the service, Allanby sent few details back to London about where he was living or even what he was calling himself, for fear that his reports might be intercepted. It was often necessary for agents to change addresses frequently and even to change their identity. Since Allanby had been working as a tailor, he was presumably living in the lower town and not up at the citadel, unless – it suddenly occurred to me – he had secured himself a position as a tailor to the military, which would have given him better access to the kind of information Walsingham would want him to seek out. It would be difficult enough for me to go ashore into the chaos of our soldiers' wild rampage through the streets of the lower town. To gain access to the citadel would surely be impossible. The one thing which might work in favour of my going into the town, although it was damaging to our expedition, was the continuing west wind which Drake had feared would drive us ashore on to the French coast. As long as it continued to blow so fiercely, and until we could round up our drunken troops and load our provisions, here we would stay in the harbour at Coruña. The longer we stayed, the more chance I might have of going ashore.

I would need to think of some reason which would convince either the captain of our ship or one of the senior army officers to authorise such a venture. Sir John Norreys had met me briefly the previous year in Amsterdam, when Andrew Joplyn and I had discovered the conspiracy to supply arms and transport barges to Parma's Spanish troops. I thought I had noticed a nod of recognition from Norreys when I had joined in the discussion about bypassing Santander and coming directly to Coruña. Perhaps, when he had managed to get the army under control, I should approach him. I could not tell him the details of my mission, for that must remain secret, but he knew I worked for Walsingham, and that might prove enough. Or I might think of some other reason for landing.

In the meantime, there was little I could do but wait and watch with the rest of the Portuguese party on deck. Norreys, in any case, had returned to his own ship before we reached Coruña and was probably now on shore himself, attempting to gain control over the rioting soldiers. He had been known for ruthlessness in his younger days, in particular against the Irish, but from all I had heard from discussions in Seething Lane, he conducted more orderly campaigns now. In any case, he would never sanction the kind of wild disorder we were witnessing in the town, which was a serious threat to his authority and that of his officers. I had seen some squadrons of the Low Countries troops disembarking and beginning to march through Coruña. I supposed they were attempting to round up such of the disorderly soldiers as were still on their feet and able to roll barrels to the quayside for ferrying out to the fleet. What the fate would be of the men lying insensible in the streets of the town, I could not imagine. Such flaunting of orders would normally call down the most severe of punishments, either flogging or even death, but so many of the soldiers were involved in the riotous behaviour that we could not afford to lose them all. Ever since the desertions at Plymouth, before ever we set sail, the number of our troops had been reduced below what had originally been planned.

Toward dusk some sort of order was beginning to be restored. A few barrels and sacks were loaded on to the vessels small enough to be able to moor at the quayside: skiffs and some of the smaller pinnaces. These then ferried the provisions out to the larger ships. A smell of cooking began to drift across the fleet. Either that, acting on hungry stomachs, or the actions of the professional soldiers, had brought some sort of discipline amongst a portion of the rabble. Others continued to roam the port. Soldiers from our own ship returned, dirty, smelling of drink and unsteady on their feet. Some, perhaps those caught in the worst acts on shore, were chained down below. The others were fed, harangued, but, for the moment, unpunished.

There was one fine Spanish galleon in the harbour, of the type Drake enjoyed sailing home to present to the Queen, laden with gold and silver from the Spanish conquests in the New World. I thought we should see Drake putting a crew aboard her, and sailing her across to join the rest of our fleet, once they had finished setting fire to the smaller, less desirable vessels in the harbour, but for some reason Drake had not acted swiftly to secure the galleon. I had been idly watching it, for it was less gruesome than watching the activities ashore, when I noticed half a dozen men leap from her to a skiff, row in haste to the quay, then run up the hill towards the citadel. Our soldiers paid them no heed.

Suddenly there was an explosion that seemed to rip the very air apart, and such a blast of wind did it make that I was knocked down and lay sprawling on the deck, unable to hear. For a few moments I was so dazed I did not know what had happened. One of the ship's officers pulled me to my feet and pointed across the harbour.

'That's a grievous loss in booty for us,' he said.

Where there had been a galleon there was now a mass of torn canvas, broken spars and burning timber. A vast cloud of dust and smoke and broken splinters of wood had risen up into the air from the wreck. It spread out over the whole harbour and fragments of debris began to rain down on us, amidst a choking smell of burnt tar and gunpowder. As I stood gaping, a forge-hot piece of metal landed on my left shoulder and I jumped about, shrieking, trying to shake it off, for it was burning right through my doublet and shirt to the skin beneath.

'Jesu!' I cried, 'I'm branded like a slave!'

The officer grabbed a marlinespike and knocked the metal off my shoulder. Where it landed on the deck it began to burn the wood until he managed to lob it overboard. As it hit the water it hissed and a gout of steam rose briefly from the sea.

'Are you hurt?' he asked, his face pale with horror.

I gasped. I was shocked and frightened. But for his quick action I would have been seriously injured.

'Not too badly.' I managed to keep my voice fairly steady, though my heart was pounding and I felt dizzy. 'It will be a nasty burn, but I'll fetch some salve.'

'You were fortunate it wasn't your head.'

I nodded. 'Aye.' I managed a weak laugh. 'Fortunate indeed.'

As I ran to fetch my satchel of medicines so that I could salve my shoulder quickly, I thought that 'fortunate' was an unfortunate choice of words. But I remembered Andrew, injured by a musket ball at the siege of Sluys, which had skimmed the side of his head, but killed the man standing behind him. He too had thought himself fortunate. Dame Fortune has sometimes an ironic touch when she spins her wheel. My clothes were charred in a round patch on my shoulder, and through the pain I could smell the very burn itself.

The stench of burnt human flesh is something you do not forget.

Chapter Six

Coimbra, Portugal, 1582

My mother and I had been in the prison in Coimbra several weeks and we thought the Inquisitors had forgotten us. Guards brought us food every day, enough to keep us alive, though we grew weak from the scanty diet and the lack of air and light. I realise now that they prefer their prisoners to remain alive, to make a greater spectacle at the auto-da-fè. If a prisoner dies while awaiting judgement, all that can be done is to throw his bones on the fire, which makes a poor show for the audiences, who flock in from miles around in the hope of gaining the great spiritual benefits they are promised from attending.

At last, however, they came for my mother. She had warned me that when it happened I must keep to the furthest and darkest part of the cell, in the hope that they had forgotten me. So when three guards came to take her for questioning, I did as I was bid, crouching down in the corner opposite Francesca, who blinked in the shaft of light which came in with the guards, weaving her head to and fro, trying to see if they brought Jaime with them.

The guards stripped my mother stark naked, and fondled her, and made lewd gestures. She crossed her hands over her breasts and hung her head so that her hair concealed her face. Then someone called from beyond the door and she was pushed out into the corridor. They did not take her far. The chamber for interrogation must have been close by, and they left the cell door ajar. Perhaps they thought Francesca too helpless to try to escape.

Or perhaps they did remember that I was there and took pleasure in forcing me to listen.

They have taken my mother away.
Screaming.
Again and again.
I wrap my arms around myself, as if by clutching my body I can somehow hold my soul there intact. For it is struggling to escape. If it can break free, if I can lose myself in death, the sound of the screaming will stop.
I cover my ears, but the screaming goes on.
My mother. My mother's voice pleading.
A horrible gurgling noise. Inhuman.
Chains rattling and the sound of water pouring.
I vomit into the refuse and the excrement that cover the floor.

I do not know what she said which eventually persuaded them to stop, for that day at least. Perhaps they had merely grown bored or tired. I had passed into a kind of coma myself, and I am sure hours had gone by before the same three guards dragged her back to the cell. She was too weak to stand and collapsed on the floor. They took it in turn, the three of them, two to hold her down while the third raped her. She tried to struggle, but she had no more strength than a cloth doll. When they finally left and barred the door at last, I rushed to her, weeping. I tried to dress her, but it was like trying to put clothes on a corpse. Francesca seemed to have returned for a time to her senses and watched with bright eyes.

'Don't worry, boy,' she said indifferently. 'She will grow used to it.'

Chapter Seven

Coruña, Spain, 1589

The landfall at Coruña, according to the original plan – or rather according to the second version of this plan – was for the sake of swift provisioning as well as firing the Spanish ships in the harbour, but we stayed there two interminable weeks. And for the first four days the new recruits continued to run riot. At last Norreys managed to muster the regular soldiers into some kind of order and set them to attacking the citadel. Drake, in overall command, had once again disobeyed the Queen's orders, but he clearly knew that if he brought back enough treasure, then, as so often before, she would forgive him. He was already losing sight of the original mission.

Lisbon! That was our goal, and it was as far away as ever. The main strategy of the whole expedition, which our leaders seemed to be choosing to forget, had been to sail *directly* to Lisbon, immediately after burning the Spanish fleet, in order to surprise the occupying Spanish garrison there, while Dom Antonio's loyal subjects would throw open the gates of the city, kneel at his feet, and welcome him with tears of gratitude. That was the plan, and as a result we carried no siege cannon, only light ordnance. There was nothing in the original plan about mounting a siege. So when the regular soldiers – those who had joined us from long experience against the Spanish in the Low Countries – when these soldiers were sent to take the citadel of Coruña, they had nothing but small arms.

They fought bravely, and paid for it. In the meantime, the gallant first-time volunteers were roaming the surrounding countryside, having wiped out most of the town of Coruña.

'That rabble,' Dr Nuñez told me, 'they have already jeopardised our mission. Soon they will destroy it.'

'What have they done now?' I asked, even though I dreaded to hear.

'They have triumphantly burned down a monastery and slaughtered those of the monks they could catch. And they have been feasting on the animals they've stolen from the nearby farms. They have been massacring peasants they have found hiding in the hedgerows.'

Even as he spoke, on the deck of the *Victory* we could watch the plumes of smoke from burning villages rising like vast umbrella pines to the heavens.

'What will happen to our own countrymen when these butchers reach Portugal?' I said. 'And it will not take long for news of events here to reach the Spanish court.'

Dr Nuñez grimaced. 'All hope of a surprise attack on Lisbon must have been lost by the end of our second day here at Coruña.'

The Dom and his master strategist, Ruy Lopez, were powerless. They had handed themselves over to Drake and Norreys, believing the agreed plan would be carried out. But Drake, as Sara Lopez had said on more than one occasion, was a pirate, and answered to no one when he was drunk on the prospect of looting. I was certain he did nothing to curb the behaviour of the rioting men, but used it as a cover for his hand-picked sailors to carry out more discriminating plunder on his own behalf. I believe Sir John Norreys gave his best endeavour, but not even he could mount an effective siege with his small number of trained but poorly armed soldiers, hampered by that much larger rioting crowd of vicious men.

And those trained soldiers were suffering injury and death in their futile attempt to attack the citadel with their inadequate weapons. In the end, after several days of desperate fighting, it was this which gave me the opportunity I was looking for. I sought out Dr Nuñez.

'I want to go ashore,' I said bluntly. 'Norreys's men are in need of medical care. I find it shameful to lurk here in safety aboard the ship, out of range of the Spanish cannon, when I could be relieving their suffering. Will you give me leave to go ashore and see what I can do to provide help?'

'How is your own injury?' he asked. 'Your shoulder? Surely it still pains you.'

'Aye, a little,' I lied, my hand stealing involuntarily toward my left shoulder. 'But it is healing.' I had smothered the burn with a cooling salve and left it open to the air at night, when it kept me awake with acute pain. During the day I covered it with a soft pad under my patched shirt and doublet.

'In truth, I should be glad of some occupation to distract me from thinking of it,' I said. 'There will be men amongst our besiegers who are suffering far worse, and we both know that the naval surgeons are much less skilled than we are, except in sawing off limbs. Let me go and see what I can do.'

He got up from the chair where he was sitting in the elegant cabin allotted to Dom Antonio. The Dom himself was presently relaxing under an awning on deck, reading, as if all that was happening on shore was of no concern to him.

'First,' Dr Nuñez said, 'let me show you what I have arranged.'

He led me out of the Dom's cabin to the slightly smaller cabin next to it, which he occupied, and opened the door. I had not been in here before, but I saw that it was fresh and airy, with a glass window open to the breeze, like a gentleman's study. Everything was in immaculate order, a few books on a shelf, his satchel of medical supplies hanging on a hook next to his physician's gown.

'Here,' he said, opening a door. 'This was storage space for spare linen and tableware used in the captain's and officers' cabins. I have had everything removed and stored elsewhere, and the shelves taken down.'

It was a narrow, windowless space, though there was a small grill opening through into the cabin to allow air to circulate. Perhaps it was sometimes used to store food. A cot had been fitted inside, filling most of the floor, though there was a hanging cupboard over the foot of the cot and a pisspot under it.

'It is a poor enough cabin for a gentleman physician,' he said, 'but perhaps you would be more comfortable here than in that fox's den you have made for yourself on deck.'

He was smiling and I smiled back, full of gratitude.

'I won't inconvenience you?'

'Not at all. I am more likely to inconvenience you, for Beatriz swears I snore like a pig.'

I laughed. 'So does my father.'

It took very few minutes to move my few possessions and my blankets into this cubbyhole, my blankets on to the cot, my clothes and books into the cupboard, apart from my gown, which I hung from a nail on the back of the door. I felt almost overwhelmed with relief. Here I would be safe and private.

Once I had arranged everything to my satisfaction, I found Dr Nuñez on deck and tried to thank him, but he brushed my words aside.

'Proper provision should have been made for you before, but I am afraid everyone has been caught up in other affairs,' he said. 'Now, about your request to help the soldiers attacking the citadel.'

'I may go?'

'Aye, but I shall come with you. Between us we should be able to offer some comfort to those poor fellows.'

I did not know whether to be glad or sorry. If he came with me, it would be much easier to go ashore and reach the men, but it would be difficult, or even impossible, for me to go looking for Titus Allanby in the town, or what was left of it. However, all I could do was go ashore and spy out the town as best I could. Later, I might be able to return alone.

We both equipped ourselves with our medical satchels and commandeered one of the *Victory*'s small attendant pinnaces to take us ashore. As we walked along the quay and stepped down on to the harbour paving, I realised that, for the first time in my life, I was walking on Spanish soil. It gave me a curious feeling, partly fear, partly a kind of exhilaration that I was nearer to fulfilling the first of my missions. Serving Walsingham had begun to work upon me once again and I was aware of a familiar sense of half-guilty excitement.

69

We had been given an escort of four trained soldiers, who led us a roundabout way through the cracked and broken streets to avoid the direct line of fire from the citadel's cannon mounted in the walled upper town. The lower town and port appeared deserted, yet I was aware of watching eyes. When I turned my head to seek them out, there was nothing but a kind of quiver in the air, which sent a tremor along my spine. Most of the inhabitants were dead or escaped into the surrounding country, but I was sure there were others hiding amongst the damaged buildings, the very old and very young, and those who would not abandon them.

Everywhere, there were bodies, lying disregarded in the roadway or glimpsed through the broken doorways as we passed. Men, women, and even small children. A few mangy dogs were scavenging in the kennels of the streets through which we were making our way. A black and white cat watched us, slit-eyed, from a window where the shutters had been half torn away. Some of the damage to the buildings was too severe to have been inflicted by our drunken soldiers, even if they had been carrying muskets. This was artillery damage. In firing down on our besiegers, the Spanish garrison was wreaking havoc on their own civilian town.

The streets were pitted and strewn with abandoned possessions – clothes and cookpots and broken crockery. I saw a single child's shoe, lying on its side next to a torn head veil. Somehow that shoe was more poignant than the derelict buildings. The air was thick with dust and the stench of gunpowder, trapped between the walls of the crowded houses by the heat. There had been a lull in the cannon fire when we came ashore, but now it started up again, so that instinctively we ducked and the soldiers hurried us on, past a church whose doors gaped open on a rubble-strewn interior, where the tower had collapsed into the nave. That was certainly not damage done by us. It could only be the result of heavy artillery.

At last, after a steep climb up through the rubble-strewn streets that left Dr Nuñez breathless, we reached the English outpost, securely placed close under an overhanging rock face, protected from the line of fire raining down from above. A group of soldiers came in just ahead of us, their faces patched with dirt, their clothes torn, and their eyes blank with exhaustion and a kind of dumb resignation. They knew that it was impossible for them to take the citadel by force against such superior fire power. All they could do was to try to wear down the garrison by making constant attacks and cutting off their supplies of food. Some of the soldiers carried muskets, the rest crossbows, and I saw that in one corner of their makeshift camp fletchers and smiths were at work making more arrows, quarrels and musket balls. Otherwise, their only attack artillery was some small ordnance the soldiers had sweated to carry up the hill to within the necessary close range of the citadel. Too close for safety. To be sent to man these guns was a death sentence, for the Spaniards could easily pick off the gun crews.

As we had expected, there were wounded men here who had not been able to return to the ships and Dr Nuñez and I were soon at work dealing with direct injuries from arrows and shot, and the many indirect, peripheral wounds from shattered stone flying from the impacts of cannon fire. There were several broken limbs as well, mostly caused by rocks falling from the walls, dislodged by shot, which we were not equipped to treat here in this makeshift camp. Dr Nuñez organised a relay of men to carry the more seriously injured to the harbour, though they would have a hazardous time of it, exposed in places, as we had been, to the guns of the citadel, and not easily able to dart out of the way.

The injuries I dealt with in the camp were similar to those of the soldiers brought back from the fall of Sluys, though, kneeling on the stony ground, with the sound of the cannon overhead, I felt that the crowded ward at St Bartholomew's was a haven of peace compared with this. My head rang with the constant explosions of cannon fire, so I understood how the sheer unremitting noise must exhaust men in battle and leave them without the will to carry on fighting. At least the wounds we found here were fresh and had not had time to become infected or gangrenous.

When we were done, and had passed the less seriously injured men as being able to continue on duty, Dr Nuñez and I started down through the shattered streets of the town again, accompanying the last stretcher carrying a man with a broken leg.

As we drew near the harbour, I stopped. I had caught the sound of sobbing from one of the few quayside cottages which was still partly intact. I laid my hand on Dr Nuñez's arm.

'There is someone in trouble there,' I said. 'It sounds like a child. I am going to see.'

'Nay, Kit! You must not! It could be a trap.'

'There are no Spanish soldiers here,' I said. 'They took care to flee to safety. And very few people. How can I come to any harm? When our soldiers have delivered the injured man to the boats, they can come back and protect me.'

He hesitated, uncertain. We could all hear the desolate crying. It was certainly a child.

One of the soldiers, one of the trained men from the Low Countries, said, 'We're not barbarians, like that rabble who wrecked the town. We don't make war on children.' He turned to me. 'We'll be back with you in no time, Doctor.'

Dr Nuñez was persuaded at last and they moved off to the quays where the boats and smaller ships were moored. I did not wait for the soldiers to return, but went to the doorway of the cottage. The door itself had been ripped from its hinges and lay on the ground at my feet.

'Is someone there?' I called out softly in Spanish. 'Do you need help?'

It was a fisherman's cottage, for there were traps and nets bundled up just outside the door. I could make out little in the gloom within, for we had spent a long time up at the camp and the evening was drawing in. Though I could see not see much, I could still hear the sound of a child crying, though an attempt had been made to suppress it, and it came to my ears now in spasms of gulps and gasps of drawn breath. As my eyes grew accustomed to the dimness, I made out three figures. In front of me crouched a girl in a torn dress, perhaps eight or nine years old, rubbing her face with the back of a dirty hand. In a corner a boy of about three sat on the ground staring vacantly into space, his mouth hanging open like an idiot child. There was another figure lying on the dirt floor behind the girl, and it was clear that she was trying to shield it from view.

I stepped inside the cottage and crouched down until I was in front of the girl, close to her, but not touching. I could see now that it was a woman lying behind her. At first I thought she was dead, but then she gave a low moan and began to writhe. The child uttered a low cry and spread out her arms as if to bar the way to the woman.

'Is it your Mama?' I said gently. 'Is she ill? I am a doctor. I'd like to help you if I can.'

She looked at me with eyes full of mistrust and did not answer.

'My name is Christoval. What's yours?'

'Teresa,' she whispered at last, reluctantly.

'And is that your brother?'

She nodded.

'What's his name?' It was like trying to gentle a frightened horse.

'Carlos.'

'And Mama is ill?'

Her eyes welled up with tears again. 'The baby won't come,' she said. 'And they killed Señora Perez, who makes the babies come. I don't know what to do. I think Mama is dying.'

I slipped the strap of my satchel off my shoulder and unbuckled the flaps.

'I'm sure I can help.'

Even as I spoke, she shrank away with a cry. Something had darkened the doorway. I glance over my shoulder and saw that the soldiers had returned.

'No need for you to stay,' I said in English. 'It is a woman in labour and two small children. You are frightening them. Go back to the camp.'

'You're sure?'

'Aye, there's nothing to fear here.'

I did not watch them leave, but the shadows vanished from the doorway and I saw the child Teresa relax a little. The boy continued to sit without moving.

'Do you have a lamp?' I asked. 'Or a candle? I need to see what Mama needs.'

'There is a lamp.' She got to her feet and fumbled about on a small table near the little boy. I heard her struggling with the flint and tinder but did not interfere. It was better for her to have something to do. At last she had the lamp lit, a rough pottery cruse with a wick floating in cheap oil, but it would serve. She handed it to me and I found a ledge for it above where the woman lay. I saw she was not directly on the floor but lay on a thin palliasse, not much more than two fingers thick.

'Now, Teresa, can you find me some water, and a cloth? Then I want you to bathe Mama's face and give her a drink. See how hot and tired she is? And I will see if the baby is ready to come.'

Once given something to do, the child stopped crying. She brought a bucket of water and a crude wooden cup and a cloth. While she tenderly bathed her mother's face and lifted her head so she could drink, I turned back the woman's skirt, which was soaking, and checked to see how far she was dilated. The baby was nearly ready to come, but it was clear the woman was almost at the end of her strength. I had feared that the baby might have been badly presented, but its head was in place. The woman lay inert and flaccid. Perhaps she was already dead. I was afraid I might have to cut the baby free, and I could not do that in front of the child.

Then the woman's body gave a convulsive shudder. It was still suffering contractions, though the woman seemed barely conscious.

'When did you last have something to eat?' I asked.

'Before the bad men came,' the girl said.

'Have you nothing? Something to drink? If we could give Mama some ale or some wine, it would make her feel better.'

'Paolo might have some.'

'Paolo?' I looked around. There was surely no one else in the cottage, which had only this one room, with a ladder to a loft above.

'Next door.'

She scrambled to her feet and darted out of the cottage. The woman arched her back and gave another low moan.

In a few minutes the child was back, carefully carrying another wooden cup in her two hands. 'Paolo gave me this.'

'He is your neighbour? He is coming?'

'He can't walk. The bad men beat him. But he says the wine is good. He had it hidden.'

It was a dark red. I dipped my finger in the cup and licked it. It had a fierce kick, but it should give the woman a little strength. With some difficulty I managed to get my arm under her shoulders and lift her enough so that she could drink. Her eyes flickered and she fixed them on Teresa, who knelt beside the palliasse, watching anxiously.

'You must drink, Mama. The doctor says so. Paolo sent you the wine.'

She drank, then. Some of it dribbled from the corners of her mouth down the front of her dress, but most of it went down her throat, in small gulps. She coughed a few times, but I could see it reviving her.

After that, everything happened very quickly. The woman had already borne two children, probably more, given the difference in age between the two here. The baby was ready to come and she had a little strength now, at least for a short time, to respond to the rhythmic convulsions of her body. It cannot have been more than half an hour later that the baby slithered into my hands, a girl. Healthy enough, though small. Teresa found a piece of torn blanket and I let her wrap the baby in it and hand her new sister to her mother.

When I had finished tending the woman, I got stiffly to my feet, after kneeling all this time on the earth floor, and gave Teresa a hug. 'You see, you are almost a doctor yourself. Now you must help Mama look after the baby. I will send you food.'

She smiled up at me, the smile transforming the pinched dirty face. 'You are good man, Doctor Christoval.'

'My friends,' I said, 'call me Kit.'

I packed up my satchel and swung it on to my shoulder.

'It is late now, and you must all sleep, but in the morning I will bring you food.'

As I ducked out under the low lintel of the door, I found Dr Nuñez sitting on a quayside bollard opposite the cottage. He looked tired, but alert.

'You should not have waited for me,' I said, stretching my arms above my head and flinching as my shirt caught the half healed burn on my shoulder.

'Oh, I have not been here all the time. I have been back to the *Victory*, and dined, and come ashore again. It was a woman in labour, was it?'

'Aye. Babies do not know to wait when a town is destroyed in battle and a siege is under way. Their midwife has been killed. By our soldiers. The child was terrified and the woman at the end of her strength. Is this how we make war?'

I felt bitter, feeling that I was tainted by association with this wicked violence.

He rose to his feet and we turned together to where we could board a boat to take us out to the *Victory*. After the incessant din of the daylight hours, the silence and the clear air felt like a blessing. The wind was still blowing from the west, bringing with it the fresh scent of the ocean. A few lights shone from some of the ships, with their reflections dancing in the waters of the harbour. Overhead the sky was blue-black and clear of cloud, so that the stars sparkled as vividly as the jewels on a monarch's robes of state.

'I care for this no more than you do,' Dr Nuñez said, 'but there is little we can do, we are in other men's hands.'

We climbed down into one of the skiffs moored at the end of the quay and a sleepy boatman began to row us out to the ship.

'One thing I can do,' I said, 'is to take that little family some food tomorrow. The child said they had eaten nothing since the bad men came. I thought we were supposed to be taking the food stockpiled for the Spanish navy, not leaving civilian children to starve. There was no sign of a father. I suppose he is either dead or escaped from the town.'

'Or joined the garrison.'

'Perhaps. But I think he was nothing but a poor fisherman. Probably dead. There is a man next door who has been so badly beaten by our soldiers that he cannot walk. I will visit him as well.'

'Have a care, Kit. You must ask for permission before you begin to act on your own.'

'I will ask the Dom himself, then. Let us see whether he has the compassion a ruler should possess.'

That night I slept in luxury in my tiny cabin. After so many uncomfortable nights on deck, the strenuous journey through the town to the English camp below the walls of the citadel, and delivering the baby in the fisherman's cottage, I fell into a deep restoring sleep free of dreams and woke late to find Dr Nuñez already gone from his cabin. After a hasty breakfast at the table where the ship's officers and gentlemen passengers took their meals, I sought out the Dom.

I found him on the forecastle, in conference with Ruy Lopez and Captain Oliver. Dr Nuñez was nowhere to be seen. I had to wait until I could interrupt them, but the Dom bent a condescending smile on me.

'Dr Nuñez has told us that you have done valiant work caring for our injured soldiers.'

I bowed my head slightly in acknowledgement.

'They are suffering a good deal, but so too are the few civilians left in the town, with whom – surely? – we have no quarrel.'

'I understand you assisted at a birth,' he said.

'Aye, a woman in one of the fisher cottages along the shore. It seems our men have murdered the town's midwife.'

He had the grace to look somewhat ashamed at this, so I pressed home my request.

'If you are agreeable, Your Grace, I should like to take food to the woman and her small children. And I am told there is a badly injured man in the next cottage, injured also by our soldiers. It was too late last night, but I should like to see if I can help him, or any others of the poor folk who are still left in the town.'

He considered for a moment, then gave a nod. 'I see no reason why you should not. It will demonstrate that our quarrel is not with the common people of Spain, who may be our friends in future. Our quarrel is with the overreacher Philip and his army.'

This was delivered in ringing tones, as if he saw himself already upon the throne and addressing the *Cortes*. That the desolation of the town was mostly the work of our own ungovernable army, I did not mention. I did, however, draw attention to another problem.

'Your Grace, there are many bodies lying unburied in the streets of the town. Some have been dead for several days now. If we are to remain here any longer, we ourselves risk disease from them. A burial party should be mustered to deal with the dead. It is not merely common humanity. It is an urgent necessity.'

Ruy Lopez eagerly supported me. He was well aware, as I was, what dangers could arise from the noxious fumes given off by the unburied dead. The Dom turned to the captain.

'Can you arrange it?'

'I will speak to Sir John,' he said.

I left them to their discussions and went in search of supplies to take on shore.

In the fisherman's cottage I found the woman propped up, with her back against the wall, nursing the baby, who looked the strongest of the family. Someone, probably Teresa, had washed and tidied the boy and cleaned the bed place, removing the bloodied covering of the palliasse and replacing it with another, threadbare but clean. I gave her a parcel of food to set out on the table while I examined the woman, who was in a better state than I had feared. She thanked me, stumbling over the words and clutching the baby tightly, but she was interrupted by Teresa exclaiming over the food.

'Fresh bread, Mama, see! And cheese and sausage and – what is this?' She held up a greasy packet.

'Some cooked meat,' I said. 'Mutton. I was not sure whether you would be able to cook fresh meat.'

'I can cook,' she said proudly. She was a different child now the fears of the night were over. I could see that she was well able to care for her mother.

'There are olives as well,' I said, 'and some dried plums. And here is a flask of small ale.'

Her eyes glowed as she held up the food for her mother to see. Even the little boy seemed more animated than before.

'Before you eat, Teresa,' I said, 'will you take me to Paolo? I want to see whether there is anything I can do for him.'

She looked longingly at the food, but led me willingly to the cottage next door, which was another almost identical, though even more bare of possessions.

'Paolo,' she said, 'this is the doctor who helped Mama. He says he can help you.'

I saw a big man seated on a stool beside the far wall, where he could lean against it for support. He clutched a heavy stick in his hand which I suspected he might have used to club me if I had tried to come here without Teresa. There was a dirty cloth wound round his head as a bandage, one of his cheeks was cut and bruised, the eye above it surrounded by blackened and yellow flesh. The stick, I guessed, was to help him walk, for his left leg, bare below his workman's tunic, was deeply slashed, almost certainly by a sword. The torn flesh was crawling with flies.

At a nod from me, Teresa slipped away and I drew cautiously nearer to the man.

'I am Dr Christoval Alvarez,' I said. 'Thank you for the wine last night. It gave Teresa's mother enough strength for the final effort.'

He grunted. 'The babe will survive?'

'Aye, she's strong and healthy.'

'So were we all before you came.'

'I am no part of what has been happening here.'

'You're Portuguese,' he said. 'I can tell from the way you speak.'

'I was. I live in London now, where my father and I serve at a hospital for the poor.'

'So what are you doing here?'

'I'm a physician, as I said, and I would like to help you if I may. Has anyone looked at those injuries?'

'Not likely, is it? If you want, you can.'

He leaned his stick against the wall and began to unwind the dirty cloth from his head.

For the next hour we exchanged few words as I cleansed and treated his wounds. The head injury was unpleasant, but relatively clean. The sword slash needed stitching. The black eye and the cut cheek, once salved, could be left to heal. Through it all he endured the pain stoically, only grunting a few times.

When I had finished, I unloaded the rest of my basket, for I had kept some of the food for the injured man. He merely nodded his thanks, but I saw the gleam of hunger in his eyes. As he fell upon the bread, tearing off great chunks and stuffing them into his mouth, I packed up my satchel and spoke casually, not looking at him.

'Do you know of a tailor in the town, by the name of Titus?'

It was a risk, but I would have to take risks if I was to find Walsingham's man.

He considered, chewing the bread, then breaking off a piece of cooked mutton and studying it, before it followed the bread into his mouth.

'No tailors in this part of town.' He spoke through the food. 'Folk down here, the women make their clothes. Men like me, who don't have a woman, buy from the market stalls or trade with a neighbour.'

'But there are tailors?'

'Up there.' He jerked his head, indicating the higher parts of the town. 'Where the rich folk live.'

His expression showed his opinion of rich folk.

'Not living safe inside the walls, not if he's a tailor, you may be sure. But just outside. There's a street of tailors' shops near the wall of the old town. So the great folk need not soil their satin shoes by walking far to place their orders.' He leered at me, so I could see the fragments of meat and bread sticking to his strong teeth. 'Though for all I know, those people may summon the tailors to their houses and not stir a step. There's likely no one left there now.'

He threw a handful of olives into his mouth, then spat the stones, one by one, on to the dirt of the floor. 'Portuguese like you, is he? Titus an't a Spanish name.'

'I know very little about him,' I said cautiously.

He considered a moment. 'I did hear, two-three weeks ago, some craftsmen were sent for to go up to the citadel. Carpenters and such. Don't know if they wanted tailors.'

There was a note of contempt in his voice. To a working fisherman, a man who plied a needle could hardly be called a man.

I left the basket and the remains of food with him, and made my way to the top of the lower town, just below the walls, to the quarter where he said I would have found the tailors before the town was ransacked. There was still occasional firing from the citadel, but it seemed they were saving their gunpowder for the next assault by the English troops. Nevertheless, I did my best to keep walls and buildings, such as were still standing, between me and the line of fire. As far as I could see, our own troops were lying low as well, for it was nearing the heat of midday, when it would be exhausting to make an attack. They would probably wait until the cool of the late afternoon.

The lower town, however, was not deserted. Burying parties had been sent into the streets, so the captain must have spoken to Sir John about the danger from unburied corpses. The men appeared to be some of the untrained soldiers, under the command of experienced officers. All of them had cloths tied around their faces as some small protection from stench and disease. They had good reason, for the merciless sun was turning the town into a charnel house.

I was sweating profusely by the time I reached the quarter where Paolo said the tailors had their premises. This street was not so badly damaged as some. Like the English camp, it was protected by an out-thrust spur of rock from the cannon fire. Nor had it been much troubled by our looting soldiers. Most of the food and drink would have been down near the harbour, either in the naval warehouses or the town market. There would have been few portable valuables to be found here either. Churches had gold and silver candlesticks and crosses and church plate. Wealthy houses, if the soldiers had managed to find any, would have yielded all manner of small, rich items. Here in this street there was little but the tools of the tailors' trade, and I could not imagine one of the looters carrying off a heavy bolt of cloth when he could pocket a gold and silver pyx worth a hundred times its value.

The shops were mostly intact, but deserted. I went from door to door, knocking and calling out in Spanish, but got no reply. I was near to giving up when I met an old woman stumbling up the steep street with a string of onions. When she saw me, she clutched them to her breast like a precious child. I held up my hands, palm out, conciliating.

'I mean you no harm, Señora,' I said. 'I am looking for a man called Titus. Someone told me he lived near here.'

She glared at me suspiciously, as if she did not believe me, but when I made no move to steal her onions, her face eased a little.

'Señor Titus, aye, he lived here until a few weeks ago. He's with the garrison, lucky bastard. Sent for to make new uniforms before the foul heretics came.'

'He's up in the citadel now?'

'He will be, unless he ran away, like every able-bodied man in this part of the town, the cowards. They left those of us who couldn't run to fend for ourselves.'

There was no answer for that.

'Do you think I could gain admission to the citadel?'

'I don't see why you should.' She was looking suspicious again. 'None of us can, the poor townsfolk. It's only the rich folk up there. Who are you, anyway?'

'I'm a physician, and I have a message for Titus, but I could offer my services to aid their wounded.' I paused, thinking fast. 'Do you know the name of the commander?'

'Why should I?' She shrugged. 'No concern of mine. A crowd of cowards, that garrison, just like the men who ran from the town. They went dashing for the citadel the moment they saw *El Dracque*'s flag, like a flock of sheep running from a wolf, leaving the rest of us to face the heretics and die.'

She glared at me. She still wasn't sure whether I might be one of the heretics, despite the fact that we were speaking Spanish.

'The only name I know is Captain Pita,' she conceded at last. 'He has a house in the upper town. Through there.' She gestured to where the tailors' row ended and a heavy gate closed the way through the substantial walls. 'His wife, Señora Maria, orders garments from the tailors here. I know her by sight. I haven't seen her since the invasion, so I suppose she's with her husband in the citadel for safety.'

'Are you a tailor yourself?' I asked, though I knew most tailors were men.

She snorted and gave a toothless grin. 'Do I look like a tailor? I clean and cook for two of them, or I did. I'm living in one of their houses here, with my old father, since our house was smashed by our own guns.'

I thanked her, though I was not sure for what. The information that Titus Allanby was probably in the citadel was bad enough news. I had the name of one officer, but I hardly believed that would enable me to find my way in. As I turned and started to make my way back down to the harbour, I thought of how Andrew Joplyn and I had broken into the locked storehouse in Amsterdam last year. That was no more than a child's game compared with trying to gain access to the citadel of Coruña. I would have been glad of Andrew's help now, but if he had joined the expedition at Dover, or with the soldiers coming over from the Low Countries, I had seen no sign of him.

I took an indirect route back to the ships, in case the old woman was watching. There was no harm in taking precautions. I might need to come this way again. From here I could explore the perimeter of the walled citadel, where, soon, I would try to bluff my way in.

Chapter Eight

*A*fter our first visit to care for the injured soldiers besieging the walled upper town, Dr Nuñez and I went every day. Sometimes I went alone. On those occasions, before I returned to the ship I explored the perimeter of the wall, clambering over fallen masonry and awkward corners of rock where the walls had been built to take advantage of the steep terrain. Although it had now become a citadel for the embattled garrison, it also enclosed the homes of the richest citizens, located up here where the breezes from the ocean would mitigate the heat of a Spanish summer and where the delicate noses of wealthy merchants and their families would not suffer the stench of the fishing fleet and the commercial harbour from which their wealth was drawn.

It was an ordinary town wall which encircled this upper part of Coruña, not very high, not very new, not the wall of a great fortress like the one being erected on the island. Moreover, as the town had grown over the years, forming an outer ring of houses and businesses outside the original settlement, the wall had not always been maintained in perfect condition. The English attack was being concentrated on one of the weaker portions, to one side of the main gate. I found that there were others. Here and there private citizens had knocked through the wall to extend their own properties. And apart from that main gate, which I had seen from the street where the tailors had their shops, there were three postern gates. All of these were guarded, but by only a handful of soldiers, since it was clear that our small attacking force was being deployed in full strength against the weak area of the fortification, where they had already done some damage with their small portable cannon. It was there that all the fighting was taking place.

It would not be possible to gain entry through one of the guarded posterns, but if I could somehow manage to trick my way inside the citadel, it might be possible to leave through one of them, or through one of the private properties. One, in particular, had drawn my attention. The substantial house was three storeys high and thus projected above the top of the wall. At some not very recent time the owners had knocked down a portion of the town wall in order to extend their garden out beyond it another fifty yards or so. The stones salvaged from the town wall, with additions, had been used to build a wall around this extended garden, and the garden wall was a good three feet lower than the original town wall. I reckoned I could climb it. If I could get into the citadel, if Titus Allanby were there, if I could find him, then we might succeed in making our escape that way.

There remained the unlikely prospect of entering the citadel without being killed by either our own forces or the enemy's. Walsingham's instructions were always to keep our activities secret unless absolute necessity drove us to take someone into our confidence. In this case, I decided that I must confide in Sir John Norreys. If he agreed that I should make the attempt to reach Titus Allanby, he could order the English troops not to fire on me as I approached the citadel. Everything else would rest with me.

I decided that I must also explain to Dr Nuñez what I planned, for if I did not return, it would be up to him to tell my father. Having made up my mind, I had one of the skiffs row me over to Sir John's ship, the *Nonpareil*. Fortunately, he was aboard and agreed to see me at once in his cabin. When I had explained what Walsingham had asked me to do, and how I meant to go about it, he ran his fingers through his beard. He was still wearing his helmet, having just returned from the camp. Taking it off and setting it on a table, he scrubbed at his sweat-stained hair.

'It is a mad scheme, but it might just work.' He cast an approving eye at me. 'I like young men who show some courage and imagination. You have done so before. You say you can pass for Spanish?'

'I am sure I can. I grew up speaking Spanish as easily as Portuguese.'

'Hmm. Well, I suppose it is worth a try. But you understand, do you not, that if they suspect that you are a spy you will be tortured, probably killed?'

I swallowed. Of course I understood that, but I had been closing my mind to it, knowing that the knowledge would undermine my resolve.

'I understand,' I said. 'But I shall go in as a doctor, unarmed. And I shall treat their wounded, you may be sure. I cannot forget my calling, even amongst the enemy.'

'I suppose you must, to maintain your disguise, though I would have you not treat them too well. The more wounded there are, the fewer remain to fight against our men.'

I kept my tongue behind my teeth. I would treat the men because they were in pain, not simply to maintain my disguise. And I would not stint my care of them.

'When do you want to make the attempt?'

'Tomorrow,' I said. Best to act while my courage was fresh. 'At first light.'

'I will send the order now. You will not be able to say when or how you will return.'

'Nay.'

When I reached the *Victory* again, I sought out Dr Nuñez and told him what I was going to attempt, swearing him to secrecy.

His face had gone very white and he laid his hand on my arm.

'This is a very dangerous enterprise, Kit.'

'It may be that the Spanish garrison will not admit me at all. Or if they do, I may not find Titus Allanby. He may not even be there.'

'And how do you expect to leave, in company with another? They will not allow you to walk out of the gates.'

I explained about the house with the low garden wall. 'Look, you can almost see it from here.'

As usual we were standing on the foredeck, and I pointed up at the citadel. 'There, off to the left of the town walls. Can you see where it bulges out a little, just before it turns round to the south? That is the garden.'

He screwed up his eyes and shook his head. 'Nay, I can't see it. But I will keep a watch on that part of the wall and send up my prayers for you.'

I rose before dawn the next morning and was taken ashore over the dark waters of the harbour. The birds on land were already awake and singing. On a post at the end of the quay a cormorant watched us come alongside, and only raised itself lazily into flight as I stepped ashore. I wore nothing which would identify me as coming from the English invading force, merely my usual somewhat nondescript doublet, breeches and hose, with my physician's satchel. Before approaching the fortified main gate of the citadel, I took care to advance in a roundabout way, having first taken the precaution of checking that the soldiers in our camp had received the order not to shoot me.

While I was exploring the area around the citadel during the previous few days, I had noticed that there was a postern gate at the top of a precipitous path which descended to the sea, not to the main harbour but to a narrow bay on the opposite side of the island on which the new *castillo* stood. Even as I had watched from the higher ground early yesterday morning, I saw a pinnace pulling away from the end of the path leading down from the postern, where there was a wooden jetty. So it was evident that the garrison was not entirely cut off. Supplies were being brought in by night. Our armaments were inadequate to take the citadel by force and there was clearly no possibility of starving them out while they could be supplied thus clandestinely. The siege was as pointless as I had always supposed.

I had given some thought as to how I could approach the fortress without being shot on sight. It would be obvious to any watchman that I was unarmed, but a nervous sentry might not care to take the risk. Shoot first and ask questions afterwards. Therefore I had provided myself with a large square of white cloth, the universal emblem of peace, and could only hope that the Coruña garrison would interpret it accordingly. I felt physically sick as I stepped on to the broad street leading up to the main gate of the citadel. At that moment my plan did not seem like courage but an act of gross stupidity. My heart was pounding so hard it that it dulled my sense of hearing. I could, I suppose, have abandoned the search for Titus Allanby as impossible and stayed aboard the *Victory* until Drake and Norreys decided to leave Coruña, but at the back of my mind I was haunted by the memory of Mark Weber.

Last year, Walsingham had sent me in search of one of his agents, Mark Weber, who had gone missing in Amsterdam. I had found Weber, it was true. But he was already dead. Although by all the signs he had probably been killed before ever I reached Amsterdam, yet I could not quite shake off the feeling than somehow, if I had been able to find him sooner, he might still be alive. I did not want the same fate to befall Titus Allanby. He had reported to Walsingham that he feared he might have come under suspicion. Had he still been in the town when we arrived, he would probably have contrived to reach one of the ships. Since he had not, it seemed that what the old woman had said must be true, that he had been summoned to the garrison before we reached Coruña and was still there. That summons might have a quite innocent explanation. Or it might mean that the officers of the garrison were indeed suspicious and wanted him under their eye, where he could not pass information to England.

I took my stand some yards from the gateway, holding up my white cloth. There was no reaction at all from the fortress. No figures appeared on the walkway above the gatehouse. No cannon was swung down to take aim along the street. No musket or crossbow was thrust out from one of the firing positions on the ramparts.

I took a step forward.

Nothing.

Two more steps. Three. Four.

Suddenly there was the twang of a crossbow, and a quarrel, fast and deadly, whined over my head like a monstrous bee. Instinctively, I ducked, but far too late if the bolt had been aimed at me. Whoever was shooting had aimed deliberately over my head. It was a warning.

I stopped. What should I do? If I advanced further, the bowman might aim lower and I would have no chance. I wore no armour. A crossbow bolt at this range would pierce me from breast to back and I could not live more than a few minutes. It was too far away to shout, to explain why I had come. I could turn tail and walk away. Or I could go on.

Holding my white cloth above my head, I went on.

Another bolt shot over me and this time I thought I really would vomit, but I kept walking in a kind of numb trance, until I was near enough to make myself heard.

'Don't you see my white flag?' I shouted. 'I am a doctor. The English have allowed me to come through.' This time I was careful to speak in highly educated Spanish, allowing no trace of a Portuguese accent to creep in. 'I have come to help tend the wounded.'

It was a dangerous ruse, but I was counting on that disorganised and panicked rush to the citadel when they had first seen *El Dracque*'s standard. There might have been one resident physician in the island fortress before the garrison abandoned it, but had he fled here with the soldiers? There would have been no time to organise adequate medical care. If I was lucky, there might not even be a single physician with the soldiers.

No one answered, but there were no more shots over my head as I covered the rest of the distance to the gate. Confronted by the massive double doors of the gatehouse I stopped and waited, hoping that someone was fetching an officer. At length, a voice called from above. I stepped back and tilted my head. A man leaned over the parapet, wearing the distinctive helmet of a Spanish soldier, with its almond-shaped crown and curled brim.

I repeated what I had said before, holding out my arms on either side, so that he could see that I wore no sword and carried no musket.

Even at this distance his suspicious frown was clear to see, but he did not immediately dismiss me. I could feel the pulse beating in my throat and I had to concentrate hard not to let my hands tremble.

'Very well, we'll have a look at you.'

After a moment, the wicket gate opened in one of the heavy doors and I was allowed through. I was inside. It might not be so easy to get out again.

I tucked my white rag into my belt and followed the soldier who gestured to me to cross to the base of a stair which must lead up to the wall-walk. A man was coming down, the man who had spoken to me. He looked me up and down.

'You are over young for a physician.'

At nineteen I no longer considered myself so very young to be practising medicine, but I suppose my smooth cheeks made me look younger. I laid my hand on the buckles of my satchel. Immediately the other soldier leapt forward and grabbed both of my arms from behind.

'I was merely going to show you the implements of my calling,' I said mildly. I must remain calm and pleasant, and show no fear.

The officer – for he was clearly an officer – stepped forward and unbuckled the straps of my satchel himself. He poked about amongst the contents, then stood back and nodded to the soldier.

'Release him. He is carrying nothing but a physician's equipment.'

The man let go of my arms and with shaking hands I buckled the straps again.

'I have been treating the injured in the town,' I said. 'Not that there are many people left. And I was told my help might be needed here. A woman who knows Captain and Señora Pita said I should come.' It was near enough the truth to carry conviction.

The officer relaxed. He nodded to the soldier to leave. 'Follow me,' he said.

They did indeed need medical help and my luck was in. There was no other physician with the garrison. If there had been any physicians resident in the upper town, they must have fled with the other deserters. The officer took me to a run-down cluster of buildings which had served as their old quarters before the new fortress was built. There was a central building, a small, squat keep, surrounded with outbuildings – stables, kitchens, an armoury from which could be heard the ring of mallet on iron. Their injured were laid out in the hall of the keep with no one to tend them but a few women – ladies, rather, officers' wives, I assumed, who were willing enough but had no idea of how to care for men with bullet wounds. Our English attackers might be lightly armed, but they had certainly been able to inflict injuries. I rolled up my sleeves, called for boiled water and raw wine to clean the wounds, and set about my work.

I had no objection to treating these men, even if they were Spaniards and our enemies. A wounded man is a wounded man whatever his nation, and my calling was to care for the sick and wounded. The injuries I treated here were identical to those I had been treating in the English camp, bullet and crossbow wounds for the most part, and the men were suffering the same pain. Some were delirious with the heat and their wounds. As part of my plan, I had deliberately carried no bandages with me, so once bullets had been extracted and wounds cleaned and salved, I asked the women to find me cloth for bandages. They seem puzzled, looking about them as if they expected to find cloth ready to hand.

'Do you have seamstresses?' I asked. 'Perhaps your sewing women will have something we can use?'

I knew it would be unlikely. But then one of the women spoke – I had learned by now that she was that very Señora Maria Pita of whom the woman with the onions had spoken.

'There are no seamstresses here,' she said. Her voice was contemptuous. A fool of a physician could not be expected to know that ladies would not bring their women servants to the citadel. 'But there are two tailors who were engaged in making new uniforms before the attack came. They may have something you can use.'

'Could someone perhaps take me to them?' I asked humbly. 'Then I can see for myself whether there is anything suitable.'

'Come with me.'

She strode ahead of me out of the keep, ignoring the sound of cannon and musket fire which had started up more intensively than ever from somewhere behind us and over to the right, where I knew the weakened area of the wall lay. The woman might be arrogant but she was courageous, marching across the open courtyard where occasional arrows and crossbow bolts from the English besiegers were falling. She led me to one of the outbuildings backed into the town wall and flung open the door.

Two men looked up, startled.

'You see,' she said, on a note of pride, 'even under siege we keep up the work of the garrison. These men are busy making

91

new uniforms for the soldiers to replace those damaged in the fighting.'

'Indeed,' I said. I turned to the men. Which of them was Titus? If he was here? 'I am Dr Christoval Alvarez, physician. I am treating the wounded and I need some light-weight cloth to use for bandages. Such as you might use for shirts.'

I did not look round, but I was aware that the woman had left.

'Luis de Cantor,' the older man said, standing and offering me his hand. 'Aye, we have some shirt cloth you can have.' He walked through into a back room, where I could hear him moving bolts of cloth.

'And you are?' I asked the other man.

'Titus Mendes,' he said, keeping his face bent over his stitching.

'Not Titus Allanby?' I said softly in English.

At that his head snapped up and his mouth fell open.

'Quickly,' I said. 'There isn't much time. I have come from Walsingham to fetch you out of here. Meet me at dusk in the southeast corner of the citadel. There is a large house there. Three storeys. The only one that large. Wait near there.'

He had just time to nod when Cantor came back with half a bolt of shirt cloth.

'That is excellent,' I said. 'Just what I need.' I bowed my thanks to him, ignoring Allanby, and returned to my wounded.

I had hoped that the day would proceed as previous days had done, with a relatively ineffective exchange of fire between the garrison and the besiegers. I would then meet Allanby at dusk and proceed to the next part of my plan. Unfortunately, Norreys had other intentions for that day. Unknown to me, he had decided upon an all-out assault on the half-demolished section of the wall, in the hope of breaching it. The English troops would throw everything they had at this least defensible side of the citadel. Everything they had in their armoury consisted of nothing more than muskets, crossbows and fire-arrows, with the two very small cannon unloaded from one of the armed pinnaces and man-handled up the steep hill. These small cannon could do little damage at that distance, but they would give courage to the soldiers, who would need to rush the breach and attempt hand-to-hand fighting. A few of the smaller ships would try to provide some fire-power from the inner end of the harbour, where the larger ships could not go, but their guns would barely reach so far. If they did, they would be in danger of hitting our own men.

It was only the suddenly increasing noise late in the afternoon that alerted me to what was happening. Soon more wounded men were being brought in. One of the ladies, less squeamish than the others, stayed with me, ripping the shirt cloth to make bandages and wrapping the dressed wounds under my direction. Most of the others had retreated to the upper floors of the keep. We could hear their occasional shrieks echoing down the stairs. Señora Maria – to give her her due, she was no coward – had gone out again into the main courtyard, behind the defending troops, where her own husband was among the fighting men and where she could reload muskets for them.

The constant fighting and the roar of cannon and the crack of musket fire deafened us even inside the keep and showed no signs of diminishing. The garrison servants themselves were out there, behind the crumbling rampart, and I saw the tailor Luis run past, a pike in his hand. I saw nothing of Titus, but thought what a fine irony it would be if he and I died here on the Spanish side, at the hands of English soldiers. When there was a brief respite from my work with the wounded I stepped outside the keep and saw that the darkening sky was lit up by flames, where the English troops had shot fire arrows into the timber houses near the wall and set them alight.

At that moment I heard a howl of grief, and saw Señora Maria bending over a man lying on the ground, a pike still clutched in his hand. Around him the Spanish troops wavered. They were no longer firing muskets. Either they had run out of shot or a decision had been made to reserve all the gunpowder for the cannon, the weapons which must, inevitably, tip the balance of the battle in favour of the Spanish.

'It is her husband, Captain Pita.' A voice at my elbow. The woman who had been assisting me. 'They are very devoted. Is he dead?'

From the crossbow bolt lodged in his head there could be no doubt. I nodded. Why must men rip each other apart in war? We bring them into the world and when they grow to manhood, this obscenity is what they wish on each other. What was the point of this battle? We should have been gone from here days ago. The purpose of the expedition had been to place Dom Antonio on the throne through the loyal support of his people. Yes, we would burn Spanish ships on the way, but ships are nothing but wood and iron and canvas. This slaughter was never meant to happen. On the other side of that crumbling, burning rampart our own men were dying, just as men were dying in front of me.

The woman suddenly gripped my arm. 'Look!'

Señora Maria had wrested the pike from her dead husband's hand and climbed on to a pile of rubble which had fallen in from the wall. Across the gap in the defences a young English soldier, an unarmed standard-bearer, was holding aloft the banner of Dom Antonio. Maria Pita lunged at him with the pike, striking him deep in the neck, just where one of the major arteries lies. I caught sight of his startled look before he fell backwards and vanished from sight. The woman had retained her hold on the pike and now raised it in the air.

'Anyone who has honour, follow me!' she cried.

After a moment's shock, the defenders crowded in behind her and I heard another boom from the cannon. As long as the Spanish had cannon balls and gunpowder, there was little chance the English troops could take the citadel.

The other woman had gone from my side. Despite the fire, which continued to burn, it was growing dark. I had seen nothing of Titus. He might be dead or caught up in the fighting, but it was now that I had arranged to meet him. The southeast corner of the town wall was well away from this fighting by the partial breach in the wall. I hoped that meant even the soldiers who had been patrolling beside the postern gates in that far part of the town would have been drawn to the defence of the weakest part of the citadel.

I had had no chance to explore the town in order to find my way to the house I had picked out from the outside of the wall, and it was growing darker every minute. All I had to provide me with any sense of direction was the light given off by the burning buildings, which must lie almost diametrically opposite the position of the house. With this as my sole guide, I set off running through unfamiliar streets, my satchel flapping at my side, passing darkened houses and stumbling over broken cobbles. As I ran, I realised two things. Many of the inhabitants of the upper town were probably still here, but lying low in their unlit houses, for fear of attracting the attention of the attackers. And the streets were so damaged not from cannon fire – our little cannon could never have reached this far. Nay, the best rounded cobbles had been prised up to be shaped into cannon balls. Even as I came to this conclusion I tripped over one of the holes in the street and came down on my knees, my ankle twisted under me.

Cursing, I scrambled to my feet again. I had certainly sprained my ankle, for pain shot up my leg at every steps I took, but I was sure it was not broken. However, it was going to hamper me.

At last I saw the tall house looming ahead against the night sky. I stopped to catch my breath. My heart was pounding and I must wait and think calmly. I had not been able to detect from the outside of the town how the garden was reached from this side. There might be a way into it from the street, or – and this was what I feared – the only entrance might be from the house itself. Now that I was on the far side of the town from the fighting, the fires could only be seen as a distance glow. There was no more than a sliver of moon tonight, and that little was hidden most of the time behind cloud. The house in front of me was dark like all the others, but that did not mean it was unoccupied.

Something moved over to my right. I laid my hand on my small dagger, the only blade I carried, then I risked a whisper.

'Is that Titus?'

'Aye.' A shadow drifted toward me. 'I do not know who you are.'

The tone was reserved. He had every right to be suspicious. Had he not seen me welcomed by the Spanish garrison and working all day amongst their injured? I wondered whether he carried a sword.

'I am Christoval Alvarez,' I said in English. 'Kit. I work as a code-breaker with Thomas Phelippes.' My voice was no more than a breath. 'Sometimes Sir Francis uses me for other missions. As I was coming with Drake's expedition, he asked me to try to find you and bring you out.'

I racked my brains to find some way of reassuring him. We must not stand here much longer, whispering in the street. How long before my absence from the soldiers' bedsides was noticed, and someone began to question my all-too-opportune appearance? Then I remembered Titus's last despatch to Walsingham, which I had been shown.

'Listen,' I said, and quoted to him the first few sentences of his despatch, as well as I could remember them.

There was a stirring in the shadows, which I hoped was Titus relaxing.

'We can easily climb over the outside wall of the garden behind this house,' I said, trying to ignored the pain in my twisted ankle. 'But I'm not sure how easy it will be to get into the garden from this side.'

'There is a gate just behind me here,' he said, 'but it is locked.'

I moved closer. I could just make him out now, and behind him an ornate, gilded gate of the kind often seen leading to noblemen's houses. This was an even grander place than I had imagined, perhaps the home of the town mayor or the governor of the province. The gate was indeed locked, as I quickly ascertained, but the scrolls and bars of the ironwork offered easy footholds for climbing. Without saying anything further to Titus, I seized hold of the gate and began to hoist myself up. Every time I put my weight on my right foot I nearly cried out from the pain, but I clenched my bottom lip between my teeth and continued up until I reached the top. There I paused for a moment, then eased myself down the other side, not daring to jump on to my damaged ankle. While I caught my breath, I could hear Titus climbing over behind me and dropping down from the top of the gate.

I looked around to get my bearings. At the far end, on the left, I had noticed that the wall was stepped down and lower than the rest of its length, but the land beyond fell away in a steep, rocky cliff. If we tried to go that way there was a danger we might fall. We would have to attempt the higher portion. It was lower than the town wall, but still a considerable height. Over to the right there was a shrubbery up against the wall. That might give us some purchase.

I did not speak, but pointed that way and Titus nodded. I realised I could see him now because the cloud had cleared, letting a little fitful moonlight shine down on us. It made it easier for us to see our way, but it also meant anyone looking out from the house would also be able to see us. We began to run softly across the garden, which was laid out in the very formal Spanish style, with a geometric pattern of gravel paths, interspersed with beds of flowers and herbs. We dared not step on the gravel, so we had to make our way awkwardly across the beds, trampling down the plants. It would be all too clear in the morning where we had been.

Halfway across, Titus grabbed my arm and halted me.

'What's the matter with you? Are you lame?'

'Twisted my ankle on the way here.' I spoke through gritted teeth, for the pain was getting worse and it was a long way back to the ships.

'Can you climb the wall?'

'Needs must,' I said, and set off again.

Somehow we reached the wall at last. I was right. A large bush of yew grew up against the wall, enabling us to reach nearly halfway to the top of the wall by scrambling up its branches. Titus now insisted on going first and I happily gave way. He was not some helpless civilian. As one of Sir Francis's agents, he would know how to look after himself. When he reached the top of the wall I was already seated in the upper branches of the bush. Without speaking he pointed out hand-holds to me and when I came within reach he grabbed my wrists and hauled me up the last few feet. As we sat on the top of the wall, assessing the far side, a light came on in the house. I tapped his arm. Perhaps we had not been as quiet as we thought, crossing the garden.

'Jump,' he said, 'I'll break your fall.' And he jumped down to the ground below the wall.

I dared not risk it. Painfully I began to feel my way down, until I felt him grip me around the waist.

'Now,' he breathed.

I slithered down the last few feet and managed to land with my weight on my left foot.

'Thank you,' I whispered, disengaging myself and hoping he had not felt the shape of my body too clearly in those few moments. 'This way.'

'I know where we are now. This isn't far from an alley that runs through to my street.'

I let him lead the way, limping along behind. When we reached the street of tailors' shops, he stopped.

'There are some things it would be wiser not to leave behind,' he said. 'I'm going into my house for a few minutes. You can go on ahead.'

I shook my head. 'If you can give me something for a bandage, I'll strap my ankle before we go any further.'

'Some shirt cloth?'

'Aye.'

We both laughed. It was relief at having escaped from the citadel, but there was still a long way to go, down through the dark and dangerous streets of the town. When we reached it, we found that Titus's house had been broken into and stripped of every crumb of food. I realised I was suddenly hungry, for I had eaten nothing since leaving the ship before dawn. He was able to find me some cloth for a bandage and while I strapped my ankle tightly he went upstairs, where I could hear him apparently moving furniture. When he reappeared, he was tucking a small book into the breast of his doublet.

'My codes,' he explained. 'I had them hidden under the floorboards, but once it was noticed I was gone, someone might have come looking.'

I nodded. He had lit a candle so that I could see what I was doing and I now had my first good look at him. He was older than I had realised, well into his late thirties, with some grey just beginning to show in his hair. But he was slender and wiry, and, as I had seen, quite able to climb difficult obstacles.

'So you're the young code-breaker,' he said. 'I've heard of you. Portuguese? That's how you managed to pass yourself off as Spanish. I'm glad to get out of there. They didn't only want me to sew uniforms for them. Some awkward questions have been asked, and if they hadn't been so occupied defending the citadel I was facing interrogation under torture.'

He shuddered.

'I was watched all the time. I'm not sure I could have got away tonight if it hadn't been for that fresh attack. Luis was set to keep me under guard.'

'I thought the attack was by chance,' I said, 'but Norreys knew I was coming. Perhaps he intended it as a diversion.'

'Whether or not, it was timely. I'm sorry I can give you nothing to eat.'

'Let's go. The sooner we reach the ships, the better.'

I got up from the stool where I had been sitting to strap my ankle. Testing it gently with my weight, I found the strapping eased it a little. Titus turned and blew out the candle.

'Why do you think they were suspicious?' I asked, as we left the house.

He shook his head. 'I'm not sure. I've been wondering if I might have been betrayed. Not here. I am the only agent in this part of Spain. No one knows me here. Could there have been careless talk at Seething Lane?'

I gave him a startled look. 'I don't know. But let us discuss this later, once we're back with the fleet.'

I knew I would be slow, but Titus had found me a tailor's yard to use as a stick and we began our descent of the streets. I was glad to see that as well as his code book he had equipped himself with a sword. Somehow the lower town seemed less deserted than it did by day. We heard furtive footsteps. Shadowy forms slipped into alleyways as we passed. Once a group of three men barred our way, but I spoke placatingly in Spanish and slowly they drew back, letting us pass, though they remained watching us, so that the hairs of my arms stood up, and I had to force myself not to look back.

At last we reached the harbour. I was sweating with pain, but would not give in to it, not until I could stretch out in my own cabin. It took a long while to rouse a boatman from the cluster of skiffs tied up beside the quay, but at the cost of some grumbling he rowed us out to the *Victory*.

Someone was waiting on deck as we climbed aboard, awkward for me with my strained ankle. The downwash from the riding-light showed a weary Dr Nuñez seated on the bench which Dom Antonio normally occupied when he took the air.

'Ah, Kit,' he said, 'so you are safely come back.' That was all, but I could read the relief on his face.

'This is Titus Allanby,' I said, 'and if you want perpetual reward for your good deeds in the hereafter, you will persuade one of the cooks to wake up and find us some food.'

I sank down on the bench as the two men bowed and shook hands.

'Kit has sprained his ankle,' Titus said, 'but he has managed to spring me before the trap closed.'

I remember little after that. Some food was found and I suppose I must have eaten it, but at last I was in my cubbyhole, stretched out on my cot, with my painful ankle propped up.

That night I dreamt of fire and darkness and wounded men crying out in English and in Spanish.

Chapter Nine

*A*s the fruitless siege continued unchecked, I grew restless with impatience. I would never be able to carry out my plan, my own private reason for coming on the expedition. I even thought of going ashore here at Coruña and riding south through Spain, but it was much too far. Besides, I needed to wait until my ankle healed. It was not a bad sprain, but I had not improved it by all the climbing and walking I had done that same night, as Titus Allanby and I escaped from the citadel.

Whatever it cost, I would have to wait until we reached Portugal. At night, I fretted sleepless in my cramped quarters, kept awake by worry and by the pain in my ankle and in my burned shoulder, which grew fiercer at night. The kind of cupboard, leading from his cabin, that Dr Nuñez had arranged for me to occupy was airless and dark, and increasingly hot as we drew nearer to summer, but I was thankful that I had not been forced to lodge with the men, for it would have been near impossible to maintain my disguise. At first I worried about living in such close proximity to Dr Nuñez, but I managed to keep to my cupboard, using the pisspot in privacy. He never troubled me there.

Intermittently, I slept during those nights moored off Coruña, a sleep troubled by dreams that remained with me by day only as dark and troubling shadows, in which I seemed to be hunting through the squalid alleys of London for someone . . . Was it Simon? I thought I caught glimpses of him, always turning a corner far ahead, always out of reach. I could not understand why I should be haunted by such a persistent yet meaningless dream.

Titus Allanby was accommodated aboard the *Victory*, sharing a cabin with two of the junior officers. He was accepted by all on board as an Englishman trapped in Coruña and anxious to go home. No mention was made of his assumed occupation as a tailor, nor of his true position as an agent of Walsingham's secret service. Instead he let it be understood that he was a merchant, and I backed up this impression whenever I had the opportunity. For the most part no one was interested, having more important matters on their minds. Dr Nuñez, of course, realised Titus's real identity, but he would not reveal the truth. Norreys knew as well. The day after Titus came aboard, Norreys sent for him to be rowed over to the *Nonpareil*, where he questioned him closely about the dispositions of the garrison in the citadel, the strength of their troops, and the supply of arms.

'I answered him honestly,' Titus told me when he returned. 'Any information I could give him that would help his endeavour to take the upper town, but of course he will not succeed.'

We had been granted the use of Dr Nuñez's cabin for a game of chess, which we were setting out on the table as he spoke.

'As for any other matters?' I asked, lining up the chessmen. It was a beautiful set given to Dr Nuñez by one of his grateful patients. Delicately carved from whalebone, the white pieces had been left the natural creamy colour of the bone, the red pieces had been stained with madder. The board was inlaid with matching squares of plain and dyed whalebone. I coveted it.

'As for matters intended for Walsingham alone,' Titus said, 'he did not press me and I did not volunteer them.'

I nodded. 'Sir John is aware that I work for Walsingham,' I said, 'as is Dr Nuñez. No doubt they will have guessed that you are also in his employ, but unless it should have some bearing on this expedition, I doubt if they will question you further.'

He poured out two tankards of ale and sat down opposite me, looking grave.

'It is ill-conceived, this expedition, Kit.'

'I'm well aware of that.' I shrugged. 'I have known it from the start, but you will not convince men to abandon their dreams.'

'And now this attempt to capture Coruña. For what purpose?'

'None, as far as I can see. For loot? For a brief triumph against Spain? Even if we were to capture it, we could not hold it. We have no means to leave an occupying force here.'

'And in the meantime, the expedition falters.'

'Exactly so.' I sighed, and took a swig of my ale. 'The problem lies in the divided aims of the leaders. The Portuguese exiles want to drive the Spanish out of Portugal and put Dom Antonio on the throne. On the other hand, Drake wants to inflict the greatest possible damage on the Spanish, especially the Spanish navy, so he can seize their treasure from the Americas. He cares not a farthing what happens to the Portuguese crown. I think Norreys set out with the intention of promoting the Portuguese mission, but he is easily diverted and has fallen in with Drake's plans.'

'All of which is very damaging.' He set down his tankard. 'It is you to move first.'

I moved one of my pawns.

'We are here not only to play chess,' I said, 'but to discuss in private what you mentioned to me, the night before last. Before I left London, I was told by Sir Francis that you thought you had fallen under suspicion, and you said you thought you had been betrayed.'

He moved a pawn and I moved another. I had only half my mind on the game, but I did not wish to make any careless moves. In the past I had often played with my mathematics tutor Thomas Harriot, though there had been very few opportunities in recent years. Sometimes I played with my father, though his increasing inattention had meant it was no longer enjoyable.

'You said,' I reminded him, 'that you did not believe you had been discovered or betrayed locally, but that something might have occurred at Seething Lane.' I shook my head. 'I do not see how that could be. I would trust them all – Sir Francis himself would never endanger one of his agents. Nor would Thomas Phelippes or Arthur Gregory or Francis Mylles, none of those who work at Seething Lane. I am sure of it.'

'I put it badly.' He grinned. 'We were somewhat distracted at the time, you will recall. When I said Seething Lane, I did not mean at the centre of the service itself. The whole organisation has many branches, many agents, many – like your Dr Nuñez –

who provide occasional assistance or information. That is partly the danger. Too many people, some of whom may have divided loyalties.'

My heart gave a sudden lurch, *divided loyalties*, and I hesitated, my hand holding one of my knights over the board.

'When did you first begin to think you were under suspicion?'

'It must have been in March.' I had placed my knight carelessly and he captured it with his queen. 'It was then that the commander of the garrison summoned me to the fortress, the new fortress on the island, the Castillo de San Antón. At that time the garrison was still quartered there.'

'You were interrogated?'

'Nothing so obvious. I was told I would be commissioned to make a number of new uniforms for the soldiers of the garrison. It was a valuable order, so I must understand how important it was that they should know more about me. It was all done in a most friendly, jovial way.'

'And?'

'All the time I have been in Spain, I have passed myself off as half Irish, half Spanish, and a Catholic. In truth my mother was herself half Irish, and *her* mother was Spanish. I simply skipped a generation. I called myself Mendes, my grandmother's name. She had much of my early rearing, after my mother died, so I am fluent in Spanish. She also started my training as a tailor. My father, of course, was English and I lived with him in Winchester from the age of seven. He felt that tailoring was a useful trade, and had me apprenticed, though I have never earned my living as a tailor at home, having abandoned it to become a merchant's clerk. I regard myself as English, but my mixed background made me useful to Walsingham.'

'Yes, it would. Like mine.' I studied the board, planning my strategy, and set out to lay a trap for Titus's queen. I moved my remaining knight more carefully and decided how I would deploy my bishops and one of my castles.

Titus had not seen through my intentions and moved a bishop in a way that would not threaten them.

'March,' I said. 'I know of one man who gained his freedom in December from the Tower. A man I would not trust.

There has always been a kind of mist obscuring the true nature of his loyalty. Walsingham still continues to use him, though I am not sure how far he trusts him. I know Thomas Phelippes is deeply suspicious of him. I have my own reasons for knowing that he is a liar and a dangerous man.'

His head had jerked up when I mentioned the Tower, and his next move, after my careful one, was made while hardly looking at the board.

'The Tower? You mean Robert Poley? He has been released?'

'He was released just before Christmas.'

He let out his breath on a long sigh. 'Do you know where he is?'

'I have only seen him once since his release. That would have been early in March, I think. Yes, also March. He had been in the Low Countries and was about to leave for Denmark, carrying despatches.'

'You are thinking what I am thinking?'

'Aye.'

'If he was in the Low Countries early this year, he could have made contact with the Duke of Parma.'

'It would not be difficult, for a man with Poley's experience. Besides, many people still believe Poley was really part of the Babington conspiracy, though he pretended to have been infiltrated into their company on Walsingham's behalf, to spy on them. I know that he lied about that.'

He looked at me inquiringly. We had stopped playing.

'I had seen him, quite by chance,' I said, 'months before, on intimate terms with Anthony Babington, though he claimed to Walsingham that he did not know him.'

'So he may still be working for the enemy, though for the Spanish now instead of the French.'

'The French are too much weakened at the moment,' I said, 'by the struggles between the Guise faction and the Huguenots led by Henri of Navarre.'

I seized his queen with my knight, and he clicked his tongue in annoyance at himself for leaving her unguarded.

'Spain has been weakened too,' he said, 'by the failure of the Armada.'

'Aye, but Spain has two great advantages over France – a strong and ruthless leader in King Philip and all the riches of their New World conquests to put money in their pockets. Plenty to buy ships and armaments. Plenty to maintain a large standing army.'

'I agree,' he said, moving a pawn carelessly. I captured it.

'But I still do not understand.' He drummed his fingers on the table. 'Poley has a good position with Walsingham. I am sure he is well rewarded. He is an Englishman, and England will suffer if he betrays her secrets. What has he to gain?'

'Money,' I said grimly. 'Power. He enjoys power over other people, and through betrayal he gains power.'

I narrowed my eyes, thinking of Poley and all I knew of him. 'Revenge.'

'Revenge?'

'Revenge. He has been shut up in the Tower for more than two years. However comfortably he lived there, however politic it was to maintain a fiction, he cannot have taken it kindly. He might well want to take revenge on Walsingham by damaging his service, provided he can conceal his own involvement, acting by stealth. He will want to stay privy to its secrets. Do not underestimate his talents and his cunning.'

'You hate him.'

'I have my reasons. I think you will find – if ever the truth can be laid bare – that Robert Poley passed word to Parma, who in turn passed word to Coruña as to your identity.'

'You are probably right,' he said. 'But in that case, why merely have me watched? Why not arrest and torture me?'

I smiled. 'Well, you can be thankful for that.' I moved a bishop to a strategic position.

'Perhaps they trust Poley no more than we do,' I said. 'They had you watched, hoping to catch you out, but wisely you sent no more despatches after warning Walsingham.'

He nodded. 'I stayed quiet and plied my trade. That kept me safe. Then the English fleet arrived and you sprang me from the trap.'

He moved one of his castles. A mistake.

I made my final move and smiled at him. 'Checkmate,' I said.

We had no proof of Poley's involvement, of course, and probably never would have, but we agreed that when Titus got back to London he would give Walsingham an account of our suspicions. He did not intend to travel on to Portugal with the expedition but would return to England whenever the next ship was sent home with despatches. In the meantime he stayed on board the *Victory* and we had a few more games of chess. When we were not distracted, we found we were pretty evenly matched.

Although I was still troubled and in pain from my burn, which was gradually growing less, and somewhat hampered by my sprained ankle, it was nothing to what was taking place on land. During the following days more and more of our skilled soldiers died needlessly during the fruitless attacks on the citadel. Norreys's own brother, Sir Edward Norreys, was desperately wounded, not as a result of enemy fire, but because, in the confusion and exhaustion of the siege, he tripped over his own pike and injured himself very severely, the blade burying itself deep in his skull. It was an injury likely to prove fatal. He was one of the most senior officers on the expedition, in command of one of the five squadrons, led by his galleon ironically called *Foresight*.

The first we knew of what had happened that day under the ramparts of the citadel was when we caught sight of a party of men proceeding slowly along the harbour road which led down from our army camp, located on the highest ground of the lower town.

Dr Nuñez called me over. 'It looks as though someone is seriously injured, Kit.'

I shaded my eyes against the glare of the sun.

'That is Sir John himself in the party,' I said. 'He is carrying someone. But – I can't see very well – there are so many of them.'

The group of men all seemed to be moving together, step by step. As they reached the water's edge, it became clearer why. Sir John was carrying the wounded man in his arms, but two other men walking close beside him also seemed to be holding something. More men were right behind them. The men with the injured soldier had great difficulty, clustered together, climbing down into the skiff. Even from a distance it was obvious that there was something seriously wrong. The skiff began to row slowly toward Sir John's *Nonpareil*.

'Someone is certainly badly hurt,' I said. 'Should we row over and offer our services?'

'Aye,' Dr Nuñez said. 'Fetch our satchels.'

I limped to our cabin. With firm strapping around my ankle, I could now manage without a stick.

We reached the *Nonpareil* while they were still lifting the wounded man on board, and I could see now why the burden was so awkward. The blade of a pike was embedded in his skull and the two soldiers helping Sir John had been taking the weight of the shaft, to try to prevent its doing further damage. At least they had shown the sense not to try to drag it out until there was a physician at hand to stem the bleeding. And I saw now that the man was Sir John's younger brother, Sir Edward Norreys.

Sir Edward was carried at once to the main cabin, and we followed closely behind. Sir John was wide-eyed with shock, for the wound looked mortal, but his brother was not dead yet. His eyelids fluttered and he moaned. He seemed barely conscious as he was laid carefully on Norreys's own bed so we could examine him.

The next hour was a desperate time.

'You will need to hold the patient's head rigid for me, Kit,' Dr Nuñez said, in the calm, impersonal tone he used when dealing with a medical crisis. There was no hint in his voice that this was a friend and a valued officer, as well as being Norreys's much loved younger brother.

Two of the soldiers who were not supporting the handle of the pike lifted the bed and its occupant out into the middle of the cabin, so that there was room for me to stand at the top of the bed and grip Sir Edward's head tightly on either side. It was difficult to hold it rigid as Dr Nuñez required, for on the side with the injury his hair was soaked with blood and more blood poured over my hand as I held him. Everything was slippery. I bit down on my lip, trying to keep my hands firm.

'Now,' Dr Nuñez said to the two soldiers holding the pike handle, 'I want you, you nearest the patient's head, to release the handle when I tell you – very gently, careful! – and take hold of the back of the blade. Whatever you do, you must not move it back and forth. That will enlarge the wound. And you,' to the other man, 'you must take all the weight of the pike as he moves his hands.'

The first man did as he was told, but he was sweating with the fear that he might cause further injury. The other soldier's eyes bulged with the strain of holding the pike steady.

'Good.' Dr Nuñez took a deep breath.

'Now you must both pull the pike blade straight out, along the same angle at which it entered. Do you understand? Not yet! I will count to three. On three you will do it. Straight and careful. Understood?'

They nodded. I am not sure which of us in that confined space was the most worried. Certainly I feared I would lose my grip as they pulled.

'One. Steady now. Two. Three.'

They pulled the blade out of the skull. I managed to hold it firmly, but the blade did not come out easily, for it was buried deep in the bone. As soon as it came free, I laid Sir Edward's head gently down and seized a handful of dried moss and the bandage cloth we had set ready and pressed it against the wound, for the blood spurted out like a fountain. If we did not act quickly, the man would bleed to death. Then Dr Nuñez took over with fresh cloths as I dug in my satchel for the salve of *agrimonia eupatoria* and *achillea millefolium*. These are the most efficacious coagulants. Even our troops call *achillea* 'soldier's woundwort', for it has been used to staunch wounds since ancient times. Achilles was said to have used it during the Trojan War, which gave it the name of *achillea*. Country folk call it 'yarrow'.

Still, despite the known properties of the two herbs, I wondered whether anything could possibly stop the bleeding from this terrible head wound. There was a great loss of blood. Examining the injury I could see that the skull bone itself had been cleft. It was a clean cut, without the shattering and fragments of bone that occur from shot, but it went deep and there might be damage to the brain itself. It was a fearful sight.

The soldiers were thanked and dismissed and went away in gloomy silence, for Sir Edward was a popular man with the troops, less severe in discipline than his brother. Sir John himself stayed, handing us what we asked for like an assistant apothecary, saying never a word until we had done all we could – salved and bound the injury and laid the patient down on his bed. The gash could not be stitched, for there is little enough skin and flesh on that part of the skull and that little had been torn and damaged.

'Will he live?' Norreys's voice was harsh and I realised that he cared deeply for this younger brother of his, despite the rigid control of his face.

Dr Nuñez was washing the blood from his hands in a basin that a servant had brought. We were both blood-bespattered.

'At this stage, I cannot tell,' he said gravely. 'The wound has been treated as soon as possible, that is in his favour. But it is very deep. He may live, but still suffer from its effects.'

It was his way of avoiding the issue. Sir John was not misled.

'You mean he may be mad or childish hereafter? His mind affected?'

Dr Nuñez winced. 'We will pray not, Sir John. The next few days will be crucial. If he does not take a fever . . . he is a strong healthy man.'

Norreys did not look reassured, but he thanked us both warmly and saw us on to his private pinnace to be taken back to the *Victory*.

We visited Sir Edward several times a day after this. He regained consciousness on the second day and gradually began to recover, although he suffered acute pain. It was so severe we could only partially relieve it with poppy juice. Had we given him enough to defeat the pain, it would have ended all his pain for ever. He was very weak, but his brain did not appear to be impaired. However, he had no memory of how the accident had happened. It was only from those who had been nearby that we heard how, in scrambling amongst the rocks and fallen masonry below the citadel walls, he had tripped over the pike he was carrying. Like Sir John he did not order his men to go where he would not go himself. He faced the same dangers and had suffered for it. Perhaps now, I thought, Norreys would abandon this pointless siege.

'It seems a kind of emblem of our whole venture,' I said to Dr Nuñez. 'It is descending into disaster and farce. Sir Edward's injury came not from the enemy but from his own weapon.'

He shrugged. There was no need to answer. More and more, events spoke for themselves. As matters had become more catastrophic, he had begun to spend more time in my company and to avoid Dr Lopez and the Dom.

'We can do nothing but endure in patience, Kit,' he said.

Another tragedy soon followed. Our troops had finally succeeded in making a major breach in the walls of the citadel, and continued to throw themselves at it with immense courage, in the face of the defenders' cannon fire. During one of these charges a mass of loosened masonry fell outwards, crushing Captain Sydenham. He was not killed outright, but was pinned to the ground by four huge boulders lying on top of his legs and lower body.

I heard the story later from one of the soldiers on our ship. Originally, he had been amongst the new recruits, but, different from so many of the others, he was a responsible man, prepared to do his duty as a soldier, as faithfully as the regular troops from the Low Countries. Unlike some of the men who were present at the disaster, he had survived, although he had been shot through the shoulder with a crossbow and I dressed it.

Afterwards he sat wearily on the deck, too exhausted even to drink the ale which stood in a tankard at his side.

'He was a decent man,' he said, 'Captain Sydenham. He knew it was hopeless, what we was trying to do, up there, take their damned citadel. Still he had his orders. And he always led the lads from the front.'

'Drink your ale,' I said. 'You've had a bad time.'

He looked at the ale as if he had not seen it before, swallowed a mouthful, then put it down again.

'We went in where there's a partial breach, see. Getting bigger. The wall is broken. God's bones, I don't know how we done it without cannon. Torn half the stones down with out own bleeding hands.'

I could see that he meant this literally.

'Anyways, the wall was beginning to collapse, see, then suddenly a whole section came away when we wasn't expecting it. Came down like a landslide, and there was Captain Syndenham underneath it. All of him, from the waist down, pinned under these b'yer lady great rocks.'

He wiped his face with both hands.

'We wasn't going to desert him. Most of the lads there was the troops who fought the Spanish under him in the Low Countries and they wasn't going to leave him to die under the rocks and that sun like a firebrand, on some stinking Spanish hillside. Nor was I. He treated me decent, even if I wasn't one of his regular lads.'

He looked vaguely at the ale, then drank the rest of it down.

'Over and over we made sorties under cannon shot and crossbow fire to try to rescue him. The Spanish just sat up there and picked us off. Would they stop long enough for us to rescue an injured man? Like Hell they would. Over and over they picked us off, them filthy misbegotten Spaniards. Before he died this morning, a dozen more of the lads was killed trying to save him. Dunno how many was injured like me. Jesu, I hate the bastards!'

Alone in my dark cubbyhole that night I wept for Captain Sydenham and a dozen other men and all the useless slaughter of this terrible futile siege of Coruña.

Chapter Ten

*A*t last, after two weeks of unnecessary death and injury, it became clear even to the leaders of the expedition that we had not the means to overpower the citadel with our puny artillery. Their minds were further persuaded by a fortunate change in the wind, which began to blow in our favour from the northeast, the very wind to carry us down the coast of Portugal. The soldiers were ordered back to the ships, loading what provisions they could and destroying what little was left in the town. It would be a long time before Coruña recovered. There were a good many wounded men amongst those who had served in the attacks against the citadel, including even some of the recruits who had finally been forced into service. Along with the provisions, the injured were loaded on to the ships, to survive or die while we sailed south, as Fate should decree.

Before we left, I paid a final visit to Teresa and her family, and to Paolo, whom I had kept supplied with food all the while we had remained in the harbour.

'You are leaving, Dr Kit?' Teresa asked. She was a different child now from the terrified creature I had first seen. The cottage was kept as clean and neat as anyone could contrive, given its dirt floor and the sand that blew in from the foreshore. Probably Teresa had been hard at work. I had persuaded one of the ship's carpenters to replace the door and to make some repairs to Paolo's house.

'Aye, we are leaving,' I said, 'and you will be glad to see us go.'

'Nay,' she protested, 'you have been kind. Without you the baby would have died, and Mama too. And we would have had nothing to eat.'

Her mother was still weak, but she was growing stronger. Nevertheless, it was always Teresa who was in charge and who did most of the talking.

'I shall be sorry to say goodbye to you all, Teresa, but you will be better off when we are gone. Paolo will be recovered soon and says he will fish for you.'

I had learned from Paolo that Teresa's father had been lost at sea just two months before our arrival at Coruña. The little family would have been destitute but for the kindness of neighbours, for the mother had never been strong and the little boy was simple-minded.

'I will look after them,' Paolo had said to me in his gruff voice, giving nothing away. It would not surprise me if he moved in with them and they became one family.

'May I see the baby?' I asked now.

Teresa's mother smiled and held the baby out to me. She rarely spoke, but on my second or third visit she had asked me if I would give the child a name, so that I should always be remembered. I was embarrassed and could say nothing at first.

'Caterina,' I suggested at last, 'if that pleases you.'

'Caterina.' She tried it on her tongue. 'She will be baptised Caterina, as soon as we can hold a service.'

As soon, in other words, as the priests who had abandoned their flock returned. Well, although Caterina Alvarez was no longer, this little Caterina should take her place. She promised to be a fine healthy child like her sister. She was warm and soft in my arms, long eyelashes lying quietly on plump cheeks. She, at least, would have no memory of what had happened here.

When I bade them farewell, Teresa hugged me about the waist, pressing her face against my doublet, and I kissed the top of her head. I would not let them see the tears in my eyes, for their suffering at our hands far outweighed any good I had done them.

Paolo was standing in his doorway, leaning on his stick, as I went out into the street.

'So you are leaving, then.'

'Aye.'

He spat juicily, but had the grace to turn to one side.

'I wish you well, Paolo. The town will recover, in the end. I have nothing but sorrow and regret for what has happened here.'

He grunted.

'They will be glad of your help.' I nodded toward the other house.

'Aye, well, there will be none from *them*.' As once before, he jerked his head up, indicating the upper town.

'You'll be glad to see us leave,' I said.

'We will.'

There was nothing else to say, but as I was starting to move away, he cleared his throat and, surprisingly, looked slightly ashamed.

'This is for you.'

He thrust a grubby fist toward me and something small dropped into my outstretched hand. Then he turned his back on me and limped back into the house, slamming the door behind him.

It was a model of a seal, about four inches long, beautifully carved from some glossy wood. The eyes were filled with a look of innocent curiosity. Even the whiskers betrayed inquisitiveness. I closed my fingers over it, then I too turned my back and walked away.

Drake and Norreys sent despatches home to London, and with them I sent a coded report to Walsingham on all that had happened, including such information as I had been able to glean about Coruña and the surrounding countryside. It was carried by Titus Allanby, returning to London on one of the fast pinnaces, who would make his own report in person. Before he left, he shook my hand, and thanked me again for extricating him from the besieged town.

'You would probably have contrived an escape yourself,' I said, 'even without my help.'

He shook his head. 'I was too closely watched. And even had I done so, the English fleet might already have left. I owe you a good deal, Kit.'

Awkwardly, I tried to brush aside his thanks, but did ask that he would take my greetings to my father.

'Tell him I am well,' I said, 'and please do not mention the burn or the ankle. Both are nearly recovered now.'

'Very well, but I *shall* mention them to Sir Francis. Those who sit comfortably in Seething Lane do not always understand what we endure, who are out in the world, following their orders. I will also tell him all that we have discussed concerning Robert Poley.'

'Aye, do that,' I said. 'Though we have no proof.'

'It may plant a seed of doubt.'

He grinned and stretched, as he shouldered his pack before climbing down the rope ladder to the pinnace.

'I am growing too old for this game,' he called up to me, from where he stood on the deck of the smaller ship. 'I think I shall buy a small farm and grow pigs and cabbages.'

I laughed, and raised my hand as the pinnace rowed clear of us and hoisted her sails. Part of me – nay, much of me – longed to be going home with her.

The next morning we set sail on that strong north-easterly, which carried us round the rest of Cape Finisterre and on towards Portugal at last. Away from Spain and Coruña, I began to breathe more easily. Looking around, however, I saw that the fleet seemed to have shrunk. I stopped one of the sailors.

'Where are the rest of the ships?' I said. 'Have they fallen behind?'

He grimaced. 'Not they. Most of the sixty Dutch *vlieboten* have abandoned the expedition and turned for home. And taken some three thousand men with them.'

I caught my breath. The *vlieboten* were small ships, like the pinnaces, not great warships, and they carried only light-weight armaments, but they were very useful, moving between the larger ships and able to navigate the shallower waters along parts of the Portuguese shore or in river estuaries. The three thousand men were also a substantial cost to the expedition, on top of the hundreds left buried in Spanish soil at Coruña.

Despite the loss of the Dutch ships and all those men, it was good to be on the move at last. The weather was hot, but tempered by the wind, and the rest of the fleet sailed smartly out round Finisterre and then south along the coast, although on the second day the wind dropped somewhat, so that although it continued to blow from a favourable quarter, it was not strong enough for us to make much speed. The soldiers, however, welcomed the respite as the fleet sailed on slowly. The provisions which had finally been procured meant that food and drink were in plentiful supply, although the ship's officers ensured that there should be no gorging and no drunkenness. There had been far too much of that already. For the most part the injured soldiers made good progress toward recovery, so my duties as physician were light.

Four days out from Coruña, on the thirteenth day of May, I was standing once again with Dr Nuñez in the bow of the ship.

'Is that a galleon, Kit?' he said. 'Further out to sea but heading on a slanting course to intercept us? Your eyes are keener than mine.'

I shaded my eyes with my hand and looked where he pointed.

'Aye. It seems to be one ship on its own, not a Spanish fleet.'

A man on the masthead was calling something down to the captain, and pointing.

'Is it English?' Dr Nuñez asked.

'Too far away to tell.'

I kept my eye on the approaching ship, so I did not at first notice the brightly painted fishing boat which had come alongside the *Victory*. Then, just before it dropped astern, I saw that Ruy Lopez was leaning over the rail and talking to the fishermen. Dr Nuñez went aft to see what news it had brought, for a fishing boat in these waters must be Portuguese. We were not far now from Ilhavo, where I had once hidden long ago amongst the fishnets.

As the fishing boat turned away, I saw that Dr Nuñez and Ruy Lopez were talking to Norreys, who had joined our ship that morning to discuss our strategy when we reached Portugal. It seemed they were reluctant to impart whatever news the fisherman had brought.

'Has something happened?' I asked Dr Nuñez when he returned to the foredeck, looking gloomy.

'A treasure ship has put in to the harbour at Peniche.'

I was puzzled. Why was this such bad news? A single treasure ship, laden with spoils from Mexico and Peru, would not trouble our fleet of warships.

'Why does that worry you?' I said.

'They are signalling the news now to Drake,' he said, pointing up towards the string of flags that a sailor was hoisting. 'And as soon as Drake hears of a treasure ship, to Peniche we will go.' He banged a fist against his forehead.

'Peniche cannot be much more than sixty miles from Lisbon,' he said, 'but it might as well be a thousand. By the time we come there, King Philip will have had warning enough to move his entire army from Spain to garrison Lisbon!'

I had taken my eye off the approaching ship while we had been talking, but now I saw that it was much nearer.

'That's an English ship,' I said. 'There is the flag, clear enough now, and another standard. I'm not sure . . . '

'Can you see her name?'

I screwed up my eyes. '*Swiftsure*.'

'Essex,' said Dr Nuñez. 'The Queen's errant golden boy. That rash idiot. He will want to go galloping about the countryside, imagining himself one of King Arthur's knights, and lose us the war in the process.'

He stamped off below decks and shut himself in his cabin.

Our commanders did not exactly welcome Essex, for they were carrying furious letters from the Queen demanding that he should be sent home at once. If they allowed him to join the expedition – and it would be difficult to say him nay – they would themselves incur a share of her wrath. On the other hand, he had a sound ship, provisions and arms, and well-trained regular soldiers. It was not difficult to foresee what decision they would make after our severe losses at Coruña.

Essex did join us, and demanded that he be put in charge of the next landing party. Dr Nuñez, as so often before, had been right.

I had never encountered Essex myself, but all that I had heard about him made me dread his addition to the leaders of the expedition. The spoiled and indulged favourite of the Queen – arrogant, wilful, accustomed always to grabbing whatever he wanted no matter at what cost to others – he was the last person to be given a part in the councils of the expedition. The Queen had forbidden him to come, yet he had defied even the Queen herself, no doubt envisaging some glorious heroic role for himself. He seemed to have no grasp of reality, but to live in an imaginary world of chivalry which bore no relationship to the nature of war as I had experienced it, both at first hand and through the suffering of men I had cared for. It was this mindless, hare-brained glory-seeking which had brought about such disasters when he had served in the Low Countries. I was full of dread at what further blight might be cast on our affairs by his presence.

Although it was not yet full summer, the southern sun soon became much stronger than Englishmen are accustomed to, particularly as in recent years our summers had been cold and wet, the winters bitter. The makeshift army, which had nothing to do while the seamen handled the ship, took to hanging about on deck, instead of staying cooped up below in the suffocating quarters they had been allocated. Most of the soldiers had overcome their seasickness by now, and they lay about, getting under the feet of the sailors, who tripped over them and kicked them and swore at them to move. Now that the food supplies had been augmented at Coruña, the soldiers were less apt to break out in open riot, but the quarrels between soldiers and sailors never ceased.

The soldiers stripped to the waist in the heat and – unlike the sailors, whose skin was permanently darkened by years at sea – their white English shoulders and noses turned the red of London bricks, then began to blister and peel. I found myself with some serious cases of sunburn to treat, and one or two of sunstroke. The worst of the raw red patches of skin I bathed with a cool infusion of *urtica dioica* and *stellaria media*, then I applied a salve of made from a strong decoction of *calendula officinalis*, *stellaria media*, and *coriandrum sativum*, blended with purified lard.

However much I advised them to keep to the shade, within an hour they would be back, lying in the sun, so I left them to suffer from their own folly.

A week after departing from Coruña, we were nearing Peniche. Another fishing boat had been sighted and detained, its crew apparently less ready than the first to pass information to the English fleet, despite the Dom's huge standard at our masthead. I lingered nearby.

'Aye,' said the older man, while his boy glowered at us where he squatted, gutting sardines. 'There was a treasure ship from the Spanish Main in Peniche.'

'And?' said Dr Lopez, giving a worried sideways glance at the Dom.

'Well,' said the fisherman, and spat over the side of his boat, 'word got around that she was loaded with a million crowns in gold. If you believe what they say. Not that we'll see one *real* of it in Portugal. But she isn't still here.' He laughed grimly. 'Once they heard *El Dracque* was coming, they cleared out, heading south.'

On learning what the fisherman had said, Drake decided to put in to Peniche anyway, instead of proceeding to Lisbon. Why, I am not certain. Perhaps he believed that some of the treasure had been off-loaded there. Since the treasure ship had left, I would have expected him to follow it, even deserting the rest of the fleet, the way he had abandoned the English fleet during the early encounters with the ships of the Spanish Armada. However, Drake was in command of the fleet, and to Peniche the fleet would go. The agreed goal of our mission seemed to be retreating further and further from us.

Ruy Lopez and the Dom were asked to explain the lie of the land at Peniche to Norreys, who once again had come on board our ship. His brother was making a good recovery, which he partly attributed to the skill of Portuguese doctors, so Norreys was readier to take into account the advice and wishes of the Portuguese party

'The town is loyal to me,' the Dom asserted. 'So this should prove an excellent landfall. There will be a small Spanish garrison, but the remainder of the inhabitants will be Portuguese, and loyal. There is opportunity here, at last, to begin rallying my people. We must move in swiftly, take the fortress, and plant my standard. As soon as word goes forth, my supporters will rush to my side and defeat the Spanish.'

'Aye, aye,' said Norreys, impatient with all this airy talk. He wanted hard information. 'What is the position of the fortress, and where can we best land?'

'The easiest place is the sheltered quay beside the fortress itself,' said Ruy Lopez eagerly. I could see his eyes light up at the prospect of his moment of triumph. 'The only other place is about a mile away, the Praia da Consolação, further to the east.'

'Is there deep water there?' said Norreys. 'How close can we bring in the ships?'

Lopez and the Dom exchanged glances. They had planned for Lisbon. They had no real knowledge of Peniche, nor were they men of the sea.

Norreys watched them and sighed. 'Very well, if you do not know the depth of the water, we will need to send the soldiers ashore in longboats. The loss of the Dutch *vlieboten* will cause us some difficulties here. We will try for the quay; failing that, we will make for this Praia da Consolação.' He went off to signal to Drake and to Essex, who was to lead the landing party.

Before long we caught sight of the remarkable Nau dos Corvos, the Ship of the Crows, a strange rock formation which lies off the tip of the peninsula on which Peniche is built. From a slight distance it looks like a ship heeling over in the wind and I suppose crows may perch there, though as we approached it was a flock of gulls and terns I saw diving for fish. A pretty scene but a dangerous one, for more rocks lie hidden about it below the surface, stirring up whorls and spouts of spume, and it is a notorious wrecker of ships.

After days of heat and strong but steady winds, the weather was shifting. Clouds were building up out to sea, and there was the crackle of lightning in the air. The wind was gaining in strength, and we had to fight our way round the south side of the peninsula through heavy surf. The fort stood guarding the inner curve of the harbour, so our fleet kept well off shore, out of cannon-range, while the officers of the army decided how to deploy their men. The wind continued to rise, so that once we had dropped anchor at the far eastern end of the harbour, the *Victory* tugged and jerked at the chain like an impatient dog. Some of the lubberly soldiers began to look green again, but when they were told to arm themselves for landing, their cheer increased. Perhaps Peniche would offer as many picking as Coruña had done.

A fleet of longboats was launched, rowed by sailors and crammed with two thousand soldiers. Before they were halfway across the bay, we saw a contingent of Spanish soldiers, in their distinctive armour and carrying the Spanish flag, emerge from the fortress and deploy around the safe landing place just below it. Dr Nuñez had come from his cabin and stood watching beside me, his knuckles shining where he gripped the rail.

'Pray God our men have the sense to attack the Spanish soldiers and leave the Portuguese alone,' he said. 'Though after Coruña I put little faith in them.'

'I think Sir John has given clear orders to his officers,' I said, though without much conviction.

'Let us hope you are right. What are they doing now?'

For the oarsmen had back-watered and most of the boats were changing direction.

'I think Essex has seen the Spaniards. He's making for the Praia da Consolação.'

The boats rowed off across the choppy waters, some of them becoming entangled with each other and rocking perilously as the great breakers rolled in from the Atlantic, driven by the rising storm. The boats were dangerously overfull. At last they sorted themselves and began to head towards Consolação. The Spaniards made no move to head them off. They must have thought a landing there was impossible. The boats pressed on, however, the one bearing Essex's standard in the lead. As they neared the shore, we saw Essex get to his feet and stand in the bow, his tall figure impressive, despite the bobbing and dipping of his craft. Then suddenly he was gone.

'What's happened!' cried Dr Nuñez.

'He's jumped overboard!' I said, 'Dear God, he's up to his neck in the waves. It must be near six feet deep there.'

We could see Essex's head, all that was visible, bobbing across the water towards the shore, like a pig's bladder from a boys' game of football floating on the surface.

'Oh, look, the fools!' I cried.

'It's too far away,' he said. 'I cannot see.'

Bravely, the men following Essex had jumped in after him, taking no account of the fact that he was exceptionally tall. Most of them disappeared from sight, too short and too burdened by their armour to follow his magnificent stride as he rose from the waves like some travesty of an ancient sea god, streaming with water from every joint of his armour, his helmet encircled with seaweed. A few men scrambled out of the sea behind him, but the rest never reappeared. I felt sick

In the confusion the seamen were shouting to the soldiers to stay aboard until they had beached the boats, the soldiers were standing up, uncertain whether to follow their commander or obey the sailors, the boats were rocking perilously and ramming into one another. Only Essex and a few of his followers had gained the shore when one of the other boats capsized, overloaded as it was with a cargo of landsmen who knew nothing of how to behave at sea, tipping soldiers and sailors alike into the bay, well off shore. We watched helplessly as they were swept away to the ocean by a powerful undertow.

Eventually, the remnant of the soldiers reached the shore, and we noticed then that Norreys had kept to the fortress side of the bay and was landing his disciplined men. Whether alarmed more by the mad heroics of Essex or by the calm determination of Norreys, the small group of Spaniards immediately took to their heels. We learned later that they had retreated across the isthmus to the hills opposite the peninsula.

Then to our joy and relief we saw Dom Antonio's standard climbing above the ramparts of the fortress and the gates being thrown open, spilling out a riot of civilians – women and children amongst them. Standing in the prow of the ship, the Dom had out his handkerchief and was wiping his eyes. Ruy Lopez was ablaze with triumph. Dr Nuñez turned to me with a smile that was wry and affectionate at the same time.

'Well, it appears, Kit, that not even Essex has been able to ruin our return to Portuguese soil. I wish your father could have been here.'

I nodded. Despite all my doubts about the expedition, I had to hold back my tears. I am not quite sure why I was weeping. Was it because we had reached Portuguese soil without being met by armed force? Was it because the dreams of these old men were about to be realised? But what of the men who had just died, needlessly, before our very eyes? Yet again the poor leadership of the expedition had cost the lives of the common soldiers and sailors. The senseless folly of Essex in leaping out into deep water had brought the deaths of his loyal followers. Overloaded boats had cost more lives. The failure to teach the soldiers how to behave in a boat had led to still more death. While those on shore were cheering and the Dom was weeping for joy, men's bodies were being sucked away irredeemably by the ocean, while others, weighed down by armour, were even now sinking into the mud and sand at the bottom of the harbour.

There seemed to be some little flurry on the shore. A man of commanding figure was in conference with Norreys and both were gesturing emphatically. Within a few minutes, a longboat put off from the quay and rowed out to the *Victory*.

One of Norreys's officers called out to us as they came alongside.

'The Portuguese garrison is commanded by one Captain Aruajo, who is Dom Antonio's man. He says that he will surrender to no one but the Dom himself. I am to take you all ashore.'

With some difficulty the three elderly men scrambled down into the heaving boat, and I scrambled after them, with hardly more dignity. At the quay Dom Antonio was helped ashore, and the rest of us behind him. As one, the people of Peniche knelt down, on the wave-washed quay and the sodden sand, and raised their hands and their tearful faces to their king. The tall man, Captain Aruajo, drew his sword. Holding it flat across his two palms, he offered it to Dom Antonio who took it, murmured something I could not hear, then handed it back, The captain sheathed his sword again, then took his king's hand and kissed it.

After Plymouth, after Coruña, Peniche seemed like a paradise. A throne stood ready for the returning king. The rooms were luxuriously furnished, the fortress amply supplied with food and drink. The storm rolled in over the town soon after we landed, turning the evening skies to midday with flashes of sheet lightning and making the very buildings vibrate with the reverberations of thunder. Despite the lashing wind-borne rain, we felt we had reached a safe haven. That evening we sat down to a Portuguese feast such as I had not seen since the last night in our own home in Coimbra. The tables were laid with elegant Turkey carpets and heavy silver. There were rich tapestries on the walls and braziers scented the air with regal frankincense and sweet lavender. We drank the finest wine from Venetian glass. They had killed and roasted a whole ox, and I was reminded suddenly of a story I had heard, at the church of St Bartholomew, about a long-lost son returning to his father's house. The noise and laughter were overwhelming.

Although the taste of the food was real enough, as was the slight dizziness I experienced after three glass of exceptionally strong wine, yet the whole evening had about it the quality of a dream. After the horrors of Coruña, this eager, joyous reception seemed unreal. When I went to bed that night, in a proper bed with two feather mattresses below and sheets of the finest linen, I thought with wonder that all our misgivings since leaving Plymouth had been groundless. The people of Portugal were, after all, eager to welcome Dom Antonio back and to drive the Spanish out of the country. For the first time in many days, I dreamt peacefully. I thought I was at home again in Duck Lane, in the parlour with my father and Thomas Harriot, who had come to play music with us. As is the odd way with dreams, Harriot had brought his virginals – I know not how – and I was playing. When Harriot picked up my lute and my father raised his recorder to his lips, my dog Rikki began to howl, quite melodiously, in tune with the music. I woke up laughing.

The next day, success did not look quite so easy. I was invited to join the party of English Portuguese, if I may call us that, at breakfast. At once I noticed that although they were relaxed and cheerful, their conversation was not as optimistic as it had been last night.

'Captain Aruajo,' said Dom Antonio, 'had one piece of bad news for me. Because we put in to Coruña for provisions, and stayed there two weeks, King Philip received word of our arrival before ever we sailed from there.'

We exchanged glances. We knew that Drake and Norreys had made serious mistakes over the Coruña affair. We knew all chance of surprise had been lost.

'Because of this–' The Dom hesitated, and I realised that something concerned him deeply. 'Because of this, the Spanish king has ordered the execution, without trial, of every noble who is suspected to be of my party. Merely suspected.'

Dr Nuñez groaned in horror and Ruy Lopez covered his face briefly with his hands. I felt myself go cold. *How many? Dear Lord, how many?*

'The nobles King Philip has managed to arrest and execute,' said the Dom, 'will not now be able to raise their own followers and bring them to join us.'

I felt a sudden swift stab of anger and gasped aloud at his calculating tone. Dom Antonio was indifferent to the deaths of these men, who had risked so much to remain faithful to him. He cared only for his lack of troops. It was the previous day all over again, a single-minded self-interest which set aside and ignored the tragedy of other lives, except as it affected his chances of claiming the throne.

Ruy sat up. As always he tried to persuade the Dom that all would be well.

'Yet see how you are welcomed here in Peniche!' he exclaimed. 'We may lack the nobles, but the common people and the merchant classes only await your coming to rise up and follow you.'

At this the Dom looked more cheerful, and nodded his head. All those undeserved deaths, deaths brought about by our ill-conceived and ill-managed expedition, were forgotten at once.

I soon left them to their deliberations and set out to explore the town. It was a strange feeling to be speaking Portuguese, not amongst an exiled community, but here in the country itself. The place seemed prosperous enough, not as though it was suffering under Spanish rule. There were fishing boats in the harbour and some larger merchant vessels. I found a market where there was abundant food and other goods for sale – cooking pots and dishes, lengths of cheap fabric, even children's simple toys. In a way this made it all the more surprising that the people had seemed so eager to welcome Dom Antonio.

The leaders of the expedition decided to remain for a short time in Peniche before advancing on Lisbon. They would wait for the Portuguese people to come in, to swell the ranks of our army, which was now heavily depleted by desertion before we left Plymouth (and since), by injury and death at Coruña, by the withdrawal of the Dutch *vlieboten*, and by the drownings here at Peniche. While King Antonio sat in state, blessing his people and settling disputes they brought before him, I sought out Dr Nuñez, whom I found at an apothecary's shop in the town, replenishing his supplies. I took the opportunity to buy healing herbs myself – febrifuge herbs, and those for the treatment of sunburn, since most of mine had been exhausted, and a small amount of poppy syrup, which was inordinately expensive, in a country where the poppies grew abundantly, as I knew very well. Perhaps the local people had begun to realise that they might do some very profitable trade with this sudden influx of strangers. Dr Nuñez and I walked back to the royal residence together.

'Dom Antonio,' I said, 'I mean, King Antonio – he means to stay here at least a week, does he not?'

'That is his intention at the moment.'

'Do you think . . . might I be given leave to absent myself for a few days?'

'Where would you go?'

'There is business I need to attend to at home.'

He stopped in the road and laid his hand on my arm.

'Do not suppose, because Peniche has declared for Dom Antonio, that it is safe to ride about the country, Kit. You might be known in Coimbra. You might be taken by the Inquisition.'

'It is seven years, and I was a child then. I don't think they would know me. But I do not mean to go into Coimbra itself. I want to visit my grandfather's *solar* a short distance away, to enquire after members of my family.'

'Kit, your grandfather will surely be dead by now. Your father is not much younger than I am.'

'Nay, my mother's father. She was twenty years younger than my father, and my grandfather was not much past twenty when she was born. So he would be, perhaps, only three or four years older than my father. Of an age with you, sir.'

'I see.' He thought for a moment, as we resumed our walk along the sea front. 'If you will promise me to keep away from Coimbra, and take great care where you go and who you speak to, I suppose you might go. I feel responsible for you to your father.'

'I will be careful,' I said. 'You need not fear on that score. I have no wish to fall into the hands of the Inquisition again.'

That evening I secured the loan of a horse from the Portuguese garrison, which had taken over sole control of the fortress at Peniche, and I packed my satchel with food. Walsingham's purse, which he had thoughtfully filled with Spanish and Portuguese coinage, was hidden inside my shirt. I was tense with apprehension, laced with excitement. How I wished for a companion, someone with whom I could share both my hopes and my fears. Andrew had joined in more than one adventure with me. But, still haunted by those odd dreams, I knew Simon would have been the very companion of my choice. Bold, cheerful, he would have steadied my nerve and relieved my fears. But nay, with his fair English looks and his lack of Spanish or Portuguese, he would have drawn attention and suspicion at once. This was something I must undertake alone. Before dawn the next day I left Peniche and headed north through the Estremadura towards Coimbra. The last time I had seen the town of my birth it was rank with the smell of burning flesh.

Chapter Eleven

Coimbra, Portugal, 1582

The auto-da-fè took place at the end of November. By then Francesca had been taken away and we never saw her again. My mother had been put to the question six or seven times before they were satisfied that she was a penitent. We were dressed, my mother and I, in long yellow robes with a black transverse cross, the *sambenito*, and each given a lighted taper to carry. This is the dress which is appointed for penitents. I knew now that my mother and I would be allowed to live, for the moment at least, whatever pain and abasement still lay in store for us. They put a kind of mitre on our heads and led us out of the cell and up some stairs into the blinding light of dawn. I had managed to hide inside my breeches the purse with our few bits of jewellery in it. After so many weeks in the darkness of our underground prison, my eyes could hardly bear the light.

I had not been put to the question. I knew that children as young as ten had been tortured and I can only suppose that my mother saved me from it by surrendering her body. By the time we joined the procession to the auto-da-fè she knew she was with child. After the torture and the repeated rapes, she could barely walk. I tried to help her, but was struck aside by one of the officials.

The ceremony went on from early morning until evening, and all the while we stood under a relentless sun in the great central square where the ceremony took place. There must have been at least two hundred of us, and several thousand citizens seated on banks of benches all around, eagerly watching the spectacle. As the penitents were assembled together before the rostrum where the Inquisitor General and his officials were sitting in their magnificent robes, I caught sight of my father. Like us he was wearing the *sambenito*; and once I would have cried aloud with relief, but lately I had learned much. I pressed my lips together and bit down on them to keep myself silent. His confession had been accepted. If he had been sentenced to be burned, he would have been wearing a robe painted with devils dragging heretics down to Hell. There were perhaps thirty of these, men and women sentenced to be 'relaxed' – a strange term, loaded with irony – that is, handed over to the civil authority, because the ecclesiastical authority was not permitted to carry out the sentence of death. It was decreed that the death of the condemned heretics must be accomplished without effusion of blood, so the victims would be burned alive. No blood would be spilled.

But my father, thank God, was not amongst the relaxed. As confessed penitents we would all be severely punished, my mother, my father and myself. All our property would be confiscated. My father would never again be allowed to practice medicine or work in a university. We would suffer some humiliating penance. But we were alive. At the time it seemed to me that was all that mattered.

Then the burning began. I dream of it still. The screaming. The smell. Dear God, the smell. And the greasy fragments flying through the air, like a shoal of tiny fish swimming in the smoke, and settling on our hair, our clothes, lying on our tongues with the taste of defilement, filling our lungs with the ashes of our countrymen.

As the cold November dusk set in and the formal ceremony of the auto-da-fè came to an end, we were escorted to another prison, a large chamber with windows high up in the walls. About fifty of us were confined to this one room, and we were told that our penance would be carried out the next day. We were to be stripped to the waist and paraded through the streets of Coimbra while we were scourged, as a warning to the populace. My father worked his way across the room as discreetly as he could and stood quietly beside us. He touched our hands briefly, but we did not embrace, for any sign of affection would have caught the attention of the two guards by the door. If he was surprised by my hair, hacked short and caked with filth, and my boy's clothes, he gave no indication.

'Christoval is well, Baltasar,' my mother whispered, laying a slight emphasis on my new name. 'Your son has shown himself brave and patient in all we have endured.'

I coloured with shame. I had endured nothing in comparison with her. Soon she would have to tell my father that she had been raped, but it was not my place to do so. I did lean close to him and whisper, 'Mother was tortured, Father, the *strapado* and the half drowning. She has suffered. You also?'

As we had walked from the auto-da-fé to our new prison I had noticed how he limped, setting each foot down as though he walked on hot coals. He nodded, and gave my hand a squeeze.

'I too had the *strapado* and the water, and also the burning of the feet. But they will heal, they will heal. They will let us go after the scourging and I will be able to salve them.'

'They will not let us go home, Father,' I said. My voice caught in a sob which I could not suppress. 'All our goods, all your books and instruments and medicines, everything will be taken away or destroyed.'

'We have friends,' he said gently. 'We must go to them secretly, but they will help. I think we will leave the country, go perhaps to Antwerp.'

We dared not talk any more, for we were attracting the notice of the guards.

The next morning they formed us up into a procession not far from my father's university, outside the Cathedral of Coimbra, the Sé de Coimbra, which has the appearance more of a fortress than a church. With the sleet-laden wind howling down from the north it made a grim backdrop to our shame. They forced us to strip to the waist. Then began the longest walk of my life. We went barefoot, stumbling over the wet cobbles, along the main streets of Coimbra, up and down the ancient alleyways, our feet cut and bruised by the stones, retracing our steps to the cathedral and starting off in a new direction. The whips they used to scourge us had several thongs of thin leather, and at intervals along these thongs were sewn small pieces of broken bone as sharp as knives. The men who carried out the work were skilled at it; the lashes fell on the back with a harsh crack and then were drawn slowly downwards, so that the splinters of bone gouged the skin like a plough breaking the earth. Then the lash was whipped back behind the scourger's head, the better to swing it down again with greater force.

At the first lash I screamed with pain. I could not stop myself. My father had set his jaw tight as a locked box and would not cry out. My mother, who was staggering as if she were sleep-walking, began a dreadful low moaning which went on and on, as monotonous as a dying animal, for the whole of that dreadful parade. I thought, at the first blow, that I could never experience worse pain, but that was a foolish thought. As my back became one bloody mess of torn flesh, the scourge could not find any new areas of skin – and the men were conscientious in seeking it out. Again and again the leather and bone scored deeper into flesh already broken and bleeding. After several hours, a kind of insensibility set in. I was nothing but a scalding fire of pain, so that I stumbled along in a trance. It came to an end at last. We were driven into the cathedral and made to kneel, which we did thankfully, for we could barely stand, and we were led by a priest in prayers of penitence and thanksgiving.

I felt the world swimming around me and barely stopped myself from sprawling on the floor, but I knew I must not be taken up unconscious, for I feared that if they discovered I had concealed my sex they would punish me even more. I concentrated my gaze on a chipped paving stone, trying to trace patterns in it. Why did the Inquisition stipulate so precisely that blood must not be drawn from those who were to die, yet all day they had drawn blood in rivers from the penitents? Was this some privilege to be enjoyed only by those accepted as Christian? My upbringing and religious teaching had been a mixture of old Jewish and New Christian doctrine. We attended both church and secret synagogue. From what I had been taught of the kindness and humanity of Jesus, I could not comprehend the practices of the Inquisitors. Did it make one a good Christian, truly faithful, to suffer as we had suffered?

After that interminable service, shuddering from pain and shock, we were given back our upper garments, and turned out into the night, where a cold wind from the ocean was carrying more sleet inland. I screamed again when the rough cloth touched my back, but my father took my hand, held my mother up by the arm, and hurried us away. All around us, the other penitents were slipped aside down dark alleys, eager to melt into anonymity. We staggered along as best we could, until we came to a small door in a high wall that I recognised as the garden door of a house belonging to one of my father's Christian colleagues from the university.

The rest of that night is confused. We were given a place to sleep above the stables, in case it was not safe to come into the house. Our backs were salved by Dr Soiero, another New Christian professor of medicine who had not been taken up for questioning, but had gone into hiding. My mother seemed barely conscious and could not eat, but I managed a little broth, then lay on my face, unable to sleep for the burning pain, while the men talked far into the night. They spoke of some fishing village, and a ship due out from Porto to London, but my mind was too blurred to understand their talk.

The next morning the owner of the house, Dr Gomez, came out to the stables. He brought a bundle for my father, some of his precious medical texts which he had bribed a guard at our house to give him, and my father's satchel of medicines.

'Just before the city gates shut at dusk tonight,' he said, 'a fisherman will bring his cart round to the alley and you must hide under the empty baskets. He will take you down to Ilhavo, where his brother will smuggle you on to his fishing boat. On the third day from now, when he is well out at sea, he will meet the *Santa Maria*, sailing from Porto, which will take you on board. It belongs to Dr Hector Nuñez, one of the leaders of the Portuguese community in London. Once away from Portugal you will be safe.'

My father looked uncomfortable. 'They have taken everything we have. I have no means of paying for our passage, Dr Gomez.'

The other man shook his head. 'Dr Nuñez will expect nothing. He has often helped others fleeing from persecution, and when you reach London he will help you. I will find something to pay the fishermen for the risks they take.'

I whispered in my father's ear that I still had one of my gold ear-rings, if he wanted it for the fishermen. I did not want to see him shamed, like a beggar. He nodded and told Dr Gomez that we would give the gold ear-ring as payment to the fishermen for their help.

'That is all arranged, then. The three of you, and Dr Soiero here, will be safe at sea three days from now.'

'But what of Isabel and Felipe!' I cried. 'We cannot leave them behind!'

Dr Gomez and my father looked at me.

'We have talked of this already . . . Christoval,' my father said. 'Our friend is riding up to your grandfather's house today to fetch them. They will meet us at Ilhavo in two days' time.'

The plan, which was so simple that we might have been detected at any moment, succeeded perhaps by its very simplicity. My parents, Dr Soiero and I made the night journey buried in a stinking nest of fishnets and osier baskets, jolting over small country roads in the rough cart the fisherman used to bring his catch to the market in Coimbra. My father was rapidly recovering, and benefited from not having to walk while his bandaged feet began to heal. My mother, now she no longer had to remain strong to protect me, had lapsed into a lethargic silence. She ate and drank little, and when we spoke to her she seemed to come back from somewhere far away inside her head.

When we reached Ilhavo we climbed aboard the fishing boat, which was larger than most of the other boats in the village. Though still the traditional shape, like a peasecod, it had a rough cabin amidships, and the fisherman, whose name I never learned, told us that he regularly ventured further out to sea than his fellows, so it would not arouse suspicion when we sailed out to meet the *Santa Maria*. Until she put to sea, the boat was kept dragged up above the high water mark on the beach, and we hid in the cabin.

We waited for Dr Gomez to come, and when at last he did, on the evening of the third day, the fisherman was growing anxious about leaving. He came alone.

'Where are the children?' cried my mother. It was the first time she had spoken voluntarily since we had left Coimbra.

Dr Gomez sat down on a heap of nets in the bottom of the boat and put his head in his hands.

'I went to your father's house, Senhora,' he said, 'but there were none but servants there. 'Three weeks ago, the Inquisition came for your mother. They would probably have taken your father too, were he not such a power in his own *terra*. He has gone now to Lisbon, to try to buy her release from the governor.'

He sighed and ran his hands through his hair. His face was lined with exhaustion, and I could see that he did not want to go on.

'Before he left, your father placed his two grandchildren with an Old Christian family, tenants of his, in the next valley, beyond the forest. The da Rocas. Do you know them?'

'Certainly,' said my father. 'They are poor, but good people. He thought they would be safer there?'

'Yes. So I rode on there. I found . . . ' he looked at my mother, then bent his head and fixed his eyes on the nets beneath his feet. 'I found that all the family had become ill with the bloody flux. Your son . . . your son Felipe died last week.'

My mother cried out, then stuffed her fist in her mouth, biting on her knuckles to mask any further sound, rocking herself back and forth as the mad Francesca had done.

'My daughter?' said my father, choking on his words. 'Little Isabel?'

'She is very ill, though they think she will recover. At the moment, though, she is far too ill to travel.'

A moan escaped from my mother, and I put my arm around her to try to comfort her. She pulled away, curling herself up like an injured animal.

Surely we could not leave the country with Isabel still here? The Inquisition would track her down, and she would have to endure imprisonment and torture alone, knowing we had deserted her. I tugged at my father's sleeve.

'We must go back for Isabel,' I begged. 'We cannot leave her behind!'

His face was bleak and he seemed hardly to hear. Then he turned towards me.

'We cannot risk all these other lives, Caterina,' he said, forgetting to use my new name. 'Your grandfather will care for her.'

I sank back amongst the stinking nets and covered my face with my hands. Behind the darkness of my closed lids I seemed to see Isabel's eyes, pleading with me.

Within half an hour, a yoke of oxen had dragged the fishing boat down the beach to the sea, while we remained hidden in the tiny cabin, and we set sail, leaving Dr Gomez in Ilhavo. The fisherman set a course heading north and slightly west, where we hoped to cross the path of the *Santa Maria*. The boat, which had seemed large amongst its fellows, seemed no bigger than a mussel shell on the vast grey waves of the Atlantic, waves which threw us about like a piece of driftwood, rising up above our heads as if they would crash down on the boat and punch it to the bottom of the ocean. It was growing very dark. The fisherman said we would have to light a lantern once we could make out the ship, or she would pass us by, or even run us down. I clung to the side of the boat, terrified by the immense ocean. I had never been to sea before, and all I could think of was the depth of violent grey water beneath, with nothing between us and drowning but the thin planking of the boat.

It seemed like a lifetime later, for my fear stretched the time out, yet it cannot have been more than a few hours, when the fisherman called out to us that he could see the ship. I could see nothing, but I had been sitting with my eyes screwed shut and my stomach heaving, so my night sight was poor. My father was trying to help with the boat, while my mother and Dr Soiero sat like helpless puppets, so I was told to light the lantern and climb to the front of the boat, where I was to show it and cover it three times, then pause and show it again. I did as I was told, wondering how so feeble a light could possibly be seen on this heaving monster of an ocean, an ocean which surely stretched to the end of the world.

Yet it must have been seen. After a while, even I could make out the ship, looming up against the stars, as some of the cloud began to clear. There were lanterns hung fore and aft, lights shining from her cabin windows in the forecastle and sterncastle, and sailors taking in the sails. The ship hove to – a manoeuvre I was to understand later – and the sailors threw a kind of giant net over the side, with meshes about a foot across. We were to climb this, from our little boat, in the heaving sea, up the side of that huge ship that soared above us like the tower of the university in Coimbra. Before we left the boat, I handed the ear-ring to my father, who gave it to the fisherman, and embraced him in gratitude. They sent me up the side of the ship first – I think because they did not want me to watch, in case my mother fell and was drowned. I do not know to this day how Dr Soiero and my father got her up that net ladder. All I know is that she tumbled over the side of the ship and lay on the deck as though she were already dead. And the two men followed her.

Chapter Twelve

Portugal, 1589

It took me two days of hard riding before I neared Coimbra. Despite my need for haste, I did not dare to use post horses, even if any were to be had in this under-peopled part of the country. Besides, I needed to keep my identity and my purpose secret. My army horse was young and strong, but I must not overtax him, so I rode fast but circumspectly. There might come a moment when I would need to ride for my life, but I feared he would not have the same outstanding gift for speed as Hector, the beloved, ugly piebald I often rode from Walsingham's stables.

As for myself, I hoped that I looked like a nondescript government messenger, or some nobleman's servitor – not rich enough to be worth waylaying, but with the possible attendant risk of punishment for any assailant who might try to attack me. I wore no weapons but my light sword and my dagger. If it came to a fight, I had little hope of defending myself despite my training in swordplay at the Tower by Master Scannard. I could handle a sword now, but I had no experience of using one in anger. Beside, I had had no practice since we had left England, and I knew that my wrist was nowhere near as strong as a man's. My sprained ankle was nearly sound again, though I would hesitate to put too much reliance on it. The burn on my shoulder had healed over with thin, pinkish, delicate skin.

As I rode across the isthmus from Peniche, I wondered whether I might encounter the soldiers of the Spanish garrison who had retreated when we arrived, but I saw no sign of them. Either they were lying low or they had made their way to some other strong point, perhaps Lisbon itself, or even back to Spain. At first I followed the Atlantic coast north, skirting the towns of Óbidos and Nazaré. I kept close to the shore to avoid Óbidos, which lay somewhat inland, and took a ferry across the river mouth. The ferrymen rowed me and my horse across the estuary together with a woman and small boy carrying two pairs of chickens tied together by their legs, protesting feebly, and a dour youth with a pig which nearly overturned the boat. Riding on from the other side of the river, I looped inland behind Nazaré, which lay on the coast. There might be Spanish garrisons in either of the towns.

Only twelve when I had left Portugal, I knew little of public affairs then, being absorbed in my narrow sphere of family and studies, until my world broke apart into shattered fragments. Although I had now worked for Walsingham more than three years, decoding and transcribing despatches (ours and those of our enemies), I was more familiar with the affairs of Rome and Paris and Madrid than with the current situation in small Portuguese towns. I did not even know whether the Spanish had established garrisons in such towns, or just how dangerous it might be to enter them. There had certainly been that Spanish garrison at Peniche, but Peniche was a major port. One of Philip of Spain's principal reasons for invading Portugal had been to gain access to our Atlantic ports, so serviceable for him in plundering the riches of the New World. On my present journey I did not want to run the risk of discovering how widely the Spanish army was deployed, so I avoided all places larger than a village.

After steering clear of the towns, I headed toward the sea, threading my way through a series of small fishing villages along the low shore. The villages were all built to the same pattern: small zigzag clusters of wooden houses raised on stilts, erected directly on the sandy beaches at high water mark. The stilts provided them with some protection from the seasonal spring tides, but gave them a curiously mysterious look, like the fantastic dwellings from some fairytale. Somehow you expected the houses to gather up their fishing net skirts and walk away on their thin legs. The fishermen and their families lived in these raised houses amongst the sheds for their boats and the barns for

139

the oxen which dragged the boats to and from the sea. It reminded me of Ilhavo.

In appearance these villages were very different from the fishing villages along the Sussex coast which Phelippes and I had searched back at the time of the Babington crisis, when word had come that two traitors were to land somewhere there. The houses in Sussex had been squat but comfortable, solid and timber-framed, infilled with wattle and daub and roofed with thatch. The fisher houses here seemed fragile by comparison, hardly more than temporary shacks perched atop their stilts. Yet the people had money enough to own oxen to launch their boats. In Sussex, the fishermen and their wives had dragged the boats down the beach to the sea themselves.

Some things united the villages, however different they might seem in appearance. Everywhere, the smell of fish and ocean and seaweed and tar and the peppery scent of rope. It was as if the scents from aboard the *Victory* had been boiled down to a concentrated essence which saturated everything. I knew that when I left these villages my clothes, my hair and even my horse, would carry the smell for hours. I think if you had to search for a fisherman through the streets of a strange town by night, you could find him with your nose.

By the time I reached the shore, the fishermen had already set sail for the day, leaving the villages populated by none but black-clothed women mending nets, or gutting and salting sardines, and half-naked children playing with shells and bits of driftwood. It all seemed peaceful enough, with no sign of the Spanish in these remote parts. The oxen were tethered above the high water line, where tough sea-grass grew in ragged clumps, working their way placidly over their circles of restricted grazing until the time should come for them to be harnessed to the boats again, to drag them up the beach.

Towards noon I stopped in one of these villages to rest my horse and let him drink from the narrow stream which ran down between the houses, before it fanned out into a dozen rivulets across the beach and into the sea. The women raised their heads, watching me cautiously until I gave them a friendly greeting. On hearing my native Portuguese, their faces cleared. What might have turned to hostility was transformed magically into smiles of welcome.

'God be with you, Senhora,' I said to a plump, kindly looking woman, who had left her netting to draw three rough loaves from the beehive-shaped clay oven outside her house. 'Have you enough to spare for a traveller?'

I reached into the purse at my belt and drew out a small coin.

'Put your money away,' she said. 'I would be ashamed to turn aside a traveller from my door. Sit, sit.'

She motioned me towards the log where she had been had just been seated, busy about her work on the nets. She bundled them courteously away to one side. I was glad of a seat, already beginning to feel saddle-sore. She disappeared into the house, which was hardly more than a hut, another of those ramshackle wooden dwellings on legs, and returned with a wooden trencher piled with sardines hot from the fire.

I shook my head. 'I cannot eat your meal, Senhora.'

She waved my objections aside.

'I am cooking more. The fishing was good last night. Eat, young man, and do not argue!'

At that I grinned and fell to. The sardines were wonderful, fresh from the sea and smoky from her open fire. As I mopped up the last welcome fragments with chunks of the warm bread, I looked up to see four little boys in a row watching me, with their fingers in their mouths. Behind them, two of their sisters peeped at me through their hair. Seeing me looking at them, they all scampered away like young deer, but not too far to keep me under observation. I suspected that I was eating their midday meal.

The fisherwife brought me a mug of fierce local wine, so harsh it nearly scoured the roof of mouth to the bone, but as it began to circulate through my limbs I could feel myself being prodded out of my weariness. The children crept a little closer. I noticed that there was a hank of string lying where the woman had been at her work. Remembering how Andrew had taught a child how to make a cat's cradle when he was in St Bartholomew's, recovering from his injuries at Sluys, I beckoned the oldest boy over to me.

'Do you know how to do this?'

I hooked the string between our fingers, and began to weave the cat's cradle, hoping I had not forgotten how to do it. By the time I completed it, then showed how to make it vanish back into a simple length of string, all the children were crowding round, even the little girls, demanding to try it. The woman, who was probably the mother of some of them, had set more sardines cooking and had taken up her net mending again. Looking up from the third or fourth cat's cradle, I realised that my audience had grown considerably. These could not all be the children of one family. Every one of the children in the village had been drawn by the novelty of a stranger, and especially a stranger who could do tricks.

Long before they were all satisfied, the woman clapped her hands.

'Enough!' she said, laughing. 'Your dinner is ready and the Senhor cannot spend all day amusing you.'

Her own children fell upon the food, while the others wandered off, taking the string with them and arguing about how to weave the cradle themselves. She brought out a basket of fruit from the hut, the kind of fruit I remembered from my childhood: peaches and apricots warm from the sun and so juicy that when you bit into them the juice spurted out and ran down your chin. The fruits of the south do sometimes reach London, but they never taste like this. Either they have been picked too soon, to stop them rotting before they can be sold, in which case they are edible, but have little flavour; or else they have been picked ripe, but have developed a taste of mustiness and mould, however careful the dealer has been to wipe away any blackened surface traces.

It was pleasant sitting there at the edge of the beach, with the somnolent midday sun beating down, tempered by a cooling wind off the ocean, whose waves resounded with a deep music on the rocks enclosing the small bay where the village stood. Sitting here amidst the quiet chatter of the children, I could put aside the horrors of Coruña and close my mind, for the moment, to what might lie at the end of my journey to the *solar*. Yet I must not linger too long. The children and their mother finished eating and when I had eaten the fruit I had been given, I thanked the woman and rose from the log. Before I mounted again I tucked a *real* under the trencher which had held the sardines. As I rode on my way out of the village, a cavalcade of children ran after me, shouting their good-byes. Two of the boys were linked together by a half-made cat's cradle.

Early in the afternoon I turned somewhat east, away from the coast and found that my way led through the fringes of the vast pine forest. I had become very hot under the unremitting sun, no longer benefitting from the ocean breeze. Before I reached the forest the land was open and quite barren, with few villages or even isolated farms. As my road passed in among the trees, the glare of the sun was cut off. The trees stood tall and regal as pillars in a church, and shafts of sunlight played across the forest floor as if they fell through illuminated windows. The long heat of the day had roused the scents of the pine, heady as incense. It was very quiet amongst the trees. An occasional bird crossed my path, but there was little birdsong. I imagined that they reserved their singing for the cool of the morning and evening. The forest seemed devoid of animals too, unless they too were sleeping away the heat of the day. The coolness and the shade were like a drink of fresh water. Even the horse felt it, for he raised his head and stepped more briskly. For the last hour he had been plodding like a cart horse.

Late in the day, I found a small wayside inn north of Leiria. It was clean enough, and seemed safe enough, but after a frugal meal I chose to sleep in the stable with my horse, rather than pay extra for a bed, thus saving my money and keeping a watch over my mount. It was not the first time I had spent the night in a stable and I was content, but I slept poorly, for the hard riding and the chafing of my clothes had broken the thin skin which had begun to form over the burn in my shoulder. The pain fretted me and prevented me from driving the anxious thoughts about my plan from my mind. During the day I had been able to concentrate my mind on finding my way and covering the ground as swiftly as I could without over-tiring my horse. The brief interlude in the fishing village had raised my spirits for a time, but lying on my bed of straw and staring into the darkness, I could no longer keep at bay the worries I had thrust away during the daylight hours. Since leaving Portugal seven years ago, my father and I had heard nothing of those of our family who had been left behind. My grandfather, being one of the most substantial landowners in the area inland from Coimbra, and moreover being a pure-blood Christian of ancient Portuguese lineage, would have been safe from the Inquisition. Surely he must have been able to protect the rest of the family. Yet in all these years we had heard nothing, despite sending several letters. Under Spanish occupation, Portugal was no longer a sovereign country and perhaps our letters had never arrived. Or else they had been deliberately confiscated, though I knew my father had always worded them with care. And would their connection with us have endangered even my grandparents? These thoughts tumbled over and over in my head. The following day, or the one after, I would know the answer. In the end, the weariness of my aching body finally drove out all thought, and I slept.

The next day, as I drew even further away from the sea, it grew hotter. It was still early in the summer, but my years in England had made me unaccustomed to Portuguese weather. By midday I was sweating and wiping my face every few minutes on my sleeve. We had reached the Beira Litoral now, with its groves of olives and cork-oaks. Some of the south-facing slopes were terraced for vines, but this was not an area particularly suited to vineyards. There were no towns and few villages here, but scattered over the countryside there were some of the great *solares* like my grandfather's estate, and more humble farmhouses, with fields of wheat and barley, and, on the higher ground, sheep grazing.

Accustomed to the more melodious birdsong that filled the English countryside, I had forgotten how maddeningly monotonous the grating sound of the cicadas could be. Even over the sound of my horse's hoofs it drilled into my head. It drove me to stop early to eat. I had bought cheese, flatbread and olives at the inn, together with a leather jack of thin wine, so under the burning sun of midday I retreated into an olive grove, where there was shade for me and a little thin grazing for the horse. The heat and my growing exhaustion had driven out any desire for food, but I forced myself to eat, knowing that it was important to keep up my strength for whatever might lie ahead. It was much too hot to continue for a while yet. The horse was hobbled. I lay down in the shade of one of the largest trees, my head on my satchel, and watched the silvery leaves barely stirring in the breathless noontide.

Somehow, I fell asleep. When I woke, I could tell by the different slant of the light through the branches that several hours must have passed. The leaves above me were beginning to stir in a slight movement of the wind. I could hear the horse tearing up grass, accompanied still by that mindless scratching of the cicadas. I found I was stiff when I tried to get up – too long in the saddle and too long lying on the baked earth – but I must continue. I put on the horse's saddle and bridle again. He seemed willing enough, after his rest, to carry on.

I had hoped I might reach my grandfather's house before nightfall, but my horse was growing tired. As evening began to close in, much more quickly than in England with its long twilights, and after the horse had stumbled a third time, I reined in and looked about, trying to decide what to do. There would be little hope of finding an inn in this sparse country, unless I pressed on to Coimbra. I had promised Dr Hector that I would avoid the town, and the thought of the prison there turned me cold even in the heat. At last I headed my horse, at a slow, ambling pace, towards a grove of trees on rising land about two miles away. It would be cool under the trees, especially now as the evening drained away the heat of the day. Before heading further into the little wood, I looked again in the direction where I knew Coimbra lay. The wood grew on the foothills which lifted up to the Serra da Estrela and I could see below me the valley through which ran the river Mondego, as it flowed toward Coimbra. I would need to cross it to reach my grandfather's *solar*. There was, I knew, a bridge a little to the east and north of Coimbra. In the middle of the day tomorrow it might prove busy with beasts and carts, but if I could reach it early there would not be too many people about.

I rode a little further into the wood towards the sound of water and found a stream where both I and my horse drank. Then I unsaddled him, rubbed him down, and hobbled him again so he could graze without wandering too far. In my satchel I had bread left from Peniche – somewhat stale after two days of summer heat – some dried fruit, strips of dried beef and a small goat's cheese wrapped in vine leaves. I fed well enough on these before lying down under the trees and trying to sleep. I was tired from the long ride, despite my midday siesta, and painfully stiff, not having been on horseback since we had left London. My shoulder throbbed and was weeping a thin yellow pus. Also, my troubled thoughts kept me awake again. Until now I had not allowed myself to think what I might find when I reached the *solar*, but I would surely be there before the next day was out. My grandparents would be horrified to see me, disguised as I was, sunburnt and coarse. It might be that they would turn me away. Nay, surely they would not do that! They must have been told of our escape from Ilhavo by Dr Gomez, but would know nothing of what had become of us afterwards. All those letters sent by my father, met with nothing but silence.

My worries robbed me of sleep until far into the night. At last I slept, but woke again after a few hours, aching in every muscle and joint, and could not sleep again. I doused my head and face with cold water from the stream, ate a piece of bread and a lump of cheese, and saddled my horse.

When we reached the old stone bridge over the Montego about dawn, there was no one about but a shepherd trying to drive his flock over its arched span ahead of us. The bridge rose high, almost to a perfect semicircle, for the boats which brought produce down from the Beira Alta had to pass underneath it, and the sheep were skittish and reluctant to cross over it.

'Shy of the bridge, are they?' I said, dismounting.

He shrugged. 'Fool animals. Take them over a bridge with a parapet so they can't see the water, and they think it's a road, no matter how narrow it is. But here,' he waved at the bridge, which was wide enough for a hay cart but open on both sides, 'here they can see the river and they panic.'

'Like some help?'

'I'd be glad of it. My boy usually helps me drive them to market in Coimbra, but he's laid up with a fever.'

Between us we rounded up the sheep which had begun to run along the bank in a skittish crowd and herded them over the bridge. Once on the other side they began calmly to graze, all fear of the river forgotten.

146

'Thank you, Senhor,' the shepherd said, pulling off his cloth cap and using it to wipe his face.

'It's nothing,' I said. 'Tell me, do you know Senhor da Alejo? His *solar* is over that way.' I gestured away towards the east.

He shook his head and grinned. 'I live five miles south of here, and only bring the sheep to Coimbra three or four times a year. I'd not be mixing with the likes of such a man.'

With that he went off, whistling to his dog, who had proved of little use in herding the sheep, but had watched us, panting, from the shade of a thorn bush.

Once I had led my horse over the bridge and remounted, I turned up river and headed in the direction of my grandfather's estate. Taking the road which led away from Coimbra and into the interior, I began to recognise landmarks I remembered from childhood journeys following this same road. There on the left was the farm which always looked tumbledown and uninhabitable, yet we would see a swarm of children playing around the ramshackle barns and wonder what their lives were like, so different from ours. A little higher up, on the right, stood the mill where part of the river was diverted into a mill leet. This was the mill owned by an abbey in Coimbra, where all the local peasant farmers were obliged to grind their corn and pay a tithe to the abbey, a tax they resented. I wondered whether the tax was more severe now, under a Spanish regime, when money was demanded to maintain the troops controlling the country. There was another mill on my grandfather's *solar*, where all his tenants had the right to grind their corn. They paid no tax for the privilege. Their only responsibility was to contribute to the maintenance of the mill and the grinding, when it was necessary, of new millstones.

As the familiar fields came into sight, my throat tightened and my eyes blurred with tears. Nothing seemed to have changed since that last summer I had come with my mother and with Isabel and Felipe, to spend the hot months away from Coimbra, here where the rolling lands of my grandfather's estate rose up the gently sloping ground to the manor house. Suppose – the idea had never occurred to me before, and came to me suddenly now as if someone had struck me on the head – suppose the summons had never come from my father that summer, which fetched my mother and me back to Coimbra for a few days, so that I might be presented to his scholarly friend from Italy. How would all our lives have been changed?

In the low meadow by the river two mares grazed with their foals, but I saw no sign of my grandfather's favourite stallion. Even now he would still be in the prime of life, and I wondered whether my grandfather had ridden him off somewhere. As we climbed the hill, the morning sun was reflected from the dazzling whitewash of the main house, with its carved granite window embrasures and doorways. There was no smoke rising from the kitchen chimney, which puzzled me and stirred a faint sense of alarm. Usually there would be smoke from a cooking fire every day, summer and winter. I rode round the corner of the house to the front. At the grand double stairway that swept up to the main door, I slid from my horse and looped his reins through the hitching ring in the wall. For a moment I laid my hand against the old blue and white *azulejos* tiles that decorated the triangular wall between the two branches of the steps. They were as warm as a human hand, and I felt such a rush of sudden joy that for a moment I was dizzy with it. This was the home where I had been happiest.

I mounted the steps and pulled the ornamental handle which, through a system of wires and pulleys, rang a bell inside the house. It was at that moment I suddenly realised I must decide what to say. I had not prepared my story. A servant would answer the door. It might be one I knew, or some stranger. I would not say who or what I was, but would need to pretend to be some passing friend or a distant relative, until I was able to speak to my grandfather himself and reveal who I was.

The man who answered the great oak door was familiar to me, one of my grandmother's house servants. I thought he might recognise me, but he did not, and instead stood staring at me, speechless, in a manner that was somehow disturbing. My stomach clenched.

'Is your master at home?' I said. 'Senhor da Alejo? I am on my way to Lisbon, and bring news of his relatives in Amsterdam.'

The man continued to stare at me, then he swallowed and shook his head. He still seemed unable to speak.

'His wife?' I said. 'The Senhora?'

He looked at me as if I were mad, and found his voice at last. 'The mistress has been dead these seven years. She died in the Inquisitorial prison in Lisbon.'

He squinted at me suspiciously. 'How do you not know this, if you are a friend of the family?'

I stared at him. Suddenly I was cold, and shaking. Remembering.

That last time we had arrived here, when we three children had hung out of the carriage window, jostling to see who would catch the first sight of the house. Mama trying in vain to persuade me to behave like a lady, Felipe nearly tumbling head first over the side. Then my grandparents were there, welcoming us into the ancient stone-flagged hallway, so cool and welcome after our hot journey.

'Come, Caterina,' said my grandmother, 'you are almost a young lady. You should not tumble about like a wild boy.' But she laughed as she spoke.

My grandfather kissed me on the forehead, then held me at arms' length.

'You have grown two handspans at least since last summer, Caterina. You will be as tall as I before you are done.'

My grandmother had led us through into the high-ceilinged *salão*, with its floor inlaid with those same blue and white *azulejos* tiles. We had drunk fruit juice and eaten the fig pasties which were always Isabel's favourites. And mine too, though I pretended to be too grownup to snatch at them as she and Felipe did.

Standing here now, I looked beyond into the same hallway behind the servant, the hallway which led to the *salão* where we had eaten the fig pasties.

Their voices sounded in my head.

My grandmother concerned. 'You are pale, my dear. Are you ill?'

My mother. 'It's nothing but the heat. It came early in the city this year. I'm glad to be home here amongst the mountains.'

Minha avó. Mama.

I tried to hide my feelings, but I think I must have revealed something. So my grandmother had died at the very time that we, too, were taken.

'We did not know,' I said at last. 'The . . . the cousins in Amsterdam have written, but received no reply for many years. It is sad news I shall have to take back to them. But your master, when do you expect him to return?'

He shook his head again, and now I saw that his eyes had filled with tears.

'He went to Lisbon on business three weeks ago. We knew nothing then of this English invasion and the return of Dom Antonio. Word came yesterday. The master has been taken by King Philip's men and executed without trial. But we knew nothing here of Dom Antonio's plans, nothing – he was no part of it!'

The world seem to spin around me and I closed my eyes, leaning my forehead against the hot door frame to keep myself from sinking to my knees. I had thought, surely, that my grandfather, of all the family, would be safe. We had brought this death upon him. Dom Antonio's expedition. Drake's thirst for plunder. Our stupid blundering and delays at Coruña, our triumphal landing at Peniche. What had it accomplished but the deaths of Portugal's finest nobles, whether or not they supported the Dom? Three weeks ago he was here, my grandfather. Only three weeks ago. While I sat idle on the *Victory* in the harbour at Coruña.

And my grandmother had died all those years ago, when we had lain in the Inquisition prison at Coimbra.

Taking me firmly by the arm, the servant led me into the house and made me sit in the cool *salão* and brought me chilled golden wine.

'I am sorry to have distressed you with this news, Senhor,' he said, 'and the heat . . .'

'Yes,' I said dully. 'The heat.'

'May I know who you are, Senhor?'

'Christoval Alvarez,' I said automatically.

'Alvarez? The master's daughter married a Dr Alvarez. You are related?'

'Yes.'

150

I roused myself. There was one more person I had come seeking. Surely they could not all be dead.

'Your master's granddaughter, Isabel,' I said, hardly daring to ask, 'my . . . my cousin Isabel. Is she here?'

'Oh, nay, Senhor Alvarez. To see her you will need to go to the farm of the master's tenants, the da Rocas. Do you know the da Rocas? Their farm is through the forest. In the valley on the other side. I will give you directions.' He was a kind man, still looking at me with concern. I could not tell how much my face had given away. 'Will you take some food first?'

I refused the food, but listened to the directions, for I could not exactly remember the way. Why, I wondered, was Isabel still at the farm, where she had been placed all those years ago for safety? Why was she not here, in my grandfather's house? But my sister was alive! I would see her again in less than an hour.

Chapter Thirteen

*T*o reach the da Rocas' farm by the quickest way, I took the half remembered path through the forest of Buçaco. As a child I had loved the forest, a place which always seemed to me an enchanted realm, full of mystery. I knew that it had become the custom, in our Prince Henry's time, for his expeditions to strange foreign parts – to West and East Africa, to the lands of Arabia, to India and the spice islands far to the east, and later still to Brazil – to bring back saplings of exotic trees and to plant them here, in the native forest of Buçaco. So now our indigenous species of pine and holm oak and lesser trees were interspersed with these strange trees whose names I did not know, but which seemed to carry with them the cries of parrots and birds of paradise, the screams of monkeys leaping amongst their branches, cold-eyed snakes coiled about their feet, and predatory tigers lurking behind their trunks. In the century and more they had stood here, many of them had seeded young descendents, so that a great matriarchal tree would be surrounded by a cluster of daughters and handmaidens.

Although I had set off in haste from my grandparents' home, the forest, as always, filled me with a sense of awe, so that I slowed my horse first to a walk, and then stopped under a tunnel formed by unimaginable trees whose trunks soared far above my head, and whose branches met and intertwined in the mysterious green light. My grandfather had told us this was a holy place, where monks and hermits had lived in times past, but secretly I had disagreed. To me it breathed an air much more ancient. It was a place where myth was born, a forest from Homer or Vergil, or from the strange jumbled folk tales our nurse used to tell us.

Arthur's knights might have ridden here, but in my imagination they were not the sanctified and cleansed knights of French chansons. They were primaeval. Demi-gods amongst mortal men, who haunted such places as the forest of Buçaco still. Even now, I could not rid myself of these feelings. I dared not turn my head, for I could sense them breathing behind me.

I dismounted. There was a stream beside the path, running cold and pure down from the higher mountainside and murmuring over its stony bed with a sweet and musical note, like some voice out of those ancient tales. I led the horse over to drink from it and, pulling off my cap, plunged my head into the water. I gasped with the shock, for despite the heat of the day, the stream ran icy cold, having sprung from deep under ground. This was what I needed. A moment of chill clarity to gather my thoughts. I sat down on the bank and flung my wet hair dripping on to my shoulders.

Both my grandparents were dead. The cruel truth of it confronted me. I had clung to the hope that I would find them there, the beloved home unchanged, their arms held out to embrace me, just as they had been when I was a little girl. And even as recently as three weeks ago my grandfather had still been there. The thought of that was almost too much to bear. I laid my forehead on my up-drawn knees and at last allowed myself to weep.

I do not know how long I sat their, hugging my grief, while the horse tugged at a few sparse tussocks of grass amongst the tree roots. At last I drew breath. I rubbed my face with my sleeve and tried to gather my thoughts. There was still Isabel. My little sister would be seventeen now, but I could not understand why she was still at the farm, instead of living with our grandfather at the manor house. Unless the Inquisition was still active in this area, seeking out any person tainted with Jewish blood despite being converted Christians, so that my grandfather had thought it was safer for her to remain there with the da Rocas. But would he not have sought a good marriage for her by now? Perhaps he had been so overwhelmed by grief at my grandmother's death, that he had become senile. Nay, that made no sense. It was clear that the estate was in good order, the farmland cared for, the house immaculate, and the servants – though frightened by what had happened – were still carrying on with their duties. My grandfather had ridden on business to Lisbon, the servant had said. That did not suggest a man overwhelmed by age or infirmity of body or mind. And now he was gone. Who would inherit the estate now? Surely, it would be Isabel, for he could not have known whether my parents and I were alive or dead..

I must talk to Isabel. I had come hoping to take her back to England, to join my father and me in London, but if she was heiress to this great estate, surely Dom Antonio would ensure that she took her place amongst the Portuguese aristocracy, if that was what she chose. The Spanish Inquisition would have no power in a Portugal ruled by a half-Jewish king. Aye, she might choose to remain here, however sorry I would be to lose her again.

I caught the horse and mounted once more. I had delayed too long, time was passing. I must hurry on to the farm and discuss these matters with my sister. I did not even know whether word had been sent to her about our grandfather's death at the hands of the Spanish authorities in Lisbon, since the news had only reached the manor yesterday. I should have asked the servant, but I had been too stunned by what he had told me to gather my thoughts.

My horse and I picked our way along the path, heavy with the forest's sun-warmed spicy aromas, stirred up by his hooves amongst the leaf litter of centuries. At last the trees thinned and we emerged into the open again, where the heat struck me like a blow. I found myself looking down over a shallow valley, cleared of trees, where the tenant farm stood. Here in the north of Portugal, expensive whitewash is reserved for churches and the homes of the wealthy. Common houses are grey stone, schist or granite, and sink into the setting of the surrounding rocks. Down below me I could see such a house, huddled low amongst its barns and outbuildings.

Despite my sorrow at the loss of my grandparents, my heart suddenly lifted at the thought that I would soon see my sister again. Isabel and I had always been close as children, friends as much as sisters. She had not possessed my passion for learning, but she had loved the countryside as I did. All three of us, Isabel and Felipe and I, had swum and ridden and played about the *solar* with a freedom not often granted to children of our class, certainly not to girls. I had never thought, as a child, to wonder why. Indeed, it was only now, looking back, that I realised that our upbringing was unusual. I must ask my father. Was it my parents or my grandparents who had slipped the reins and allowed us that freedom when we were in the country? In truth it had stood me in good stead in my masquerade to conceal my sex. I was not afraid to ride or climb like a boy. Had I always been reared as the demure daughter Caterina, a part I had sometimes played in Coimbra, then the boy Christoval would have found life difficult indeed.

I held my horse back to a gentle walking pace as we descended the steep path to the farm. I did not want to make a dramatic entry and alarm the inhabitants. Shut away in this remote valley, they must have few visitors. A stranger arriving thus on horseback might mean trouble – a tax collector, perhaps, or the forerunner of a troop of Spanish horse demanding food and quartering. I did not want to find a crossbow confronting me before I could explain my business here.

The farm was not prepossessing. Indeed it was not what I had expected from valued and respectable tenants of my grandfather. There were a few scrawny sheep in a dirty pen, some mangy chickens scratching listlessly in the dirt, and a vicious dog chained up, who would have had the leg off my horse if he could have come near enough.

The whole farm appeared deserted. Could this really be the place where my sister had been lodged for seven years, since that summer when she was ten? The summer when everything fell apart. It was here, we had been told, that she and Felipe had fallen ill, and Felipe had died. It was because of those few words of reassurance from Dr Gomez, as we crouched in the fisherman's boat in Ilhavo, promising Isabel would recover, that I had clung all these years to hope. It was those words which had brought me to Portugal, to find my sister and bring her home with me. Yet I was appalled at the sight of the farm, a filthy neglected place. I had never been here before, but I knew that in the past the da Rocas had been considered excellent tenants and sound farmers. What I could see of the farm now seemed an outrage. This was no place for my sister.

I rode slowly down the last of the path, which led first to the farm, then continued on downhill past it, to the lower part of the valley, where I believed there were more tenant farms. Dismounting, I left my horse to stand at the far edge of the yard, and made my way warily in a wide circle around the dog until I could reach the front door of the house and bang on it with my fist. It hung askew, and the mean windows on either side were shuttered. Everything was very dirty, and the paint on the woodwork had blistered and peeled off long ago. No one answered my knock, but I saw a slatternly girl come out of the cowshed with a pail of milk and head towards the back of the house. She wore a ragged dress, with her hair hanging in lank tresses below her shoulders. Her feet were bare and filthy. I shouted at her, but she ignored me. I banged again on the door, beginning to grow angry. Was she deaf? Was there no one else here?

At last, when I was thinking of going in pursuit of the girl round to the back of the house, a man of about thirty emerged from one of the outbuildings and came slowly towards me, glowering. I saw him take in the sword at my side, and the quality of my mount, and my clothes, which (though far from elegant) were many degrees better than his. He wore loose dirty breeches, like the slops our sailors wore, and a sleeveless tunic which revealed thickly muscled arms, from which wiry black hair sprung. Unlike the girl, he wore heavy boots. This, then, must be the farmer, though I had expected a much older man. The girl must be a maidservant or kitchen skivvy. The man shouted at the dog to be silent, and kicked him in the ribs. The cur slunk back to a patch of shade and lay down, his eyes never leaving me. The man straddled his legs, folded his thick arms across his chest, and regarded me with much the same expression as the dog. I was relieved to see that he was not carrying a weapon.

'I am looking for Isabel Alvarez,' I said, without preamble. If this man intended to be aggressive, I could return like for like. I would not let him intimidate me, however aggressive he appeared. Like him, I stood with legs apart and let my hand rest casually on the pommel of my sword.

'And who are you?' he said, in a tone that did not reflect our clearly different social status.

'Her cousin, Christoval Alvarez,' I said. I had no intention of revealing my true identity to this man, even if he was one of the family caring for my sister. Isabel herself, of course, would know me.

'Have you proof of that?' He spat, narrowly missing my foot.

I clenched my teeth. It was not this man's place to demand such proof, but I did not intend to come to blows with him. Not if I could avoid it.

'Naturally. Though I see no need for it.' I put into my voice all the scorn of a Portuguese aristocrat speaking to a labourer. I would *not* be intimidated by this fellow. My indignation was burning in my cheeks.

I produced the passport Dom Antonio had provided me with. If this man was a supporter of King Philip of Spain, I was placing myself in great danger, but I must somehow gain access to my sister. However, here in this remote farm it was likely that the fellow took little interest in politics. If the Spanish invaders left him alone, he probably cared nothing, one way or another, who ruled the country. As my grandfather's tenant, his obligations in rent and duty would be to him, rather than to the Spanish. He took the passport, stared at it in such a way that I knew he could not read, then handed it back to me.

'You have read it?' I said blandly, aware that he had not. 'You can see that I am Christoval Alvarez, cousin of Isabel Alvarez, and I demand that you take me to her at once.' I was pleased that my voice was firm, with all the authority I had a right to, as a member of his overlord's family.

A look crossed his face which I did not like. A barely suppressed smile, a knowing smile. It gave me a brief stab of unease. With a jerk of his head he indicated to me to follow him round to the back of the house. We crossed the yard, which was no more than beaten earth, liberally scattered with dung. Broken farm tools, lengths of wood, dented buckets, and unidentifiable rubbish lay everywhere, so that I had to pick my way amongst the obstacles, though the way was so familiar to the farmer that he moved swiftly across the yard before halting before an open door. Like the front door, this one hung crookedly. It could be cold here in the mountains in winter. The January wind must find its

157

way through the house, from the gaping front door to the back, with its icy fingers touching everything. My sister Isabel was living amongst this filth and squalor and misery?

The door on this side led directly into a kitchen roofed with beams so low the man had to stoop and I could only just stand upright. The girl I had seen before was slicing onions and wiping tears from her eyes. She was cutting straight on to a scarred table of pine, so old that it dipped in the middle like a sway-backed horse. A child of about four, naked from the waist down, was playing on the floor with what I thought at first was a furry toy, before I realised that it was a dead rat. A baby was lying directly on the dirt floor, half wrapped in a filthy blanket, moth eaten and frayed. It had fallen open and the baby was naked underneath it, a girl child. She stared up at me with wide, vacant eyes. The girl by the table was visibly with child again. This must be the farmer's wife, but where were the older couple, the da Rocas to whom my sister had been entrusted? Were they too dead?

The man pointed at the girl chopping onions.

'That is Isabel Alvarez.'

When we were very young, Isabel and I shared a bed. Our nursemaid slept in the adjacent room with the baby Felipe, so there was no one to stop us whispering together on the hot sleepless nights of summer. I cannot now remember all that we talked of, what pressing concerns occupied our minds in those days. I think we complained of minor injustices and comforted each other in our sorrows. I know that when my pet sparrow died, and I cried all night, Isabel put her arms around me and cried too. We must have had plans and dreams, but these are lost now from memory, except that I remember we were never to be parted, and if our parents should marry us to husbands who lived far apart, we would run away and live together in the magical forest of Buçaco, where we would build one of our secret houses, like the ones we built every summer when we stayed at the *solar*, only bigger, with carpets on the floor. That was a point of luxury Isabel always insisted upon: carpets from Turkey on the floor. I had my own requirements. I wanted to be sure it would have a place for dogs and horses. Isabel conceded that.

'But they must not walk on the carpets,' she said earnestly, and I promised that I would make sure they did not.

When you have shared every bath with your sister and laid your head on the same pillow every night, you come to know every detail of her body as well as your own. Isabel had a tiny mole behind her left ear, not much larger than the head of a farthingale pin, and sometimes I would tickle it to wake her in the morning. I stared now at this slovenly woman with her brood of children and knew she could not be my sister. Her eyes were dull and stupid. She must surely be older than seventeen. And yet, and yet . . . There was something in the curve of the cheek, the shape of the hand that held the chopping knife.

I stepped forward and lifted the lank, greasy hair away from the girl's left ear. She flinched away, and the hand with the knife flew up towards me. I leapt back.

'What are you doing!' the man shouted, bounding across the room to me.

My heart was pounding painfully. Isabel would never aim a knife at me.

'I know how to prove if this is indeed Isabel Alvarez,' I said. I was breathing hard and I felt sickness rising in my throat. 'Tell her I mean her no harm. Tell her to put the knife down.'

I do not know why I addressed him instead of her. Perhaps some instinct prompted me.

'Do as he says,' he said roughly to the girl, then took the knife from her hand and threw it across the table. The baby began to cry, and the boy – I saw now that it was a boy – stood up and sidled behind the man who, I suppose, was his father.

I stepped forward and cautiously lifted the girl's hair again. Her whole body was tense with terror. The skin of her neck was dirty, but there, just below her hairline, was the tiny mole.

'Oh, Isabel,' I said, and I could not stop my tears, 'Isabel, what has happened to you?'

Isabel looked from the man to me and back again, her lips slightly parted and that dull, hopeless look in her eyes. I had never seen such a look of utter despair.

'You'll get little sense out of her,' the man said, with some complacency. 'She can cook, a little, and keep my bed warm, but she is no good for anything else.'

'What have you done to her!' I turned on him, shouting. 'She was beautiful and clever when last I saw her, at ten years old. Now I find her, barely seventeen, treated like a slave and bearing your brats.'

'No blame to me,' he said insolently. He leaned his shoulders against the bare stone wall and smiled again, that knowing smile. 'She and her brother both fell ill when they were placed here in my mother's care by Senhor da Alejo, seven years ago. The boy died and the girl developed brain fever. When she recovered she had become simple-minded, as you see.'

'But surely my . . . my great-uncle came for her?' I was losing the thread of my story and my pretended relationship with Isabel. 'And why did your mother betray her trust by letting you take her as your whore?' I was breathless with horror and confusion.

'As for the Senhor, he didn't want her.' He shrugged indifferently. 'Until her death five years ago my mother taught the girl to be useful. Simple cooking. How to milk the cow and grow vegetables. And she is my wife and not my whore.'

I did not believe him, with his loud voice and his shifty eyes. I knew he was lying.

How could this have happened? My grandfather would surely have come for Isabel as soon as it was safe, as soon as the Inquisition had given up their search of the area, even if her mind had been as severely damaged as the man said. But it could be that the search had continued. Perhaps he waited until the woman of the farm died, thinking her safe here from the Inquisitors, and then found it was too late. But our grandfather was dead, and now I would never know the reason. This foul villain must have got her with child when she was no more than twelve. And I did not believe he had married her, for there was something that had the ring of falsehood in his voice.

I went to the girl and put my arms around her, but she stood stiff in them, rigid as a wild animal about to run for its life. Oh, what had they done to her!

'Isabel,' I said quietly, crooning as if to a child, 'Isabel, don't you know me?'

I brushed the greasy hair back from her face, and kissed her gently on her dirty cheek. Her cheek that was still soft and childlike, though I saw that it was bruised below the eye, and there was more bruising on her neck, as if fingers had been tightened around her throat. I could make out the impression of fingers. It seemed to me that she relaxed a little as I held her, and for the first time she looked at me with eyes that had a mind behind them.

'Don't you know me?' I rocked her gently, and began to hum a tune our nurse sang to us when we were sick or fretful. She opened her mouth as if she would speak, then she looked over my shoulder and caught the eye of the man, standing watchful behind me. Her face closed down again. She shook her head and tried to pull away from me. I put my lips close to her ear, that he might not hear, and whispered.

'Isabel,' I said, no more than a breath, 'I am Caterina. Take no heed of these boy's clothes, they are simply for safety's sake. I've come to take you home.'

For a moment intelligence flashed into her eyes and she knew me. She put her arms around me and laid her head on my shoulder. So softly that it too was only a breath, she whispered, 'Caterina.'

The man jumped forward and dragged us apart.

'What are you whispering about? Leave her alone, she's my wife. You, get back to your work!'

And he struck her a violent blow on the side of the head, which sent her staggering away from me, gasping for breath, but silent. It was the silence that wrenched at my heart. She only stopped herself from falling by catching hold of the edge of the table.

At once her head drooped, her eyes became dull, and she was again the wretched whore of a brutal farmer. Mechanically, she picked up the knife and began chopping the onions again, but I saw that her hands trembled and she nicked the side of her thumb so that blood ran, staining the onions and the table. She sucked her thumb, but did not lift her eyes.

The little boy began to cry, but quietly, as if he too had already learned to suppress the sound of his grief and pain. Even so, the man cuffed him and sent him sprawling across the room, where he crouched in a corner with his hands over his head, his shoulders heaving, but silent. Even so, the baby sensed something and began the thin gulping of breath that is the first sign of tears. Isabel laid down the knife and bent awkwardly, pregnant as she was, to pick the baby up off the floor. She was clearly still stunned by the blow, but she held the child against her shoulder, stroking her back with a hand that was shaking. Her thumb left a patch of blood on the baby's back.

'I have come to take Isabel home to her family!' I shouted at the man. 'You have no right to keep her here.'

'She is my wife.' He was sneering, sure of his power over her. 'In law she is my property, as surely as my dog or my sheep or my cow or my chickens.'

'Prove it. Show me some me some proof of your marriage. Who was the priest who married you? Did her grandfather give his consent?'

He swayed back.

Ah, I thought, *I have you there.*

'Come, Isabel,' I said, 'I am going to take you home.'

He stepped between us.

'Show me *your* proof, then, *Senhor* Alvarez.' He mocked me with the word 'Senhor', as though I had no claim to it. 'How can you prove you have the right to take her from me? Has Senhor da Alejo commanded it?'

From the way he spoke, I realised he had not yet heard that our grandfather was dead.

'Yes,' I said boldly. 'He has commanded it. And you had best do as he commands, for he is your master, and if you do not obey, I shall see that you lose this farm and your livelihood as well.' My heart was beating fast and I spat out the words, so outraged that I was becoming careless.

'Then let him come. He has not come for her these five years, since my mother died.'

'The world is changing,' I said, rash in my desperate need to rescue Isabel from this place. 'King Antonio has returned, with Drake's English fleet and army at his back. He has already been hailed as King of Portugal in Peniche. I travelled with them. Now we are on our way to Lisbon. We will drive all the Spaniards out of Portugal and it will be a free country again.'

He gaped at me. Clearly no word had come to this remote place from Coruña or Peniche. He shook his head.

162

'You lie.'

'It is true, and you will hear of it soon enough, even here in the forest.'

I saw that the conviction in my tone had convinced him, or at least made him pause to change his tactics.

'You have not proved your right to take her. I do not know that you are even of her family.' His face was twisted in a sneer. 'Perhaps you want her for your own whore!'

I was so startled by this that I began to laugh, which angered him more. This was the last thing I had expected. My astonishment made me slip my guard. And then I did a foolish thing, and cast away all caution.

'None has a better right than I to take her away!' I cried passionately. 'I am her sister, Caterina. She recognised me just now.'

Isabel had stayed cowering beside the table since he had hit her, trying to comfort the baby, but she looked at me now with frightened eyes and I realised I had taken one step too far. She opened her mouth to speak, then pressed her lips together with a look of despair. The little boy had crept on hands and knees to his mother and was clinging to the ragged hem of her skirt.

'Her sister!' He leapt at me, and before I could stop him had torn open my doublet and shirt. 'A woman? You are a woman?'

I pulled away and tried to fasten my clothes. I was shaking. Oh, fool that I was!

'I can handle a sword as well as any man, so keep your distance.' I drew my sword a few inches from the scabbard and looked at him defiantly, but I knew that I had made a fatal mistake.

He stood back and folded his arms again. To my surprise, he smiled. Then laughed. It was a sound to strike fear, but I refused to show it.

'A woman. Her sister.' He gave another great hoot of laughter, then spat, so that a gob of spittle landed on the table beside the chopped onions. 'Then you must be the heretic, Caterina Alvarez. They came searching for you at the *solar* when you escaped from Coimbra. That time they took your grandmother away, that old woman, another heretic. And killed

163

her – good riddance. A true-blooded Portuguese like your grandfather should never have married a dirty Jew like that and got all this brood of heretics. He may be my *master* as you call him, but he brought that curse on himself.'

He was grinning in elation, all the long hatred of centuries distilled into the look he fixed on me.

'The Inquisition will be glad to know that you have returned,' he said, triumph and glee mixed in his voice, 'when I report you. A heretic, a Jew, and now masquerading as a man-woman. This time it is certain. It will be the fire for you.' His face gleamed with salacious pleasure as he fixed his eyes on my gaping shirt.

It was checkmate. If he did succeed in reporting me to the Inquisitors before I could reach the safety of Peniche and the protection of our expedition, I was bound for the fire. I felt sick with terror.

'Isabel!' I cried, reaching out my arms to her. 'Come with me!' Tears were running unchecked down my cheeks. My sister.

Isabel too was weeping, but she shook her head slowly, making a helpless gesture with her free hand. Behind the man's back she mouthed the words at me, 'The children.' It was unanswerable.

I was helpless. The children were clinging to her. Even if I could get her away, how could I rescue the children? And I knew, whatever I said, she would not leave without them.

At last she found her voice. 'Go, Caterina! Quickly! Go!' Her voice broke in a sob. 'You cannot help me. Go!'

Then suddenly the man leapt forward and seized the knife from the table. He sprang for me, but I was expecting it. I grabbed a stool and flung it at his knees. It was a lucky throw. I heard the crack as it struck bone. He staggered and tripped, and before he could regain his balance I was out through the door and racing for my horse, who stood where I had left him at the other end of the yard, keeping well clear of the vicious dog. I had to weave my way through all the rubbish strewn about the yard and in my blind panic I fell over a broken rake, landing on my knees and scraping my palms on the hard and gritty soil. The man was already through the door and coming for me fast, the knife in his hand. As I scrambled to my feet, I felt a sharp stab of pain in the ankle which I had sprained.

Running lopsided, I reached the far side of the yard and threw myself across the saddle on my stomach, thanking all the stars in Heaven that the horse was smaller than Hector so I had no need of a mounting block. He was already moving as I caught the reins in my left hand and urged him back along the track to the forest, even before I was able to swing my right leg over his back and find my stirrups. He was rested now, and fear of the dog drove him all the faster. He had no need of my urging to break into his swiftest gallop.

Behind us, I could hear the sounds of the farmer unchaining the dog, and yelling curses and threats after me, but I counted on his having no horse. Nowhere about the farm had I seen any sign of one. Probably he managed with a draught ox or even just a donkey. He could never catch me on my army officer's stallion. The horse could hear the animal behind us as well as I could, for it gave tongue like a trained hunting dog, so he flew down the track as if the very hounds of Hell were on his heels. Crouched low in the saddle, I left him to find his own way, for I was blinded and racked with sobs as the place that held my sister Isabel dwindled into the distance behind me, to be lost beyond the forest trees of Buçaco.

Chapter Fourteen

*A*s my horse thundered up the hill, back the way we had come, his head was lowered and his ears back, and his gasping breath beat time to the drumming of his hooves on the hard ground. My own heart pounded in my ears to the same relentless rhythm. If we did not escape this evil man, I would be betrayed to the Inquisition. I was no longer a child, no longer under the protection of a mother who would do anything, *anything*, to protect me. I would be stripped and tortured and endure all that she had endured. No confession, no penance would save me now. Everything that she had suffered to ensure that I lived would all go for nothing. I would be for the fire. I crouched low over the horse's neck, my fingers entangled in the reins and the harsh hair of his mane, which lashed against my face. My eyes closed, I could smell the stench of burning flesh.

I was only conscious of entering the forest when the heat of the sun on my back was suddenly replaced by a flood of cool air. I opened my eyes. The arms of the trees embraced me, welcoming. A soft green had replaced the harsh glare and the stony ground of the farm, beneficent as a blessing. I drew a long, shuddering breath. The horse was almost beyond control, terrified by the baying of the dog at his heels and his instinctive sense of my own terror. The dog had been left behind, but only after he had managed to sink his teeth briefly into the horse's leg. I had been barely aware of that, and of the horse kicking out to free himself of the vicious animal.

I must get the horse under control.

I straightened in the saddle and slowly, slowly, eased the horse back from his panic-stricken gallop to a slow canter. He was still gasping and his neck was dark with sweat. I thought of how the piebald Hector could gallop effortlessly on and on, but then I had never ridden him when he was as frightened as this horse was. Slower. Slower. Down to a nervous, broken trot, then a walk. He was shivering now, partly from nerves, partly from the cool forest air on his sweat-drenched coat.

We had come to the place where I had stopped before, beside the stream. I drew back on the reins. There was no longer any sound of pursuit. The man had no chance of catching us and the dog had disappeared after the horse had kicked him away. I slid down off the horse and my legs buckled under me, so that I collapsed on the ground, the reins still in my hands pulling the horse's head down with me. The ground was cushioned with the accumulation, year upon year, of leaf litter and pine needles, and for a few minutes I did not even try to get up or release the horse. We both needed time for our hearts to steady and our breathing to return to normal.

At last I clambered to my feet. My legs were still shaking and I leaned against the horse's shoulder. He blew anxiously into my ear, leaving a trail of foam on my cheek.

'Poor fellow,' I said, as calmly as I could, running my hand reassuringly down his neck. 'That was a bad moment, wasn't it?'

I unbuckled the cheek strap and slipped the bit out of his mouth, then led him to the stream. He was anxious to drink, but I would let him take only a little at first, in case he did himself harm. Strong and enduring as they may appear, horses can be delicate creatures. When he had taken the edge off his thirst, I led him back a little way from the stream, where there was a patch of grass between the trees. As he relaxed and began to graze, I opened my satchel and found a salve for the dog bite. Fortunately it was not deep. The creature had drawn blood but had not been able to clamp his great jaws too tightly, so there was no serious harm. The horse's skin twitched as I spread the salve over the wound, and he raised his head briefly from the grass, then returned to it.

Once I had seen to the injury, I tore up a handful of grass and set to, rubbing the sweat off his coat. He still shivered from time to time, but there was some warmth in this open glade between the tall trunks, where westering sunlight fell slantwise,

167

helping to dry his skin. When I felt he was at ease again, I allowed him another drink, kneeling beside him on the bank and scooping up water in my cupped hands to drink myself, for I was aware that my mouth was dry and my throat sore, as if I had been weeping for hours, yet I was dry-eyed now, though my cheeks were stiff with salt. I was aware only of a terrible emptiness where there had once been hope. I knew I ought to eat something before my strength failed me, but my stomach heaved at the thought.

I got to my feet, eased the bridle back into place, and mounted again. The only way to go at first was back through my grandfather's estate, but I would not call at the house again. The horse was calm and seemed to have totally forgotten his fright as I urged him to a slow but steady canter that he should be able to sustain for a long while. When the manor house came into sight, I turned my back on its white walls, as they flushed a soft pink in the setting sun, and rode away, my mind in turmoil, shying away from the joyous thoughts which had filled it when I had approached only that morning.

Darkness was falling when we reached the bridge over the river Montego and there was no one about, not even a shepherd with a flock of sheep. Although he had crossed it quite willingly before, the horse baulked now. Perhaps he had not quite forgotten his earlier terror after all. Or perhaps the unchancy light of a rising full yellow moon, glancing off the water like fire, alarmed him. He would only consent to cross when I dismounted and led him over, encouraging him with soft words.

I knew I could not go much further that day, nor could the horse. Wearily we climbed up to the belt of woodland where we had spent the previous night, though I could hardly believe that only a day had passed since then. I found the stream again, but lower down. It was an adequate place to spend the night. The countryside was empty all around, no light shining from cottage or farm. Once again I removed the horse's saddle and bridle and fixed the hobble so that he could graze, but not wander too far. In fact, he was well trained. He knew to stay near his rider.

The previous night I had given little thought to any dangers here in this woodland, far from human habitation, but it occurred to me now that there were likely to be wild boar in the forest, and possibly wolves as well. A boar was unlikely to trouble me unless first attacked, but I was less sure about wolves. The smell of a horse and a human would reach them from some distance and a horse is a natural prey. He could do little to protect himself. I wished I had my dog Rikki with me. He had shown himself courageous once before in protecting me from an attack – human not vulpine. I shivered. Whatever the thoughts eating into my mind, I must keep up my vigilance and my strength, and to sustain both, I must eat.

The thought of food still revolted me, but I forced myself to eat almost the last of my supplies – a little dried meat and some bread so stale I had to soak it in water from the stream before I could chew it. Despite the heat of the day, it grew chilly under the trees as darkness fell. I had no blanket, but I unrolled the cloak I had brought strapped behind my saddle and huddled into that for warmth. Even with the cloak I began to shiver uncontrollably, so that with the detached, analytical part of my brain I knew I was suffering from the delayed effects of shock. As a physician I had observed it in patients who had survived a near fatal accident. After such an experience, overpowering cold would seize the body. It could also happen to soldiers. Sustained by courage and excitement and violence throughout a battle, they would often begin this shaking after it was over. I had heard of it many times, and witnessed it for myself at Coruña. It was not fear. Somehow the body needed to restore the balance of humours after great physical effort or mental shock. I tried to regard myself dispassionately as a physician examining a patient. It did little good.

My mind recoiled from those scenes on the farm. Though I shrank from the thought of them, I must try to decide what to do. Was Isabel truly damaged in her mind? At times it had seemed so, when she looked as me with those vacant eyes. But then at other times she had clearly recognised me and at the end she had said, rationally enough, that she could not leave the children. Any mother would have done the same. And she had begged me to leave, to save myself, for I could do nothing to help her. Nay, I did not believe her mind was gone. I was sure, however, that she lived in perpetual terror of that man. I realised I did not even know his name. He must be the son of the older tenants of my

169

grandfather, so he was a da Roca, but his first name had never been mentioned.

If our expedition was successful and Dom Antonio gained his throne, it might be possible for me to secure his help in wresting Isabel from the power of that man. If it could be proved that he was not married to her, he could have no claim to own her. It might be possible. I must cling to that hope. We had still to make our way to Lisbon and seize the capital, but the Dom was confident the people would rise in his favour. So much depended on so many imponderables, but I began to feel a small glimmer of hope. I lay back on the rough grass and watched the stars, brilliant in the dark sky, growing more intense as the moon sailed over to the west and began to sink toward the horizon. At some time in the dark hours, despite my intention to keep watch, I fell finally to sleep.

The following day I continued to retrace my route back toward Peniche, but I did not seek out the inn where I had stayed on my first night. Instead, I slept again in the open. The horse seemed fully recovered now, though it was clear he was growing weary. I still found it difficult to eat anything. Although there remained an end of cheese and some dried figs and apricots in my satchel, the very sight of food turned me dizzy with nausea, so I left them untouched. As I headed along the coast, I avoided the fishing villages, shying away from the kind woman and the children, riding now with an aching head and dogged purpose to reach the expedition again. I was light-headed from lack of food and exhaustion, but there was nothing else to do but simply ride on. Once more I avoided the towns, until I came at last to the isthmus leading to the peninsula of Peniche.

Less than a week after I had left, I was back at the royal camp. I returned my good horse to the garrison stables just inside the town gate with thanks to the master of cavalry, and bought the gallant animal a feed of bran mash and the best oats, for without him I could not have regained the safety of this small kingdom of Dom Antonio's. Before leaving, I checked that the wound inflicted by the farmer's dog was healing cleanly. I parted with the horse somewhat sadly, for we had endured much together. He had provided unquestioning companionship, but I dreaded what I might be asked about my private expedition when I rejoined the English force.

The town seemed strangely deserted. When I had left, the English soldiers and sailors had been in evidence everywhere in the streets, visiting the ale-houses and brothels, buying trinkets from market stalls, eating in the Portuguese equivalent of a London ordinary and enjoying the change from ship's biscuit and salt cod. Here they would be able to eat fresh food, especially the sardines for which the area was famous. And no doubt they had been enjoying the local wine. Now hardly anyone was to be seen, not even the local inhabitants. Some children, playing in the street, looked up as I came away from the stable, sucking their thumbs and watching me in silence, wide-eyed. A young woman, carrying a baby, nodded to me, but did not smile, while an old crone, sitting on a stool before her doorway, turned on me a look that was almost malevolent. As I neared our quarters, I began to dread that our soldiers had once again gone on the rampage. It was only when I walked down to the harbour that I understood why the town, so crowded when I left, seemed half deserted now. The harbour was empty, save for a few fishing boats and a dozen or so skiffs. The entire English fleet had gone.

Had I been abandoned while I had been absent? What would I do if I found myself now alone in Peniche, with little money and no means of making my way home to England? I walked as fast as I could to the citadel, almost running in my panic. As I came within the walls of the fortress, I was relieved to see that I had not, after all, been abandoned. The whole central court was filled with our ragbag army, rounded up and milling about aimlessly. Some of Norreys's officers were shouting orders, which were mostly ignored. The soldiers were all carrying knapsacks and wearing full or half armour. A few officers were mounted, also in armour, and there were more horses tethered outside the sleeping quarters.

When I reached the rooms which had been allocated to our Portuguese party, I found Dr Nuñez sitting on a bed in his shirt sleeves, attended by his servant, who was strapping the doctor's few possessions into a knapsack.

'Good,' said Dr Nuñez, with a smile. 'I was afraid you would not reach us in time.'

171

'What has become of the fleet?' I asked, flinging myself down on one of the other beds and prising off my boots to ease my feet, for I had not taken them off, day or night, since I had left Peniche. My feet stank like rotting meat. Although I had been riding, not walking, the heat had caused my feet to swell and the stiff leather had rubbed blisters on my heels.

'We have divided our forces.' His expression was grim and it was clear that he was unhappy with the strategy. 'Drake has gone in pursuit of that treasure ship, the one which stopped briefly here at Peniche and which is now said to be moored some way up the Tejo, but down river from Lisbon.'

'But why is the army left behind?'

'Ruy Lopez and Dom Antonio – and indeed Sir John Norreys himself – think it is best for us to remain on land with the army, so that we may gather up as many of the Dom's supporters as possible while we march overland to Lisbon. That may be right. It is possible.'

He shrugged. 'But we would have travelled faster had we gone by ship. And this amateur army has no experience of long marches, certainly not across difficult terrain and in such heat. There are not provisions enough here in Peniche to carry with us for an army. We cannot strip a Portuguese town as we stripped Coruña, so we will have to march some sixty-five miles on empty stomachs and the hope that the peasants can feed us, for we cannot pillage.'

'Drake has not abandoned us?' I asked, nervously, for I could never quite trust Drake.

'He is to meet us at Cascais, on the Tejo,' Dr Nuñez said. 'The gold from the treasure ship will help us reprovision there.'

'And help Drake buy his way back into the Queen's favour?' I shook my head. 'Will he even agree to spend some of the treasure on food for the soldiers?'

His only reply was a grunt.

'And the army must march all that way in this heat? An untrained English army? They will never survive it.'

'They must, if ever they wish to see their homes again.' He got up and struggled into his doublet. 'At least Norreys does not intend any fighting, at any rate not until we reach Lisbon. It is almost certain Philip will have strengthened the garrison there.'

'We may not intend to fight,' I said, 'but should we encounter any Spanish troops, they may not see it in the same way. We will need to defend ourselves if we are attacked.'

'That is very true.' He sounded tired and I realised that this trek of more than sixty miles across the barren Portuguese terrain would be very hard on him – a man as old as my lost grandfather – even if he was on horseback.

'When do we leave?' I asked. I realised I would have to stuff my feet back into my boots, if they had not swollen too much. It would be painful.

'At once. Or as soon as Black Jack Norreys can muster that rabble into some kind of marching order.'

He nodded to his servant to carry away his belongings and turned to me.

'You had best pack your own knapsack. Did you not leave it here when you rode off? And have you eaten?' He peered at me. 'I think your mission has brought you no happiness, but we will not speak of it now. Fetch your knapsack and I will send for some food. You look as if you have not eaten for days.'

I did not admit that he was right, and I knew that somehow I must force down some food or I would be unfit for the journey. When I had collected my few belongings and returned to his room, there was a plate of cold meats and bread waiting for me, and a tankard of thin local wine, which I drank gratefully. I managed to eat the food, washing it down with the wine. Although I could barely taste it, I knew that it would sustain me. With a great deal of difficulty and considerable pain, I managed to force my feet into the unyielding leather of my boots, muttering curses under my breath.

When I was ready, we made our way out to the main courtyard, where I was relieved to learn that there were horses enough for the gentlemen and officers. Since I was exhausted from riding most of the nights as well as the days since leaving the farm, stopping only long enough to rest my gallant horse, I certainly did not think my own legs would have carried me to Lisbon. The common soldiers, however, would have to walk, and at the same time they would have to carry every piece of armour, every item of weaponry, for there were no pack mules or donkeys or carts to be had. All beasts of burden seemed mysteriously to have disappeared, spirited away by the people of Peniche. The soldiers would not, however, be burdened with food. There was none. In the short time Dom Antonio had housed his court at Peniche, our army had stripped the town of everything edible. I understood now why the few people I had seen in the streets had given me a chilly reception. The inhabitants of the town had welcomed us rapturously, indeed with cries of joy, but I am sure they waved us off with even greater rapture.

During the last week while I had made my journey to the *solar* the weather had turned from merely hot to a blistering heat. A few hours out of Peniche and across the isthmus, our makeshift army quickly began to fail, for they had never yet marched further than the distance between the taverns in Plymouth, Coruña, and Peniche (apart from their scavenging forays into the countryside around Coruña). Some men complained unnecessarily, but within the first few hours there were cases of real need. I found that I was constantly dismounting to tend to one who had fainted with heatstroke or another whose bare feet were lacerated by the stony ground. There were, of course, no spare boots.

'Cover your head against the sun,' I would say to one man. 'Not with your metal helmet. Carry that. Contrive something cool, with a handkerchief.'

However, there were few handkerchiefs amongst the men, who thought them an unnecessary item, fit only for women, when any fool could blow his nose between his finger and thumb, so I showed them how to fastened three or four palm leaves together to make a comical kind of hat, as we had done as children. There was a good deal of ribaldry at this, when they looked at one another, but they soon appreciated the protection from the sun.

To another man, I would say, 'You are not on ship-board now, to go barefoot. All the way from here to Lisbon the ground will be stony. If you do not have shoes, bind your feet with cloth.'

This presented more of a problem, as did the continued lack of handkerchiefs. Palm leaves could not provide protection for the men's feet. I wished I had some of that shirt cloth I had used in the citadel of Coruña. In the end, some of the barefoot men resorted to tearing the bottoms off their shirts and binding their feet with these, while others continued to go barefoot, as they had been accustomed to do at home in England. But this was not England.

Late in the afternoon of the first day, I heard a piercing shriek from amongst the plodding soldiers behind me, and looking over my shoulder I could see a knot of men milling about, and all the column of soldiers behind them halted.

'Doctor!' The cry was passed along the line. 'Dr Alvarez, come quick!'

I wheeled my horse about and cantered back to where I could see a man writhing on the path, his face contorted with terror and pain. I slid to the ground, unbuckling my satchel.

'What is it?' I demanded. 'What has happened?'

'A snake.' They were all talking at once. 'A great long snake, six feet at least. He's bitten on the leg.'

'Describe the snake,' I said, as I knelt in the dirt beside the man and turned back his ragged breeches. He was one of those who wore no shoes, and the puncture marks were easy to see, just above the ankle.

But no one had seen the snake clearly, or if they had, lacked the language to describe it. Not that it would have helped, for I knew little about the snakes of my native land, except that some could kill a man. I cupped my hand beneath the man's heel and raised his filthy foot to my mouth. However disgusting it was, I must not waste any time. I pressed my mouth against his ankle and sucked. Something foul filled my mouth and I spat it into the withered weeds beside the path. Again I sucked and spat, until it seemed there was no more venom to be drawn out. My lips and tongue tingled, as if I had bitten on a wasp.

The other soldiers had fallen silent, watching me with mouths agape. I heard one man mutter a hasty prayer. Several crossed themselves, in the old way. They stared at me with something like awe. I lowered the foot to the ground and sat back on my heels, feeling dizzy. The man moaned.

'There is no reason to be afraid,' I said as briskly as I could manage. When a patient has received such a shock, his very terror may stop his heart. 'I have removed all the poison.' I hoped I spoke the truth.

I salved the bite with *echium vulgare, borago officinalis,* and *eupatorium cannabium,* and gave the soldier an infusion to drink, of *avena sativa,* which strengthens the heart, and *achillea millefolium,* which is antispasmodic. I drank some myself, in case I had inadvertently swallowed some of the poison. This treatment was usually efficacious in the case of a viper's bite, but I was uncertain whether it would prove powerful enough to counter the poison of this Portuguese serpent. The other men watched me with increasing respect. The injured soldier left off his moaning and hysterical cries and I told two of his companions to get him to his feet and keep him walking between them. The leg was showing some signs of swelling, but he had no other pain, his heart had steadied, and he did not lose consciousness.

'You saved my life, doctor,' he said pathetically. He was not much older than I, and tears had made channels through the dirt on his cheeks. I patted him on the shoulder.

'Keep moving, and look where you put your feet in future. I will keep a watch on you, to see that you take no harm.'

Most of the straggling column had overtaken and passed us while I worked, so that we were now nearly at the rear of the army. I remounted my horse and stayed near the group. Although the man was pale with shock and stumbled as he walked, two of his companions helped him along. He seemed likely to take no permanent hurt. I could not be sure, of course. Sometimes a snake's venom acts so quickly that there is no time to take any action to help a patient. Sometimes it is slow and insidious. A patient will appear to have taken no harm and then, little by little, his limbs are paralysed, and then his heart and lungs. His tongue may turn black and his eyes roll back in his head as the deadly poison seizes his whole body. I would need to keep an eye on the man, in case he suffered any of these slow-burning symptoms.

The only food the people of Peniche had been able to give us was bread and a small supply of salted fish, which was all consumed by the morning of the second day, and little wonder, for the men were sorely tried by the blazing sun and their heavy loads. The salted fish was almost worse than no food, for it increased the terrible thirst brought on by the sun and the weary marching. Those of us in the group of Portuguese gentlemen ate no better

176

than the men did. I felt myself growing giddy in the saddle by mid-day. However, I observed that the group surrounding the Earl of Essex, who kept themselves apart from the rest of us, appeared to have a supply of both food and wine.

Sir John Norreys rode up to Dom Antonio and put to him a blunt choice.

'You must provide food for the soldiers, or I will not be able to stop them looting. Men will not willingly starve when they can see farms around them in the countryside.'

Dom Antonio conferred with Dr Lopez. It seemed they had no funds left with which to buy provisions. They had expected by now that the nobles and peasants rushing to join our army would bring food with them. In the end they decided that the Dom would have to beg the peasants to provide us with food on credit. Once Lisbon was seized, he would pay them back, and generously too.

Our whole Portuguese party accompanied him as he rode up to the largest house in the next village we approached. We had just crossed an area of barren, tussocky ground and reached a small valley watered by a stream – nearly dried up now, in the heat. It was a farming village, with fields and olive orchards surrounding the clustered houses. We Portuguese went in a body to show that this was not a foreign invasion, but a mission to restore to Portugal her ancient freedoms.

'So you understand, Senhor,' the Dom said, in a somewhat patronising tone, 'by supplying our army, you will be contributing to the success of our campaign to expel the hated Spanish from our land.'

He was addressing the man who seemed to be some kind of village leader, but most of the men of the village were grouped around him, listening intently. From their expressions I fancied that they were calculating, not how soon the Spanish would be driven out, but what profit they could make from selling food to the army. When it became clear that supplies would be bought not for cash but for promissory notes, they drew apart in whispering groups. In the end they agreed to supply what they could, though it was hardly an abundance. As I watched the promissory notes signed with a flourish by Dom Antonio, I wondered when these people would ever be able to convert them to coin.

This brought us a supply of the kind of food which forms the diet of peasants in the southern part of Portugal: salted fish, dried peppers and figs, strips of dried mutton, a kind of cold porridge made of rice, flat disks of unleavened rye bread, and wine so rough it stripped the lining from the roof of your mouth. I ate cautiously – some figs and dried mutton, but mostly bread, and clear spring water when I could find it. The men ate ravenously, complaining all the while and demanding hot beef and onions, pies and pottage.

Dysentery broke out.

I do not believe – as some of the soldiers believed – that the villagers had sold us tainted food. The outbreak of the bloody flux was due to a number of causes: an unfamiliar diet, polluted drinking water, unauthorised food stolen along the march, and the weakness of the untrained, ramshackle soldiers who had never been strengthened by regular army service. For on the whole it was the first-time recruits, not the regular soldiers who had served in the Low Countries, who gave way to illness and exhaustion.

All the way from Peniche, men fell by the roadside and died. Some had wounds from Coruña or from the landing at Peniche or from their own drunken brawls. With the heat and the lack of food, their wounds festered and carried them off. Some grew so weak with dysentery they could march no further. They sat down beside the road and refused to go any further. Some died. Others, I suspect, simply melted away into the countryside. Whether they were taken in by local people and survived, or died alone and unmourned, no one will ever know.

At the three first deaths, the column of march halted, while the leaders consulted over what to do. We could not carry the dead with us. Nor could we leave them lying unburied on the barren ground, prey to scavenging animals and birds. So we halted in the unforgiving heat, while a resentful burial party was named and set to digging a grave to accommodate all three. At that point we still carried spades and mattocks, intended for simple mining under the walls of Lisbon, if the garrison should attempt to hold the city against us.

The men dug a pit of reasonable size and the men were laid to rest, with the burial service spoken reverently over them by one of the army's padres, as we stood, sweating and bareheaded, at the side of the grave.

Later, attitudes hardened. A shallow groove would be scratched out, the body rolled into it, and a few handfuls of dirt scattered over, to the accompaniment of a few a hastily gabbled words. One of the padres had died by then. Finally no one even bothered to look round at the dying, for each man struggled to put one foot in front of the other and had nothing left to spare for the dead. As for those who simply sat or lay at the roadside, refusing to go further, I do not know what became of them.

Never had the land of my birth seemed so alien to me. As I rode on, light-headed under that merciless sun, I was haunted by thoughts of my sister, trapped, perhaps forever, in a cruel servitude of body and soul. Until now I had kept at bay the thought of my grandmother, dead in a prison of the Inquisition, and my grandfather, who would be alive today but for this ill-conceived and disastrous expedition.

In my state of dumb misery and feverish imagination, I found my mind dwelling on London. Despite the secrecy and danger of my life there, it seemed a cool green haven, compared with the hellish land over which we crawled, as insignificant as a column of ants, awaiting the annihilation of some gigantic boot. What would my father be doing now? Was he well enough to minister to his patients in the hospital? I wondered whether my dog Rikki still accompanied him there every morning, and whether Joan was yet reconciled to him. What would the players be performing now, in the summer season at the playhouses? Their light-hearted companionship seemed a world away from this dark company moving forward across a foreign land in shared misery. Would Simon come to visit my father in my absence? Did he ever think of me? Or would he be too preoccupied with some new drama in the playhouse and his friendship with his new companion Marlowe? I dashed stupid tears from my eyes, making a pretence of wiping the sweat from my forehead. It was useless to think of London, for I might never see it again. I might not even survive the march to Lisbon.

Chapter Fifteen

*T*hat was the first three days. With a well-trained army, accustomed to long marches, fit and healthy, properly provisioned, it should have been possible to cover the sixty-five mile distance from Peniche to Lisbon in about three days. We should have been there by now. With our poor shambling creatures, unfit from the start of the expedition and growing weaker by the day, with very little food and almost no clean water, it would take us at least two or three times as long. If, indeed, we ever reached Lisbon. Like many of the soldiers I had begun to feel that our slow crawl across the Portuguese countryside would never come to an end. Although I was one of the privileged few on horseback, I still suffered the same heat, thirst and hunger as the foot soldiers. The horses too were growing weak. We could usually find them some grazing, however poor, but they too were desperate for water. Because of their failing condition, they plodded along as if half dead, their heads hanging, yellowish drool hanging from their lips as they gasped for breath in the heat.

The Earl of Essex had chosen to accompany the army, no doubt hoping for military glory when we reached Lisbon, although his past record in battle was no very great recommendation. This time it might be different, if the people of Portugal did indeed rise in support of Dom Antonio. On our journey so far, there had been no sign whatsoever of any such support. Apart from a few men who joined us in Peniche, no one had come to swell the ranks of the army since we had landed. Whether people were frightened by the summary execution of the nobles like my grandfather, on the merest suspicion, or whether they had little faith in the Dom himself, I could not tell, but by now I had little hope that the expedition's supposed main goal – to put the Dom on the throne – would ever be achieved. It might be, too, that the Catholic people of Portugal were reluctant to be rescued from Spain by an invading army of heretic Protestants from England. The looting of churches in and around Coruña would not have gone unnoticed. In fact, on first setting out from Peniche, the army had looted some Portuguese churches before Norreys put a stop to it.

As for what the Earl of Essex believed or expected, who could tell? I do not suppose he cared two groats for Dom Antonio, though I am sure he thirsted for glory. He was not, however, a leader to inspire the men of this army. We had seen little of him. His particular party, consisting of his own officers, servants and cronies, kept to themselves. Naturally, he insisted on leading the march, so he was away at the head of the column, while I generally rode somewhat close to the rear, keeping a watch on the laggards who trailed along in danger of being left behind. Unlike the rest of us, Essex came equipped with sumpter mules and considerable baggage, amongst which I suspected that he had ensured an adequate supply of food and wine. At any rate, on the few occasions when I caught sight of him or his men, they did not appear to be suffering like the rest of us.

On the evening of the fourth day I lay down as soon as it was dark, for I was bone weary. It had been a bad day. Several more men had died and two of the horses. The ranks of the army had also grown thinner through desertions. There were those who simply collapsed at the roadside and refused to move, however much the junior officers kicked and swore at them. Then there were others who slipped away when they thought no one was looking. Raised up on horseback, I would sometimes see a solitary man, or perhaps a group of two or three, hiding in a patch of scrub, waiting for us to pass. They must have hoped for help from the local cottagers, but we never knew what became of them. Perhaps they found a life there in Portugal, perhaps they died, starving and alone, perhaps the Spanish discovered them and either executed them as spies or handed them over to the Inquisition as heretics. The remaining soldiers in our army seemed not to care, seeing how our numbers were dwindling. The fewer mouths to feed, the larger share for each of those men who were left.

The death of the two horses had at least meant some food that day. The Englishmen soon overcame their squeamish resistance to eating horsemeat and grabbed their share almost before it was cooked, roasted on spits over the campfires. I had little inclination to eat, certainly not the half-raw horsemeat, for I had passed beyond normal hunger to a dazed and abstracted state, in which I seemed almost detached from my body. I feared I was becoming feverish, and privately treated myself with a febrifuge tincture. I was sparing of it, for I had not a great deal left and was uncertain how much Dr Nuñez and Dr Lopez might have with them. Many of our medical supplies had been left aboard the *Victory* and as a result had been carried away when the fleet sailed before the two older physicians could remove them. As a bird might fly, over to the west, to the ocean, the fleet was not indeed very many miles from us, but it might as well have been on the moon.

We carried some crude tents with us, but the nights were warm and most of us were too exhausted to erect them that night, so we slept in the open air. After my only meal of the day, some stale bread and a lump of cheese from which I had to scrape long whiskers of mould with my knife, I curled up under a withered bush, with my horse hobbled nearby and my satchel as a lumpy pillow. I never let it out of my sight, for I feared some of the soldiers might steal the poppy juice and other soporifics to send them into an everlasting oblivion. Apart from my medical supplies, all it contained were the carved seal made for me by Paolo and my two books, very battered now: the small New Testament given me by the rector of St Bartholomew's church and Simon's gift of Sidney's poems. I had been too tired and too dispirited to open them for days now. The ground was baked hard and stony, the night troubled with the sounds of the army, but despite the discomfort a heavy sleep came over me quickly.

I woke suddenly with a pounding heart, unsure for a moment where I was or what had roused me. There was shouting and the clash of sword against sword, then heavy bodies colliding and crashing through the bushes near me. Men were yelling in English and Spanish. All this way from Peniche we had been untroubled by Spanish forces, but it seemed our luck had run out. Clouds which might have given us some protection from the unrelenting sun during the day had built up during the night and obscured all light from moon and stars. Apart from a watch fire some distance away, everything was as black as the inside of a chimney. I could see nothing at all.

I scrambled to my feet, caught up my satchel, and groped about in the dark for my horse. He whickered in alarm and I found him, first by the sound, then by the bulk of thicker darkness. The noises were coming nearer as I tried desperately to free the horse from his hobble. My saddle and bridle were somewhere on the ground, but there was no time to find them. I had ridden bareback often enough in my childhood.

Before I could scramble on to his back, one of our soldiers heaved up out of the darkness. Somewhere another fire or a flare had been lit and silhouetted against its distant glow I could just make out a big fellow I recognised, one of those who had helped the man with snake bite keep on the march, one of Norreys's professional soldiers from the Low Countries. He peered at me, reaching out to grope for my arm.

'Dr Alvarez? It is you! Get back here. That's Spanish soldiers attacking. Our men will see them off, but you're best out of the way.'

He tugged at my arm. He was breathing heavily. I could smell sweat and fear. His words were confident, but the hand on my arm was shaking.

'Wait,' I said, 'I need my horse's tack.'

'This'll be your b'yer lady saddle, then, that I nearly fell over.' He gave a brief bark of nervous laughter.

He grabbed something from the ground, just as I caught my feet in the bridle and sprawled flat on my face. Between us we gathered up both saddle and bridle, and I wound my fingers in my horse's mane to lead him with us. I had been sleeping a little distance away from the main body of our army, for I had an irrational fear that if I slept amongst the men, I might give myself away by talking in my sleep.

The soldier led the way in a long curve round the main part of the camp, where we could see more and more men staggering to their feet, drawing their swords and looking about them in confusion. It was still so dark it was impossible to understand quite what was happening. Torches were flaring here and there amongst the scattered English forces, but it was clear that the attack had been concentrated, on the side where, carelessly, no sentries seemed to have been posted.

My companion pointed this out with contempt.

'If we had set up camp like this in the Low Countries,' he said, 'without proper sentries, I wouldn't be here today, tramping and starving across this God-forsaken country. We'd all have had our throats cut long ago. Though the Don Juans aren't making a very good job of it tonight themselves. They should have wiped out more of us by now.'

He spoke in a tone of professional criticism which would have made me laugh at another time.

I was having difficulty keeping up with him and persuading the horse along, for the shouting and the black shapes leaping in the firelight had frightened him. He kept trying to pull away from me.

'Why had Sir John not seen to it that we were better guarded?' I was incredulous.

'Oh, he gave his orders, did the Old Man. But most of this scum pay no heed to orders, unless they have to fight to save their own skins. There aren't enough of us real soldiers to hold this rabble together. Can't call it an army. It's no better than the sweepings off the streets of London.'

'You speak the truth,' I said, 'but what's to be done?'

I could sense him shrugging. The horse tried again to jerk away and I gripped his mane more firmly. 'Come along, lad,' I said soothingly.

'Just try to survive until we reach Lisbon,' the soldier said. 'But what will happen then? Do you think they'll surrender to us? I don't. We can't attack or carry out a siege. We've no artillery. We can't starve them out. We're more likely to starve ourselves first. They'll have laid in provisions, and made sure there's nothing in the country round about for us to eat. There's more ways than one for a siege to fail.'

'I don't know what will happen,' I said. 'I really don't know. But if Drake sails up the Tejo from Cascais, he has cannon on the ships–' I let my voice trail away. Could we rely on Drake?

He gave a disbelieving snort. It was clear that his opinion of Drake was no better than mine. At home in England, Drake was fêted as a hero for his actions against the Spanish and for the treasures he carried home to the Queen and the others who financed his voyages, but those of us who served with him saw a different side to the man – the ruthless, self-serving pirate, whose first aim in life was to hurt the Spanish as much as he could, and whose second aim was to make himself the richest man in England. Or perhaps that was the first of his goals.

By the time we reached the campfires, the sounds of fighting had dwindled into the distance. Men were milling about in confusion, bumping into each other, tripping over bundles on the ground. I hardly knew whether to laugh or cry.

'Thank you,' I said awkwardly to the big soldier. 'It was good of you to come for me. How did you know where I was?'

'Saw you go off there. The lads, they're grateful for what you done for 'em.' He gave a wicked grin. 'Wouldn't rate to lose our doctor, would it? More important that Earls or Kings. That's what the lads think, anyways.'

He went off, either to join in the fight against the attackers or to help restore some order amongst the disorderly mob. I hobbled my horse again and sat down cross-legged by one of the fires. There would be little more sleep for anyone that night and it was certain my medical skills would be needed. After some time, a jubilant group of soldiers returned, having driven off the attackers with little damage to themselves apart from a few slashes – or so we thought – which I attended to, while Norreys and his senior officers rounded up men to stand sentry, after a thorough tongue-lashing to the ill-disciplined crew who had failed to keep to their duty. In any normal army, those who had deserted their posts would have been executed on the spot, but this was no normal army and our numbers were dwindling dangerously. We could not spare even the men who disobeyed orders. It was a dangerous situation for any army. Once discipline breaks down, an army becomes a violent rabble which is as likely to turn against its officers or each other as readily as against the enemy. I saw that all the victorious men who had chased off the Spaniards came from the experienced Low Countries troop.

I sent for more flares to be set up near me, and by their light I unpacked my satchel and set about seeing to the wounded. There had been no arrows or crossbow bolts, no musket shot, presumably the Spaniards thought they were too risky to use in the dark. They must have feared they would shoot their own men. Some of the sword cuts were superficial, needing no more than salving, but two needed to be stitched, difficult to do by the poor flickering light of the flares. Dr Nuñez joined me, but I saw no sign of Ruy Lopez. Together with the Dom and Norreys he occupied one of the few tents which had been erected, but I could not believe he had slept through the disturbance. Either he was too cowardly to show his face or else he was soothing the nerves of his patron. There was no sign, either, of Essex's party. I was surprised he had not seized the chance for some heroics, but perhaps he was a heavy sleeper.

As so often on this campaign, I lacked bandages, but I made do with strips torn from the shirts that the men themselves were wearing, in order to bind their own wounds. There was little spare clothing amongst us, for it had been discarded along the march.

We never discovered why we had been attacked by the isolated troop of Spanish soldiers during that particular night. Perhaps word had been carried by one of the peasants, betraying us. Or perhaps they had simply spotted our sprawling, disorganised army tramping along in the direction of Lisbon. They were indeed driven off, but we discovered with the coming of the daylight that – what with the dark and the surprise and our inexperienced soldiers' lack of skill – a number of our men had been badly wounded and killed. It seemed that a few of the better men amongst the inexperienced recruits had tried to join the regulars, but they had been surrounded by some of the Spaniards and cut down. They lay where they had fallen just beyond the camp and we stumbled upon them in the dawn. Mile by mile, our army, instead of growing by the addition of Dom Antonio's loyal subjects, was dwindling away.

I did what I could for the wounded, assisted by Dr Nuñez, but many were far gone with existing weakness and the long hours they had lain bleeding before we found them. Four died. The march was halted, except for Essex's squadron, which set off without us. The dead were buried and Dr Nuñez insisted that the wounded who could not walk should not be abandoned. Unlike so many of their fellows, they had shown courage and initiative. There were five of them. Carrying slings were contrived out of some of the remaining tents. A few of the stronger soldiers would be able to carry these, if they took it in short snatches of an hour or two. Some of the junior officers volunteered to walk part of the way, taking it turn about to ride and using a pair of their horses to carry one of the slings. At last, after some two hours' delay, we set off in the wake of Essex. Norreys was clearly angry that the Earl had divided the army, exposing us to greater danger, should there be another attack. He sent off a messenger to ride on to Essex and order him to wait for the rest of the army to catch up with his men.

That day was the hottest we had endured. There had been no springs for many miles, and the cheap rough wine bought from the peasants with promises of later payment made the soldiers thirstier than ever. When we came upon a stinking, marshy pond, they rushed towards it in a mindless mob, pushing and elbowing their fellows out of the way.

'Stop!'

I heard Dr Nuñez shouting and rode ahead to see what was happening. The men were crowding round the greenish stagnant pool, fighting each other to reach it.

'Stop!' I echoed the command and elbowed my way in amongst them, trying to pull them away. 'This is filthy standing water,' I cried. 'You *must not* drink it, however thirsty you are. It isn't safe. It will carry sickness.'

Even from a distance I caught the rank odour of it, rising out of the pond like the stinking breath of a diseased man. It was surrounded by bog plants, many of them unfamiliar to me, but others I recognised as noxious herbs. The surface was covered with a yellow-green scum, not healthy water-weed but a kind of aquatic mould. Here and there, patches of the surface were clear and it was these, catching the sun with the winking temptation of some witch's fatal brew, which had drawn the men in, driven by their almost insupportable thirst.

I might as well not have wasted my breath. Maddened with their desperate need for water, they would not listen. They threw

187

themselves on their stomachs, those who had managed to push their way to the front, and began to drink from it, scooping up handfuls of the tainted liquid, even thrusting their heads below the surface and emerging crowned with the olive-tinted slime. I noticed a group of soldiers I recognised – the man who had hustled me away from the fighting the previous night and two of the regular soldiers who had been wounded in the skirmish. They were arguing with some of the unskilled recruits, warning them against the water. One of these was the man who had been bitten by the snake. As I watched, I saw that they were successful in persuading a few of the men, more successful than I was. As experienced soldiers, they would know they must avoid polluted water, however thirsty they were, but most of the men ignored them, as they ignored Dr Nuñez and me. I knew very well what the consequences would be.

It proved as I had expected, that we were right to fear the stagnant water, for by that evening, cholera had seized the army. It is a terrible disease at any time, but on the march under unrelenting sun in a waterless land, it can be as fatal as the plague itself. Its victims raved with fever. A form of violent flux seized them, so they vomited repeatedly and vented profuse watery diarrhoea studded with white matter like grains of rice and stinking of dead fish. There was no mistaking the signs. The loss of the body's fluid leaves its vital elements desperately unbalanced so that the body craves water, but clean water was the one thing we did not have to give them. The victims' very skin shrivelled, so that the hands of young men looked like those of aged crones. Those who had friends to help them along staggered onward with us, though they were so weak they must be half carried. Others collapsed in the ditches and did not move. They were simply left behind, for we had no carts to carry them, and even if we had, most would have died within a few hours, for the fever of cholera will burn a man up from inside, consumed by an inner fire. Fortunately the wounded men carried in the slings had been unable to reach the foetid water, for they would have been the first to succumb.

'It was the honey,' the whisper went round from mouth to mouth. 'The honey that peasant gave us, the one who had an ear cut off and watched us with an evil look. The honey was poisoned.'

And any who had eaten the honey (which was pure and good, I had eaten it myself) began to fancy themselves poisoned. They would not listen when we told them that they had caught cholera from the dirty water. They had not been poisoned by someone else, they had poisoned themselves, but it is always easier to blame another man, rather than accept the blame oneself. The whole army, even the men from the Low Countries, took hold of the idea that the Portuguese peasants were trying to poison them. It was perhaps fortunate that the local peasants had taken to hiding from the army, otherwise they might have suffered some undeserved vengeance. As it was, there was whispering amongst the men, and evil glances cast at Dom Antonio and the other senior men amongst the Portuguese.

For some reason, I escaped this mistrust, having become something of a mascot amongst the men, ever since they had seen me suck the snake's venom out of the soldier's ankle with my own mouth. Even so, I was aware that the mood was dangerous and could flare up into something more serious at any time.

On the second day after the cholera had begun its attack, our numbers had been reduced again by deaths, but some of those who had been infected, by some fluke of bodily strength, were gradually recovering. By now we knew that we were no more than perhaps a day's march from Lisbon. It was with some difficulty that Norreys managed to restrain Essex from riding ahead again, in some madcap scheme of arrogant display.

That evening we set up our usual makeshift camp, though by now even the most inadequate of our soldiers understood the need for sentries to keep watch at night. There was, as usual, little to eat. The further we travelled on this seemingly endless journey, the less willing had the peasants become to sell us food in return for scraps of paper bearing the Dom's scratched signature, so that by now we saw no sign of them. Either the people of this area were more suspicious or word had run ahead of us, so that the villagers had hidden their food supplies. Had we been able to find any of them, they could claim an inability to supply us with provisions.

We were sitting slack-jointed around the watch fires as it grew dark, when we became aware of a disturbance in one quarter of the camp. It first it was no more than a murmur of sound, like a distant thrumming of bees. Then it was punctuated by shouts and what sounded like a kind of laughter, not a cheerful sound but the kind of laughter that escapes from men who are afraid or ashamed, a sort of nervous burst of hysteria. I rose to my feet and peered toward that part of the camp, trying to make out what was amiss.

'It is nothing but some horseplay amongst the men,' said Ruy Lopez.

For once, perhaps, he had grown weary of constantly dancing attendance on Dom Antonio and had joined Dr Nuñez and me, sharing our lumps of rock-hard stale bread, which we could barely break with our teeth, and what promised to be the very last scraps of the mouldy cheese.

'I'm not sure,' I said.

'Let it be, Kit,' said Dr Nuñez. 'You can care for their bodies. There is little else you can do for them.'

I sat down again, but kept my eye on a growing tumult in that quarter of the camp. Gradually it began to roll toward us, a cluster of men, shouting. At the front was a pale, gaunt figure, stark naked. I knew the man by sight, one of the recruits who had joined us at Plymouth, but I had had no dealings with him. He was older than most of the men, probably in his middle forties, his dull brown hair touched with grey and his beard – as may sometimes happen – entirely grey, almost white. This beard had grown long and straggling since we had left England and hung now halfway down his chest, so that with his nakedness and his matted hair and long beard he seemed like some half-crazed prophet from the Old Testament. He was grown so thin that there seemed to be no flesh on his bones, only the knotted outline of wasted muscle and sinew. His joints at knee and ankle and elbow bulged grotesquely out of proportion to his limbs, and his feet were as prehensile as a monkey's.

In my profession I am familiar with men's bodies, but I had never seen one so wasted as this, not even amongst the London poor or the starved survivors of the siege of Sluys. It came to me that, under the rags that were all that remained of their clothes, the other men must look the same. My own body would be wasted. I had already noticed how thin my arms had become, the skin faintly traced with a quilting of fine lines where the layer of flesh beneath the surface had shrunk away.

The naked man stumbled in our direction, pursued by the crowd, who had begun to bay like a pack of hounds, shouting and jeering and giving way to that unnatural laughter I had heard before. The man's eyes were wild as a hunted animal's, and there were flecks of foam on the parched skin about his mouth. It crossed my mind that it was strange he should have even that much of the element of water in him, for we were all become as dry as the sands of the desert.

'The Day of Judgement is come!'

He raised a withered arm and pointed at Dom Antonio's tent.

'The Lord God of Israel has brought down his curse upon you, yea, and all you sinners who are gathered here! He has laid upon you the plague of starvation, yea, and the plague of thirst such as those who dwell in the wilderness! Ye shall perish of fevers and your guts shall burn within you until ye be consumed utterly in the fire!'

His eyes glowed with madness as he staggered toward the tent which flew, even at the end of this exhausted day, the royal standard of the house of Aviz. From within the tent there came nothing but a listening silence. Reaching the tent, he tried to drag down the standard, but it was too high for him to reach.

'See where the standard of the bastard king is ringed with blood!' he cried. His voice croaked like the cry of a raven. 'So it shall be. Ye shall all perish, drowned in your own life's blood and the vengeance of the Lord shall be wreaked upon you!'

There was more foam at his mouth now, but the strength of madness which had filled his voice faltered as he fell to his knees.

'Ye shall all perish.'

It was no more than a whisper. Then he rolled over on the unforgiving ground and lay still.

Dr Nuñez reached him before I did. There was still a faint irregular pulse from a heart which could not beat much longer. A thin watery trickle of blood ran from his nose and the corner of his mouth. Dr Nuñez looked at me and shook his head. The men who had pursued the madman had stopped in their tracks. Looking anywhere but at their prey, they shuffled their feet and began to sneak away. The group of officers and gentlemen adventurers beside the fire had been shocked into silence. There was neither movement nor sound from within the royal tent.

Less than an hour later, the man died.

We hollowed out a shallow grave for him at the edge of the camp, some of those who had been in the baying crowd being the most anxious to help. Then we withdrew our several ways for what little rest we could find, exhausted in body and troubled in mind.

In this desperate state we came, the next day, over a last rise in the ground and there, about three miles away, we could see the mighty walls of Lisbon, and beyond them its clustered roofs and towers. This was where we were meant to have sailed weeks ago directly from Plymouth, without our diversions at Coruña and Peniche. Had we done so, we would still have had an army, of sorts. Though lacking in provisions, we would not have been in a state of starvation, as we were now. And here, if we had come directly, we might have found the gates opened to us by the considerable body of nobles who supported Dom Antonio. My grandfather would still be alive and could have helped me to rescue Isabel. Now he and the other nobles were dead and the gates stayed firmly barred. And I would find no help for Isabel.

The gallant Essex emerged at last from his private convoy. While the rest of the army was barefoot, dressed in rags, and as emaciated as prisoners emerging from the custody of the Inquisition, Essex still carried amongst his luggage his finest armour. He had donned a gleaming breastplate, inlaid with ornamentation in gold and polished by some page. He was fully equipped with coat of mail under his breastplate, with greaves and cuisses protecting his legs, rerebraces and vambraces enclosing his arms. His helmet, burnished to reflect the sun and blind any opponent, was topped with three magnificent plumes plucked from some exotic African bird. A sword with a jewel-encrusted hilt hung at his side and in his left hand he carried upright a spear, from which fluttered a banner bearing his motto embroidered in thread of gold: *Virtutis comes invidia.*

He was a truly magnificent sight, like some Arthurian knight from an illuminated book of romances, if, that is, one could have banished from one's mind – as I could not – the image of this gallant warrior emerging from the surf at Peniche, his head wreathed in seaweed and water streaming from every joint of his armour, while around and behind him, unheeded, men drowned. Accompanied by a bodyguard of his followers, and watched, dull-eyed, by the rest of us, Essex rode up to the nearest gate of the city and banged on it defiantly with the butt of his spear.

'Ho, within there! I challenge you to come forth and surrender the town or else be prepared to meet your end on the bloody field of battle.'

No one responded.

Unsuccessful in provoking the garrison of Lisbon, Essex nevertheless rode back to the rest of the army with a complacent smirk displayed within his open visor. Had he no understanding that this was a real war, *not* some heroic and fanciful tale drawn from the pages of a book of romances, written for courtiers and ladies?

I slid from my horse and found my legs would not hold me. Sinking down on a tussock of dried and dusty grass, I put my head between my knees. I had been in the saddle for two weeks, first to seek Isabel and then on the terrible journey to come here, to look upon our capital city. My mind was almost numb. My only clear thought was that if we could take Lisbon and drive out the Spaniards, I might still be able to return and rescue my sister.

If we could take Lisbon.

I looked around. Like me, the soldiers had simply sunk to the ground. Their faces were pinched and grey with hunger and thirst and suffering and disease. Gone was the bravado which had had them looting the provisions in Plymouth and running wild in Coruña. They looked like a company of ghosts, like the flitting wraiths that Aeneas encountered in the Underworld. They did not even raise their eyes to our goal. They lay upon the ground and slept.

Chapter Sixteen

*T*he siege of Lisbon was doomed from the outset. It had been no part of the plan, in those days of hectic excitement in London during the early spring, that Lisbon should be besieged. Dom Antonio had even been forced to concede to the Queen that the volunteer army should be allowed to loot his capital city for the first ten days. There was no other means of paying them. I never understood how this appalling concession was to be reconciled with a longed-for monarch returning to his jubilant people. I only learned of this arrangement to permit the looting of Lisbon the day we reached the city, when Dr Nuñez told me sorrowfully what had been agreed with the Queen. It seemed that the plan, so carefully devised in London, was that the authorised looting was to occur after the gates of the city were voluntarily opened to Dom Antonio by those same adoring subjects. It was assumed that there might be a little skirmishing in the streets with the occupying Spaniards, but they would soon be rounded up and despatched.

'I don't understand,' I said to Dr Nuñez, when he told me this. I knew already that Portugal was to become some sort of dependency of England, encumbered by debt, shackled by trade concessions to English merchants, with Dom Antonio no more than a puppet king, but I did not see how the plundering of the country's capital could be reconciled with a peaceful transition of power from Spain to an Anglo-Portuguese alliance.

Perhaps I was ignorant about how warfare and the affairs of kings should be conducted, but I could not comprehend how Dom Antonio – King Antonio – could hope to sit securely upon his throne by popular acclamation if he had first agreed to allow his capital city to be looted for ten days – ten days! – by an invading foreign Protestant army, and above all after the inhabitants had welcomed that army joyfully. There is no way to control an army set loose on an alien city with permission to loot. There would be not merely theft. There would be widespread destruction, rape, and murder. I did not want to be here when this happened. On the other hand, it would never happen unless the city surrendered. There was no intention on the part of our leaders to sit down to a siege.

Dr Nuñez shrugged. 'I was not party to this agreement, Kit. It was drawn up between Her Majesty, the Privy Council and Dom Antonio. If Lisbon were to fall as the result of a siege, then of course there would be looting.'

'But surely if a city is voluntarily handed over–' I said. 'And of course we are not proposing to besiege Lisbon. The city is supposed to open its doors to us.'

As a result of the original plan, we had brought with us no siege cannon, as we had been reminded again and again. We had no heavy artillery, no cannon save those that were the armaments of the fleet, and the fleet was twenty miles away at Cascais, busy about Drake's affairs. Some small-bore artillery had originally been carried on the soldiers' backs from Peniche. One by one, as the men died on the march, the weaponry they carried was left behind, for none of those poor shambling creatures could have carried two men's loads. And even those who had managed to stumble as far as Lisbon had been shedding their own burdens, piece by piece, at the side of the road. There were men with half a suit of body armour, but no weapons for attack, and men with perhaps a musket and a dagger, but no breastplate to protect them from enemy fire. Our route across the countryside of Portugal was marked by a trail of dead men and scattered arms and armour and personal possessions, a smear, a slug track, across the map which spoke all too loudly of the true outcome of this Portuguese affair.

'If the city does not surrender, then we can only take it by siege,' he said.

I nodded. 'And we can only take it by siege if Drake sails up the river, bringing his naval cannon.'

'Those are the only alternatives.'

'And we cannot sit down and starve them out.' I remembered what the soldier had said to me, the night of the attack. The city would be well provisioned, while we were starving. 'So the only possible outcomes are the willing surrender of the city or the arrival of Drake.'

'Norreys has sent a messenger to Drake,' he said, 'urging him to move upriver at once.'

'I, for one,' I said, 'will not be counting on it.'

In fact, at first we thought the city might surrender through sheer terror. Around midnight of that first night I was summoned to Dom Antonio's tent, where I found all the English Portuguese party gathered, together with Sir John Norreys, several of his captains, and – to my astonishment – seated on a gilded stool which must have been carried here by one of those sumpter mules, the Earl of Essex himself.

I slipped behind Dr Nuñez and Dr Lopez, wondering what could be so urgent that I had been summoned like this in the middle of the night. Facing Dom Antonio and the Earl was a thin, dark-haired young man, who looked both frightened and queerly elated. He was standing before the two nobles, twisting his hands together. There were beads of sweat gathering on his temples and running down his cheeks, although the night was relatively cool after the heat of the day.

'A deserter from Lisbon,' Dr Nuñez whispered in my ear, 'or a patriot, depending on your point of view. He managed to creep out through a postern gate to bring us news of what is happening inside the city walls.'

The sweating, then, was from fear or excitement.

'Senhores,' the man said, making a bow vaguely intended to include us all. 'The garrison in the city has been reinforced by six thousand troops sent by King Philip from Madrid as soon as he heard of the attack on Coruña.' He wiped his face on his sleeve. 'You have heard of the executions? Of those believed to be supporters of the Dom?'

'We have heard.' It was Essex who spoke. He seemed to think he ranked first here and could take command of the discussion, although Dom Antonio, already proclaimed king in Peniche, far outranked him, while Sir John Norreys was indisputably in command of the army, whatever Essex might assume.

'The killings have frightened many who would have been prepared to come over to Your Majesty.' The man directed his words to Dom Antonio, and I saw Essex give an irritable jerk of his head.

'Then, after the English fleet was sighted off Cascais, a rumour has spread that *El Dracque* is roaming the country with a thousand man-eating Irish wolfhounds, trained to cut down and kill anyone of Iberian blood.'

He looked around nervously, as if he expected to see a slavering beast at his heels. Someone gave a snort of laughter, quickly suppressed.

'It is no laughing matter.' Dr Nuñez had the courage to speak up, in the face of Essex and Dom Antonio. 'Such a rumour, if indeed it is believed, might keep our Spanish enemies cowering behind the walls, unwilling to give battle. However, it also means that our Portuguese friends, if we have any, will be too terrified to leave the city to join us.'

He turned to the man. 'Is it believed?'

He nodded. 'By enough people to affect how they will behave. There are others who perhaps do not quite believe, but will find it more expedient to pretend they believe, so they need do nothing.' He swallowed. 'Is it true?'

'Nay, my friend.' Dr Nuñez smiled at him gently. 'It is not true. Drake has a pet Irish wolfhound at home. I have seen it myself and it is as gentle as a babe. There are no wolfhounds, trained or otherwise, with us on the expedition. You may return and scotch the rumour.'

The young man's eyes widened, showing the white, like those of a frightened horse. 'I am not going back.' His voice rose to a squeak. 'I should be caught and killed at once. As it is, I have risked my life to come to you.'

'Of course we welcome your good service.' Clearly the Dom felt it was time he took charge of the meeting. 'You will be rewarded for your courage, and amply too.'

I wondered at such self-deception. Dom Antonio had no money to reward anyone, nor overlordship of lands to be given away. I doubted whether, at this moment in Portugal, he owned much more than the clothes he stood up in.

'Either way,' said Dr Nuñez, 'whether such a wild rumour is believed or not, Spanish and Portuguese alike will soon see that Drake is nowhere near Lisbon, but twenty miles away with his fleet as Cascais. Whether that will help or hinder us is any man's guess.'

What had Drake been doing, all the time we had been labouring overland? I suspected that he might have been indulging in a little privateering to fill in the time. There was certainly no sign of him sailing up river to join us, despite Norreys's demand.

The man from Lisbon also brought word that public executions were continuing to take place all day long.

'Any who are suspected of supporting Your Majesty,' he said, 'are killed without trial. Men are being dragged to the gallows or garrotted in the street, merely on some anonymous informer's whisper.'

The meeting in the royal tent went on for some while longer, but the man could tell us little more, save the number of the troops and the vast quantities of arms, gunpowder and food which had been stockpiled in the city while we lingered at Coruña, then made our slow way to Peniche and overland to Lisbon. It was nearing dawn by the time the meeting broke up.

'I have heard,' I said to Dr Nuñez the following day, 'that the Dom has persuaded the local priests to slip into the houses round about and tell the people that he is God's chosen ruler of Portugal, that they must come to his aid, and they will be richly rewarded, in this world and hereafter.'

We were sitting on the ground, leaning against our saddles, while our horses grazed nearby and we tore lumps out of a loaf of bread his servant had somehow managed to find for him. The bread was coarse, and I felt my teeth grate on fragments of grit, but it was fresh and I was too hungry to care.

'Well enough,' said Dr Nuñez, 'but I have never heard that priests made good recruiting officers, except in the days of the Crusades, and then they were of a more fiery disposition than those we have seen here.'

198

I was aware all at once how tired and old he looked. When we had first set out from London, he had been so buoyed up, with hope and joy at returning to his native Portugal, that he seemed to have shed his age. Now it weighed down on him, the whole burden of his seventy years.

'I also heard there was one priest,' I said, in the hope of cheering him, 'who has promised to find a way into the city and open the gates to us.'

'Aye, I heard it too. But can one man alone accomplish such a thing? I doubt it, Kit, I doubt it.'

Later that day I met the priest, Father Hernandez. I was checking the wounds of the men who had been injured during the night attack by the Spanish. There was a danger, even with the lesser injuries, that they might still fester, for the men were so weakened and the conditions in which we had lived since Peniche so poor that there was a risk of serious inflammation or even gangrene. To my relief, there was no sign of gangrene, though all the wounds were slow in healing. There being no better place to treat them, my patients came one by one to lie on the ground under a single sheet of canvas, providing a makeshift shelter. When at last I was done, I sat back on my heels and wiped my face with a wet cloth. At least here we had water from the river.

'You are over young to be serving as an army physician, my son.'

It was a priest, not more than thirty, who sat down cross-legged beside me on the ground. He had addressed me in English, but I replied in Portuguese.

'No younger than many of the soldiers,' I said. 'Or not much. Though I think many of us have aged during the march here from Peniche.'

'You are Portuguese? This march overland does not seem a wise course to have taken. Why were you not brought by ship?'

I shrugged. 'It was the decision of those in charge of the expedition. I believe they chose that course because they believed that the local people would flock to King Antonio's banner.'

'But they did not.'

'Nay.'

He held out his hand to me. 'I am Dinis Hernandez.'

199

'Christoval Alvarez.' I shook his hand, where we sat, side by side on the ground, the last of my patients having left. In this ramshackle camp, there was no formality, except perhaps in Essex's tents.

'Are you not the priest who–' I broke off.

'Aye,' he said quietly. 'I have volunteered to make my way into the city and recruit good friends of King Antonio's to help me open the city gates to his army.'

'It is a very dangerous thing to attempt.'

He smiled ruefully. 'Such times require desperate measures. I have little love for the Spanish. They killed my parents when they first invaded Portugal nearly ten years ago. My brother and my brother-in-law were amongst those executed without trial within the last two weeks. My sister and her children were in Lisbon, but there has been no word of them. They disappeared about the same time as my brother-in-law was killed. I want the Spanish driven out of Portugal.'

'Do you think you will be allowed into the city?'

'I am a priest. Why should they refuse me?'

'If indeed you succeed in entering the city,' I said slowly, 'I know that there is an Englishman held prisoner there. His name is Hunter. I have no other name for him. Before I left London, I was asked to make sure that he was brought safely out of Lisbon, once we took the city. I do not know whether that will happen, or whether I shall be able to enter the city, but if you–' I was uncertain how to continue. It seemed best not to mention Walsingham, or what manner of man Hunter was.

'If I can find him, or help him, I will do so,' he said, and smiled reassuringly.

'I am grateful, Father,' I said.

Before we parted, I wished him success in his courageous attempt, and he blessed me, saying over my head a Catholic prayer.

My fears proved right. The following morning Father Hernandez's head appeared on a spike, hoisted high above the walls of Lisbon so that everyone in our army could see it and take note. As indeed all the inhabitants of the countryside might have done also, and taken the lesson to heart, had there been any left to see. For we found, in searching the houses which had spread beyond the city walls as Lisbon had grown outside them, that none were left but the sick and the lame and ancient men and women babbling in terror and confusion. We promised to do them no harm, but they could no more help us than they could feed us. Every able-bodied man, woman and child had fled south over the Tejo, as far from us as they could.

As for myself, I turned from the sight of that terrible object above the wall, sickened and appalled at what had been done, not only to a man but to a priest. However much I tried to keep it out of my sight, it was always there, at the corner of my vision, and his voice speaking in my ear, blessing me. The dead face wore an expression of unspeakable horror, which I think will stay with me as long as I live.

The Dom soon began to grow impatient of living in the open fields under a sun which broiled us like a bread oven and whose heat even rose from the parched earth at night. Our Portuguese party (those of us who had come from London, with the half dozen Portuguese who had joined us) rode in the evening of the next day part-way along the road to Cascais, in search of the *solar* belonging to a local nobleman, whom the Dom had known in his youth. Here he would demand accommodation for us, while the common soldiers of Norreys's army remained behind, camping outside Lisbon. He would return in triumph once Lisbon was taken. I confess, I was as eager as anyone when we rode up to the long, low building, with its thick white walls promising cool rooms and shadowy rest. The memory of the young priest's head bloodily spiked over Lisbon haunted me. I wanted to put Lisbon behind me. The doors of the manor house were closed and the windows shuttered. Perhaps none were at home. Or perhaps the Senhor was one of those already taken by the Spaniards.

One of the Dom's few servants rode up to the door, banging on it with the butt end of his whip and crying out, 'Open there, in the name of Dom Antonio of the House of Aviz, rightful king of Portugal!'

The response was swift. Men rose up on the flat roof and began firing at us with crossbows and muskets. The servant, wounded in the leg, with blood running over his boot and down his horse's side, wheeled around and galloped back to us as fast as his frightened horse would carry him. The shutters on the upper storey of the house were flung open and the muzzles of muskets poked out. From round by the stables, a group of young men, also armed, rode out and made for us. They were shouting, not in Spanish, but in Portuguese.

We scrambled to turn our horses in the narrow lane and rode hard for the high road back to Lisbon, with Dom Antonio in the lead. So this, I thought, is the Dom's warm reception from his own people. They may have hated the Spanish, but they feared them even more, and with great good sense they saw that there was no hope of release from the Spanish occupiers through the actions of our dwindling, makeshift army. Even then, Drake might have turned the tide, had he sailed the short distance up the river to Lisbon, but Drake sat counting his gold crowns in Cascais, and did not come.

At the end of the next day, Norreys strode up to our silent huddle of Portuguese, followed by half a dozen of his captains. Since his attempt to find better quarters, the Dom had not dared to stray outside the safety of the English camp. Norreys's face was grim and I suppose we all knew what he would say.

'There is no profit, Dom Antonio,' he said, 'in continuing to sit in this slaughtering heat before the walls of Lisbon. We have no siege engines or cannon. We have not even men enough to cut off their supplies. The longer we wait, the greater the risk that Philip's main army will march on us from Spain and we will be butchered like beasts in a shambles. My men are wounded and sick and starving. We must make for the ships at Cascais while we still can.'

The night was coming on, in that sudden way it does in southern Portugal, so different from the long lingering twilights of an English summer evening. A sliver of moon had already risen in the sky and the birds, silent through the numbing heat of the day, were murmuring sleepily in the broken branches of the olive trees, which the men had ravaged for wood to put on their cooking fires. There were no fires this evening, for there was nothing left to cook, the very last of the stores the Dom had wheedled from the peasants having been exhausted that morning.

'We cannot leave now!' The Dom's voice choked with desperation. This was a different man from the preening peacock we had known in London. To do him justice, he was courageous, in his way, for he was not a young man, and the last weeks had been a severe trial.

'This is the key to the kingdom,' he said. 'Lisbon was our goal, and had we come here at once, as ordered by the Queen,' (he emphasised this, for Norreys was almost as guilty as Drake) 'aye, *as ordered by the Queen*, then we would have secured Lisbon weeks since and be sitting in the palace now, with food and drink enough for all.'

Norreys shrugged.

'We cannot talk of what might have been. We must talk of what is.' He spoke as if teaching a schoolboy a lesson, tapping Dom Antonio familiarly on the arm. The Dom jerked away from Norreys's touch, with a flare of anger in his eyes.

'We cannot take Lisbon,' Norreys said flatly, with finality. 'No Portuguese have come to join you. The men are dying. We must march to the ships. We will start at once.'

Ruy Lopez, ever the one to believe in the impossible, pleaded with him.

'We must have more time!' His tone was peremptory. 'Word has been sent out around the country since we reached Lisbon. Our supporters will come, and bring weapons and supplies.'

Norreys gave an angry sigh. Then he looked about him and saw, as I did, that it would soon be night, with little moon. It was only that, I am sure, that made him say:

'Twelve hours more. You may have twelve hours more. Then I move the army to Cascais. You may come with us or stay here in your country, as you will.'

He turned on his heel and stamped away, followed by his officers.

The senior men of the Portuguese party drew together in conference then, but I walked away from them. I knew that Norreys was right. The expedition had been lost from the time we stayed more than a day at Coruña. There was nothing left for us now but to retreat to the ships and save as many of the men as we could. All hope was dead. I rolled myself in my cloak and slept on the ground that night, but my sleep was troubled. From hour to hour I woke and saw, huddled together in the thin moonlight, the three old men, Dom Antonio, Dr Lopez, and Dr Nuñez, sitting with their eyes open and their ears straining for the Dom's ghost army, which did not come.

I woke again as the sky was growing light, but before the sun had risen. The three old men had gone, but their horses remained. All around me, men were crawling from the hollows and ditches they had scratched out of the hard-baked soil, to provide themselves with some illusory protection from the merciless sun and the occasional cannon fire loosed off from the city walls, which mostly fell short of the camp, established at a discreet distance from the city. The soldiers stumbled around, gathering up their pitiful possessions and hoisting their packs on their backs. There would be nothing to eat until we reached Drake, so they were in a hurry to be on their way. I was not sure that the full twelve hours Norreys had promised were yet passed, but I strapped my gear on to my horse and brought him water in my helmet, which was not likely to see any better use that day. Before long I was joined by the others of our party. We did not speak.

Before we left, Norreys sent a troop of his few experienced men to set fire to the buildings lying outside the city wall. By now even the old and infirm had departed, but in sheer frustration he wanted to wreak what little destruction he could. The smoke of the fires rose lazily into the windless sky, wreathing Lisbon with this petty gesture of spite. *At least*, I thought, *the city will not be sacked and the innocent slaughtered.*

As the army moved off, I saw that there were men who had not climbed out of their pits this morning, but there was no time and no strength to bury them. Like those who had died on the way from Peniche, they would be left to the scavenging birds and beasts, and their English bones would bleach under the hostile Portuguese sun.

I mounted and rode alongside the weary men, who did not march so much as grope their way westwards, towards the estuary of the Tejo and the promised ships waiting at Cascais. Behind me I heard a clamour – shouting and a sort of jeering laughter. Wondering what could have roused the men, I reined in and twisted round in the saddle. Essex, magnificent, ablaze once more in his full gilded armour, caught by the sun as it lifted clear of the land, was riding up to the gates of the city. He cast his lance at the gates, where it stuck in the wood, quivering.

'Come then,' he shouted, 'you cowardly Spanish! I challenge any one of you to meet me in single combat for the honour of Her Majesty, Queen Elizabeth!'

From behind the walls there came no answer, unless it was the faint sound of echoing laughter. Satisfied with his show of bravado, Essex galloped up to join us, flourishing his sword with its jewelled hilt, as though he had won a great victory.

It was twenty miles to Cascais. That seemed nothing, compared to what we had already endured. Yet to the men it must have seemed more like the sixty-five from Peniche to Lisbon, so exhausted were they, but they kept on doggedly. It was the thought of food that kept them moving, I am sure, that and the safety of the ships which would take them away from the hateful soil of Portugal on the homeward journey. When the roofs of the Atlantic port came in sight at last, late that evening, a feeble shout went up from the men, not a cheer, for they were too weakened for that, but an acknowledgement that their ordeal was nearly over. I had ridden all day in a kind of despair. I had never really hoped that we could take Lisbon, after all the mistakes and folly of our mission, but to turn our backs on it was to concede, finally and totally, that we had failed, and the taste of failure is bitter on the tongue.

Drake and his sailors looked well and cheerful. Cascais had surrendered to them at once, without a shot fired, and they had captured a flotilla of Spanish merchant ships, providing plenty of booty, although of a somewhat workaday kind, not to be compared with the treasures to be seized on the ships returning from the New World, laden with gold and silver. One of these Drake had managed to capture, while on the way from Peniche to Cascais, and he was holding the valuables under secure locks. All the time that we had starved and laboured, Drake and his men had spent in counting their loot, feasting royally, and enjoying the prostitutes in the port. I think the sight of us must have shocked them. That evening the soldiers ate well. As men will at such times, they gorged themselves, despite our warnings of the dangers to a starved belly. The next day there were a few more deaths from its effects. Now that we were gathered together in relative safety, it was possible to hold a muster of our men, and count our losses. After the fighting and looting in Plymouth, the original army had shrunk from the numbers first gathered there, but some nineteen thousand soldiers had embarked on the ships for Portugal, not taking into account the sailors. Only eighteen hundred of the soldiers had been veterans from the Low Countries. Of those nineteen thousand soldiers, barely four thousand men remained alive. And of those four thousand, at least half were sick or wounded.

As soon as Drake and Norreys met, they began to argue violently, each blaming the other for the failure of the expedition. Drake blamed Norreys for choosing to march overland, instead of travelling by ship round the coast. Norreys blamed Drake for going in pursuit of the treasure ship and then lingering in Cascais, instead of coming to our aid at Lisbon, for which Drake appeared to have no excuse. Their anger was heightened further by the arrival of a pinnace with mails from the Queen, who was furious that Essex had been allowed to join the expedition, against her express wish. I suppose Drake and Norreys were thankful that, despite all his empty heroics, her favourite Essex was still without a scratch.

The next morning, Dr Nuñez and I watched Essex's ship, the *Swiftsure*, depart for England.

'They have sent him ahead,' said Dr Nuñez, 'with letters of apology and explanation to the Queen, in the hope that he can charm her into a sweet temper before we arrive with news of our complete failure.'

'What explanation could the despatches give, for Essex coming with us?' I said. 'He has done us little enough good, caused the death by drowning of many at Peniche, and his men have helped to consume the provisions.'

'Oh, I believe the excuse will be that the winds have been constantly strong from the north-east, making it impossible for him to set sail for home.'

'And now the wind has changed?' I asked disbelievingly.

206

He gave a wry smile. 'And now, conveniently, the wind has changed.'

'When do we sail?'

'Drake and Norreys are making their final plans now. You will remember, Kit, that the expedition was sent to carry out three tasks for the Queen's Majesty.'

I cast my mind back. It was a long time since I had thought about those plans, made so eagerly back in the spring. Three tasks? I had had three tasks myself. I had rescued Titus Allanby from Coruña. I had never been able to come near Hunter. As for Isabel . . .

'Three tasks for the Portuguese expedition?' I said. 'Above all, to capture Lisbon and so regain Portugal for Dom Antonio,' I said, 'as a province of England.'

'Yes,' he said bitterly. 'As a province of England.'

'To burn King Philip's fleets at Santander, Coruña and Lisbon.'

'Neither of these two tasks we have accomplished, apart from a few ships at Coruña.'

'Nay.' I thought again. What was the third task to have been? Then I remembered. 'And to capture the Azores.'

'Yes.'

'We are not,' I said incredulously, 'we are *not* going to attempt the Azores? With ships full of sick and dying men?'

'Drake is to attempt the Azores. He will take the most able men, and all the provisions, and make an attack on the Azores. Norreys and the rest of us will load the ships with those sick and dying men you speak of, and sail directly to Plymouth.'

At first I did not quite grasp what he was saying.

'Did you say that Drake is to take *all* the provisions? Do you mean all the armour and weaponry?'

'That too. But he is to take all the food and drink as well.'

'But with the gold he has seized, we can surely provision the whole fleet!'

'There is little left in Cascais after Drake and his sailors have fed on it like locusts all this time, but, yes, I expect if we used some of the gold, we could purchase stores from the villages round about. But Drake will not part with a single coin of it. He says it belongs to the Queen. It is not his to spend.'

'This is murder,' I said slowly. 'These men of ours will not survive the voyage back to England, with nothing to eat and nothing to drink.'

'Nay, they will not. And you may salve your conscience, Kit, for we shall starve along with them.'

The men were not told of Drake's arrangement, or we would have had a mutiny on our hands. Shortly before we left Cascais, there was a brief naval skirmish. Two of our armed merchantmen were attacked unexpectedly by nine Spanish galleys. One, the *William*, was sunk, the other set on fire. Most of the men escaped to other ships, but one of the boats carrying survivors from the *William* was attacked and sunk by the enemy warships, a brutal, unprincipled action against unarmed men. The next morning, Drake, with twenty ships but barely two thousand men, set sail westwards for the Azores. We watched them out of sight, wondering whether the two fleets would ever be reunited. I noticed that one of those embarked with Drake was the big soldier who had pulled me to safety the night of the Spanish attack on our camp. I never knew his name.

Shortly afterwards, Norreys's fleet, a kind of floating hospital, as it seemed, turned northwards, with those suddenly favourable winds. The men chosen to sail to England were pathetic in their gratitude, for they believed themselves the fortunate ones, taken home to be cared for, and spared any further fighting. They did not realise that our fleet was not a hospital, but a morgue.

As we sailed out into the Atlantic I stood, not at the bow rail of the *Victory* – how ironically she now seemed to be named – but at the stern rail. I watched as the coastline of Portugal dwindled and sank into the sea. I was certain now that I would never see my sister Isabel again.

Chapter Seventeen

*E*very detail of that voyage back from Portugal is burned into my memory as a slave's brand is burned into his skin for life, yet at the same time it has also a strange quality of unreality. How could that ship of skeletons ever have made that journey and reached England? To call it a nightmare is to belittle the horror. We talk of nightmares when we mean no more than bad dreams, troublesome the next morning, but soon vanishing away. Those of us who survived that voyage were marked by it for the rest of our lives as if we had passed through the torments of Hell itself.

By noon on the very first day of the voyage, barely out of Cascais, the men began to realise the desperate state of affairs. No food was distributed to them for a midday meal, and when they called frantically for water, it was rationed out by the ship's bosun. When Dr Nuñez had spoken to me of there being nothing to drink, he meant that there was no wine or ale. There was a little water. A very little. We had ten barrels of brackish water aboard the *Victory*, and I suppose the other ships must have had the same. It was brackish because first our sailors and then the rest of our expedition had made such demands on the water supply of Cascais in the terrible heat of midsummer that every sweet well had been drunk dry. All that remained were those that were near the shore and from time to time became tainted with sea water. It was not so salt as to make us ill, but it barely satisfied thirst, even aggravating it.

Captain Oliver had decreed that the sailors were to receive twice the ration of water as that which was doled out to the soldiers, since they must remain active and sail the ship for all our sakes, while the soldiers might sit idle. At this a great outcry went up, but our sickly soldiers had no strength to fight the crew. Many of them were feverish, and as their fevers grew worse, so they cried out more pitifully for water. The ration was one small cup in the forenoon and the same at dusk.

Dr Nuñez and I did what we could to relieve the sick and injured, but had no help from Dr Lopez. Like Dom Antonio, he hid away in his cabin and we did not see them for the whole length of our voyage. Perhaps it was as well. If the men had possessed any remnants of strength, they might have turned on them as the cause of all their misery.

'I cannot endure the men's suffering,' I cried to Dr Nuñez that first evening. I thought I had suffered strain almost past bearing during the overland forced march, but this was worse, much worse. 'I am going to give my ration of water to some soldier burning up with fever.'

He laid his hand on my arm and shook his head.

'And what will that accomplish, Kit? If you share your ration amongst so many, it will amount to no more than a few drops each, and what good will that do? If you give it all to one man or two, how much the others will resent it and condemn you! And then you will yourself become ill from lack of water, and be unable to help them. It is more important to sustain your strength, as long as you can, than to make an empty gesture, however noble it might make you feel.'

He was right, of course. I was young and foolish and thought only of relieving my distress by the gesture, but it would have done no good. Nothing I could do would help the men in their intolerable suffering.

I mumbled some embarrassed agreement, for I knew he spoke the truth.

As dusk fell on the first day, the men discovered that, as well as the lack of water, there was no food on board and that they were to starve to death, unless they could survive the voyage on that meagre allowance of water. When that news became general, six men turned their faces from us and died, as much from despair as from illness. During the dark hours, the crew slid their bodies over the stern, their pockets weighed down with stones taken from the ballast. The captain said a brief prayer over each man, as we stood bareheaded and watched the bodies slip beneath the sullen grey waves of the Atlantic. I wondered whether any of the remaining men were doing the heartless calculation. The fewer of us on board would mean a slightly larger ration of water. When people are *in extremis*, the calculus of survival comes into play.

We had set off with a fair wind, but on the second day the wind dropped and the heat grew more and more unbearable. Below decks in my tiny cabin, I felt as though I would suffocate. On deck the merciless sun burnt every exposed inch of skin raw red. The men would not go below to their cramped quarters, which were even worse than mine, filled with the stench of unwashed and diseased bodies. Dr Nuñez persuaded the captain to rig up a kind of awning on deck from a spare mainsail, beneath whose shade the men who could move crawled gratefully. The rest we carried and disposed there as best we could, amongst coils of rope and other ship's gear. The sailors cursed this arrangement, which hindered their handling of the ship, but they too were growing weak now, despite their double ration of water and the period of rest and feasting they had enjoyed in Cascais. Captain Oliver called Dr Nuñez and me into his cabin during the afternoon and gave us each a little dried meat he had put by. Otherwise, he said, he had no more to eat than the rest of us.

'We must keep our physicians on their feet,' he said with a grim smile. 'For we shall all need you before this voyage is done.'

'Could we not make a broth with the meat?' I said eagerly. 'Then we could share it amongst all.'

I saw that Dr Nuñez was going to raise the same objection as before, but the captain forestalled him.

'No water,' he pointed out.

I banged my fist against my forehead.

'But wait,' I said. 'If we took each man's evening ration of water, and made broth with the meat, then at least they would go to their rest tonight with a little more than water in their bellies.'

The captain and Dr Nuñez agreed, albeit reluctantly. I am sure they thought my gesture futile, but what difference did it make, after all? We were all growing dull and hopeless with

211

hunger. Probably we would all be dead before ever we could reach England.

I carried all the strips of dried meat down into the bowels of the *Victory*, to where the ship's cook had his quarters, and explained what I wanted him to do with it. He had a cook-stove built of bricks, but there was no fire laid in it, since there was nothing for him to cook. Sitting on a stool amongst his highly polished pots and pans, he was slumped like a sack of meal, a look of total despair pulling down a mouth much better shaped for jollity.

At my suggestion that we should make a broth, his face took on a little animation. After a moment's thought he gave me a calculating look, then lifted the lid of a pottery crock stowed away under the table where he worked and drew out from it a single onion and half a dozen carrots.

'I managed to hide these,' he said, 'when Drake's men came to strip us of all our provisions for their voyage to the Azores. If we are to make one last meal, I will add these to it. There will be no further chance, for I have nothing else left but a few dried peas.'

'Let us add those as well,' I said. 'We will make it as nourishing as we can. I will help you.'

Like most cooks, he carried a layer of plump flesh built up over the years, which had not been sucked dry by the march from Peniche, since he had remained with the ship. No doubt he had also lived well during the stay at Cascais. He had a better chance than the soldiers of surviving this voyage, but he was going to suffer the same terrible pangs of hunger as the rest of us. Perhaps he might experience even more agony than we would, for our bodies had grown accustomed to near starvation during that hunger march.

I sought out the bosun and explained that Captain Oliver had agreed that the evening water ration should be used for the broth. He himself carried the buckets down to the cook's galley, as if he did not trust even me not to make off with it. While I had been gone, the cook had lit the fire in his stove and he now lifted down a great iron pot, into which the bosun poured the precious water.

212

I found one of the cook's sharp knives and set about chopping the strips of dried meat very finely, while he chopped the onion and carrots. The bosun lingered, watching us hungrily. I did not feel very sympathetic towards him. He too had rested and eaten in Cascais while we had dragged ourselves overland. As we worked, I noticed that there were some bunches of dried herbs hanging from the beam above his head.

'Can we add some of those, for flavour?' I asked. The meat and vegetables, now added to the pot, were barely to be seen.

'Aye,' the cook said, reaching up. 'There's thyme here, and marjoram.'

He chopped them swiftly with that skilled rocking motion professional cooks seem to use so casually, then stirred them into the pot. It still looked more water than broth. He placed a lid on the pot and drew it to the edge of the iron grid above the fire.

'Don't want to boil away the water,' he explained. 'I'll just keep 'un simmering very low.'

The men were grateful for our attempt to provide at least something like food that evening, patiently holding out their cups for their share. Even the sailors were too weak by now to argue or push others out of the way. Despite the thin broth, barely tasting of the meat, the onion, the carrots, and the herbs, more men died in the night, and more bodies went overboard next day. The other ships in our depleted fleet were keeping pace with us, and we could see the dead from those ships following ours to the depths of the ocean.

I began to wonder if all the ships, empty of sailors and soldiers and gentlemen adventurers, would eventually sail on by themselves over the oceans unmanned, until they fetched up on some foreign shore – the West Indies to the south, or Virginia and the Chesapeake, where my tutor Thomas Harriot had once voyaged to meet the native peoples, or perhaps far to the north, to Iceland, which I had heard was a strange country of volcanoes and earthquakes, of spouting geysers whose boiling water rose out of the snow fields, and of islands that sprang new-made from the sea. Perhaps the *Victory* would crash eventually into one of the great ice floes, inhabited, as I had read, by huge bears as white as the snows amongst which they lived.

213

By now I was growing light-headed from lack of water and food. Hunger does strange things to the body. At first no more than a whisper in the stomach it grows and grows until your whole body is filled with a gnawing pain, as a glass is filled with water. The analogy of the water glass came to me as part of a weird hallucination which accompanied the hunger, a feeling that somewhere there was both food and water, if only I could find them. I had to stop myself roaming the ship, searching. Soon that pain walked everywhere with me, so that it was difficult to think of anything else, but I must think of my patients. I had to struggle to sustain my role of physician.

My salves had been running low at Lisbon and I had had no chance to replenish them during our brief stay in Cascais. I did what I could now, for the wounded, but the men were so weak and exhausted, their bodies drying up and crying out for sustenance, that Nature's own healing power was unable to help them.

I thought with regret of the long cool wards of St Bartholomew's, with their rows of tidy beds. The sisters – as we called them, after the nuns who had served there in the past – kept the bedlinen and the patients clean and sweet. In the case of many of the patients, probably cleaner and sweeter than they had ever been in their lives before. The food was plentiful and wholesome, our salves and potions, based on my father's long and patient study of Arab medicine, were the best known to man. We had our own apothecaries, our abundant supplies of all the medicines we needed. Even in an emergency, as when the survivors of Sluys had been brought it, we were able to help most of the patients. Every week the governors of the hospital paid a visit of inspection, to check that the patients were properly cared for, were clean and fed, and that physicians, surgeons and sisters, were all mindful of their duty. That whole world of hospital medicine seemed now like a phantasmagoria, so remote was it from the squalor in which the pitiful remnant of our army lay dying and I crouched beside them, powerless.

The next morning, I knelt by the side of a soldier with a bullet wound in his upper arm that would not heal, although I had extracted the bullet days before. He was one of those who had been discovered lying injured outside the camp after the Spanish night raid.

'Do you feel pain here, or here?' I asked, probing the lower part of his arm.

He gazed at me with dull eyes and shook his head. 'I cannot feel your finger, Doctor. Not separate, like. The whole arm is too b'yer lady painful!' He tried to give me a smile, and I could have wept.

There was no fresh water to wash the wound, but I had dipped up a bucket of salt water, and that is sometimes more efficacious. I am not sure whether it is the salt, or perhaps some essence from the seaweeds that makes it so. He endured the cleansing bravely, and when I had smeared on a little of my last, precious salve, he lay back on the deck with a sigh. I could smell the unmistakable sweet scent of gangrene setting in, like fruit beginning to rot, which mingled with the sour, sweaty stink of him. The arm ought to be amputated before the gangrene reached his heart and lungs. It is no part of a physician's business to perform amputations, although I supposed I might do it if there was no other way. I knew there was a naval surgeon on one of the other ships. We could signal to him to come over to us, but I decided against it. The man was too weak to survive amputation. He would have died of shock before the operation was over. It was now simply a matter of how long it would take him to die.

I could, however, give him something to ease the pain a little. In my cabin I checked my few remaining supplies. Over the flame of a candle I made an infusion of *spiraea ulmaria*, *matricaria recutita*, and *humulus lupulus* in my own morning cup of water, which I had not yet drunk, lacing it with nearly the last of my poppy syrup, then I returned to the deck and sat down beside the soldier.

He roused himself again and tried to sit up, so I slid my arm under his shoulders and helped him drink the medicine.

'This will ease the pain,' I said, and he nodded.

Then he lay there with his head on my shoulder, looking towards the ship's bow.

'Don't suppose I'll never see England again, Doctor.'

'You must keep your spirits up,' I said. 'A stout heart is better medicine than any I can give you.' I knew that I lied, and so did he.

'Ah, but you're a brave lad, Doctor, young as you are. Once I was in my right mind again, I never thanked you for the way you sucked that snake's poison out of my leg. That was a brave thing you done, braver than any soldier.'

I looked down at him. In all the weariness and dirt I had not recognised him.

He nestled closer against me, and murmured, so quietly I could barely hear him, 'You hold me soft as my Molly. And I won't never see her neither. She warned me.' His voice had almost faded away. 'She warned me . . . not to come.'

He died within the hour, and all the while I held him. I never knew his name, or where he came from, whether Molly was his wife, whether there were more orphans made by this death. When we dropped him overboard I wept, and I shut myself in my cabin for the rest of the night. I do not know why I wept, for this one man out of so many. Perhaps it was because I had saved him once before from death, but could not save him this time. Perhaps it was because he had died in my arms, like a lover. Perhaps it was because, in his wasted, filthy, wounded body, he stood for all those other poor creatures who had died shamefully, caught between their own greed and the insubstantial dreams of old men, who were exiles from a country that no longer existed, had never existed as they imagined it.

The following day I was sitting slumped on the foredeck, partially shaded from the sun by the foresails. Captain Oliver had ordered every last scrap of canvas to be hoisted, for there was so little breeze you could have carried a candle from one end of the deck to the other and it would not have been blown out. I had spent the morning doing what I could for the sick soldiers, but we had reached a point now when I had few medicines left, even after begging all Dr Nuñez's supplies and – through a message carried by a cabin boy – those of Dr Lopez. I had cleaned and salved what I could, but there was nothing more I could do for them. If the wind did not come soon, we would all die, becalmed here, not many nautical miles from Coruña, where the whole invasion had begun.

I was sick at heart and found I could not endure the presence of those wasted men any more. Instead I had escaped up here to the raised foredeck, where I sat on the hot planks of the deck, leaning back against a coil of rope with my eyes shut and pretending that I could feel an increase in the movement of the wind. Behind me I heard footsteps approach, then pause as whoever it was caught sight of me. I opened my eyes.

'Dr Nuñez,' I said, drawing in my knees to get to my feet.

'I don't mean to disturb you,' he said. 'Please, do not move. I'll leave you to enjoy some rest. You have been overtaxing what little strength you have left.'

'Please don't go,' I said. 'It is cooler here than almost anywhere. Or at any rate, not quite as hot.' I patted the boards beside me.

With some difficulty he lowered himself to sit next to me on the deck. I could not imagine what pains he must be enduring at his age. Intense hunger brings on excruciating pain in all the joints. It had been a courageous undertaking to come on this expedition at all, given his advanced years. He had been so full of those dreams of his youth that he must have thought it within his capability. And had things gone as planned, it would have been. A swift voyage to Lisbon as a gentleman adventurer, luxuriously accommodated about the *Victory*, a ship which would take no part in Drake's firing of the Spanish fleet; a pleasant journey along the coast of Portugal and up the Tejo to Lisbon; a joyous reception in the city, followed by the crowning of the exiled king. Feasting and celebration. All of this would have made no demands even on a man of seventy.

For a time, neither of us said anything.

'It will be good to come home,' he said at last.

I smiled at him. Like me, he was now thinking of England as home. Those dreams of the past had been blown away, probably some time during the march from Peniche.

'Mistress Beatriz will be so glad to see you,' I said. 'And your children and grandchildren too.'

'Aye.' He sighed.

I knew that he suspected, like me, that we would never reach England. And indeed we would not, unless the wind came soon. The *Victory* could be propelled, slowly, by towing her with an oared pinnace, though she was not designed to travel far that way. She could not be rowed herself, as a galley is. This method of towing the ship was intended only for manoeuvring in the close quarters of a harbour, or to extricate her from possible danger, if the wind failed or else blew her on shore. It could never be used to move the ship for any distance at sea. Besides, our sailors, though not yet as weak as the soldiers, could never summon the strength now to row even a pinnace.

'Your father will be glad to see you safe home as well, Kit,' Dr Nuñez said.

I nodded. 'I am worried that he has had to carry the burden of my work at St Bartholomew's, as well as his own, all this time. I should have returned long before this, weeks ago, had the expedition been conducted as it was planned. He has never been strong, not since the Inquisition.'

'Nay.'

He sighed again, and leaned back, like me, against the great coil of rope.

'I wish I had never allowed myself to be persuaded into this affair,' he said. 'Unless Drake manages to take the Azores, we have failed of every goal.'

'Aye,' I said, and could not keep the bitterness out of my voice. 'The one goal I achieved was to rescue Titus Allanby from the citadel at Coruña.'

'Walsingham's instructions, was it? Allanby is one of his men?'

I nodded. 'Aye. He had sent word that he was under suspicion.'

I had told Dr Nuñez very little before I went into the citadel at Coruña, but there was no harm in his knowing the full story of my missions from Walsingham. He often aided Walsingham himself.

'I was also supposed to see that no hurt befell the man Hunter,' I said, 'who is being held in prison in Lisbon. If we had gained the city, I was to make sure he was brought safely out of prison and sailed home with us. Father Hernandez–' I swallowed.

218

I could not erase the memory of that dead face, spiked up on the walls of Lisbon. 'Father Hernandez promised to try to help him.'

'That was a terrible business.' Dr Nuñez patted my arm, but did not look at me.

'I know that when you rode off from Peniche,' he said quietly, 'you had some hope of finding members of your family near Coimbra, but when you returned you were distraught. Was that another goal in which you feel you failed?' He paused and smiled at me, a little tentatively. 'Do not speak of it if you do not wish.'

Nay, I had not spoken of it, but perhaps to speak of it now, to this man who had always been good to me, would be a kind of relief to the turmoil that the memory of that ride caused inside me. I had said no word of my intentions to my father, to anyone at all, except to Dr Nuñez just before I left Peniche, yet I would have to tell my father what I had discovered. Talking to Dr Nuñez might help.

'I rode to my grandfather's *solar*,' I began slowly. 'That was where we left my sister Isabel and my brother Felipe, with my grandparents, when my mother and I travelled to Coimbra to join my father for a few days. Seven years ago.'

Looking out over the oily sea, I drew a deep breath, remembering the four of them standing on the steps and waving goodbye as the carriage bore us away. I had hung out of the window for the last sight of the house and of my grandfather's prize stallion in the meadow.

'Later,' I said, 'while we were waiting to make our escape from Ilhavo, to join your ship, we heard that my grandfather had sent my brother and sister to tenants of his, the da Rocas, Old Christians, so they would be safe if the soldiers of the Inquisition came hunting for them. They both became ill with a high fever. We heard that my brother Felipe had died before we left Portugal. My sister was too ill to come with us, but they thought she would recover.'

I realised that Dr Nuñez was patting my arm again, but spared me a direct look.

'I thought I would find them there, you see, all three, at the *solar*. My grandparents and Isabel.'

'But you did not?' he said gently.

'The servant who came to the door was suspicious, because I did not know that my grandmother had died in a prison of the Inquisition at about the same time as we were taken. All that time ago.' My voice shook, and I paused, trying to steady it. 'I had to pretend I was a cousin, come from Amsterdam.'

At that moment I nearly let slip why I had needed to conceal who I was. Dr Nuñez must not be told that I was another sister who had fled from Portugal, not a brother.

'Then the servant told me that my grandfather was still alive three weeks before. He had gone to Lisbon on business. When I arrived, the household had just received word that he was one of the first of the nobles executed in the city by the Spanish, suspected of supporting Dom Antonio, though he knew nothing of this affair of ours.'

I turned suddenly, ablaze with anger, which I had not been able to express before. 'That madness in Coruña! If we had not delayed there, the Spanish would not have killed my grandfather!'

If I had not been so weak, my words would have come out as a shout. Instead they were no louder than a vicious whisper. Tears were running down my face. I realised that I would have liked to kill Drake and Norreys at that moment. I had never felt such hatred and it frightened me.

'If my grandfather had still been alive–' I gasped. I must be careful what I said. I dashed the tears away angrily with the heel of my hand.

'What of your sister Isabel?' he asked quietly.

'I found her,' I said. 'Oh, aye, I found her. Taken as a whore by the da Rocas' loutish son,' I spat out. 'The parents, who were decent people, were dead. He got her with child when she was only twelve. Now, at barely seventeen, she has two children and another on the way. She would not come away with me, she would not leave the children. And he was violent, threatening me with the Inquisition. He tried to attack me with a knife. He beats her. She was terrified of him and begged me to leave. I had to ride away, like a coward.'

'I don't understand,' he said. 'Why was she not with your grandfather?'

'I don't know!' I cried. 'And now I will never know. Perhaps the man threatened to betray her to the Inquisition. Perhaps my grandfather did not know what had happened, thinking that she was safe in hiding, until it was too late and she feared for the children.'

I ran my fingers through my hair and sat clutching my head between my hands.

'She had been very ill when we left, and developed brain fever, so the man said. She is very frightened of him, intimidated. He beats her,' I said again. 'I saw the signs. He struck her, and the little boy, while I was there.'

He said nothing for some time, but at last he spoke.

'If our expedition had succeeded, and Dom Antonio had been made king indeed, he might have been able to help you.'

'Aye, I said, 'I had thought of that.'

He sighed. 'I feel your grief, Kit, and I know there is nothing I can say to ease it.'

'It will kill my father,' I said in despair. 'He thought at least the three of them had survived.'

'Did you tell him what you planned to do?'

'Nay. I feared I might not be able to make the journey to the *solar*.'

'Then I think you should not tell him. What good will it do, except to ease your own mind by sharing the burden of the truth? I think this is a burden you must bear alone, Kit, to spare your father.'

He was wise, Dr Nuñez. I realised that it was the right advice. I would keep all these painful truths to myself and say nothing to my father, however much it hurt.

At the end of the fifth day out from Cascais, urged on with a slightly stronger wind, we finally reached Cape Finisterre, the last west tip of Spain. That was when the weather changed suddenly and the tempest caught us. As we rounded the cape and aimed north and east across the Bay of Biscay, the winds came howling down upon us and seized the ship and threw it almost over at the first blast, as if some giant's hand had grabbed the *Victory* like a fragile toy. It seemed as though we might be crushed to splinters by that giant hand. I could not tell which

221

direction the wind came from, for it seemed to come from all directions at once. A sailor up on the yardarms, trying to gather in one of the topsails and tie it down, was struck by the beating canvas and thrown out in an arc like a stone from a boy's slingshot. We barely heard his cry before he plunged into the sea far in our wake and was lost at once to sight as the ship rushed first one way and then the other, at the mercy of the storm. Those of us who were still, almost, on our feet tried to drag and carry the sick men below decks, but despite our efforts three were washed, screaming, overboard in the first few minutes.

Out at sea long columns of flame, like the tongues of gigantic dragons, shot down from the sky and seemed to link earth and heaven in some devilish bond. Moments after, deafening thunder rolled over us, so that I felt the beat of it deep in my chest, and my ears were numb. Then the rain came, rain such as I had never seen before, hitting us like musket balls. As the bosun and I lifted the last of the injured men, to carry him below decks, the wind caught the awning we had erected for the soldiers, ripped it up till it stood on end and clapped and danced like the Dervishes of the Barbary Coast, then carried it away. It vanished into the solid wall of rain which was now so heavy we could no longer see the other ships of our dying fleet.

When we had deposited the last soldier down with the others on the gun deck, the bosun clambered hastily up the companionway to the main deck, and I followed after him, but I was not welcome there.

'Get below!' one of the officers shouted at me. 'We want no landsmen on deck in a storm like this. Get out of our way!'

I did as I was told and retreated back down the companionway to the gun deck, then picked my way through the men lying there until I reached the companionway that led up to the poop and the cabins. I heard the faint sound of voices from Dom Antonio's great cabin, but I did not want the company of my fellow Portuguese. Instead I let myself through Dr Nuñez's empty cabin and into my cubbyhole. No larger than a clothes press, without porthole or any natural light, at least it was my own place. There I huddled on my bunk, weak now myself, and dizzy with lack of food for nearly a week, trying to blot out the memory, brought suddenly and vividly alive by the tempest, of my first journey north on these seas.

Chapter Eighteen

On Board the Santa Maria, 1582

When my parents and I were smuggled from the fishing boat aboard the merchant ship out of Porto, bound for London, I knew nothing more of Dr Hector Nuñez than his name, that he was the owner of the ship *Santa Maria*, and that he would help us when we reached England. I began to feel a little safer as we sailed west to gain sea room for rounding the Cape of Finisterre, and in the morning of the next day I ventured out of the cabin my family had been given, to explore the ship. During the few hours of the night that remained after we had come aboard, my parents had slept in the single bunk, and I had lain on the floor. After the months on the stone floor of the Inquisition prison it was no hardship.

My father had gone on deck before me. I followed him up the companionway and roamed about the ship, getting in the way of the sailors, and occasionally earning a cheerful cuff from one of them when I asked too many questions. I could hardly believe that my life was returning to some kind of normality. It was strange being at sea on this great ship. It was strange pretending to be a boy in the company of all these sailors. But we were free and alive, my mother, my father and I, with every hour taking us further from danger.

The previous evening, before we slept, I heard my father telling my mother what our plans should be. It would not be wise to travel on from England to Antwerp, as he had originally intended, for the Spanish King had turned his attention to his possessions in the Low Countries. Antwerp would not be safe for us. We would settle in England, where there was already a sizeable Marrano community, who would welcome us. I could not imagine what this place 'England' would be like, but I was beginning to feel hopeful. If only my sister Isabel were with us, I would almost feel happy.

After a time, the wind got up and a storm began to heave the seas about. Not a great storm, but enough to make me uncertain on my legs, so I went back down to the cabin.

I found a scene of chaos. My father's medicines were scattered about, phials overturned and smashed, powders strewn over the small table. My mother was lying on the floor, writhing like a creature in agony. I cried out in horror and flung myself down beside her.

'Mama! Mama!' I cradled her in my arms. 'What has happened?'

She looked at me with feverish eyes, and gasped. A little blood and saliva trickled from the corner of her mouth.

'I took,' she whispered, 'I took . . . things to kill the baby.'

I picked up the bottles lying near her hand. Seeds of *flos pavonis*. Leaf of *leonurus cardiaca*. Root of the rare American *cimicifuga racemosa*. Tincture of *stachys officinalis*. All the bottles were empty. Even then, I knew what they signified.

She could speak no more, for her body arched and heaved, and suddenly a great bloody mass burst out between her legs. She screamed and retched.

Terror swept over me. I did not know what to do. I did not know what to do. I seized a bolster from the bunk and wedged it under her head, then ran for my father. I seemed to hunt for hours, running up and down companionways, along the decks, until I found him at last in the captain's cabin.

'Come,' I gasped. 'You must come. Mama.' The words froze on my tongue.

I clutched my father's sleeve in both hands. If I could hold on to him, perhaps the horror would stop. Time would slip back. Everything would be as it had been, only a few hours before.

When we reached my mother she was breathing still, but the floor was awash with blood and she could not speak.

'What did she take, Caterina?' My father took me by the shoulders and shook me so I could not speak.

'Abortifacients,' I managed to say at last, breaking away from his grasp and pointing at the empty bottles. Tears were running down my face and soaking the front of my tunic. Jaime's tunic, ragged and filthy.

'But why?' His cry was terrible to hear. 'Why?'

I hung my head. I could not meet his eyes. 'She was raped,' I whispered. 'Over and over, they raped her in the prison. She told me she was with child. While we were still in the prison. And now, she said . . . now all she could say to me, was that she wanted to kill the baby.'

'She has killed herself as well!' he wailed, taking my mother in his arms.

We made her as comfortable as we could, but the blood flowed and flowed. My father helped her to drink an infusion of *capsella bursa pastoris*, which is believed to stop haemorrhage, but I guessed from his face that there was no hope. I know now that she had taken far too much of the drugs. A lethal dose. She was so desperate to kill that child which made her feel defiled.

By the next morning she was too weak even to lift her head to sip water. She asked our forgiveness, and died before noon. They slid her overboard, my mother who had disguised me as a boy and kept me safe all those months, in the prison of the Inquisition. Kept me safe by enduring all that they had made her suffer, to protect me. The sailors had wrapped a shroud about her, but not sewed it as close as they should, so that those cruel waves plucked it away and I saw her pale face looking up at me before her heavy skirts dragged her down and she was gone for ever.

Chapter Nineteen

On Board the Victory, 1589

The present storm lasted three days and three nights, and by the time it died away the *Victory* was off the Pointe de St. Mathieu in the west of Brittany. More men had died during the storm, but none of us had the strength any longer to heave them up on deck and tip them overboard, so they lay and rotted where they were. Towards the end of the next day, the ninth day since we had left Cascais – or was it the tenth? – I dragged myself up the companionway, one rung at a time. The last of the pewter-grey storm clouds lingered over France, but the Channel lay ahead of us, clear under the July sun, a kinder sun than we had known in Portugal.

The ship was making its way slowly northeast, slowly because we were under half sail, since many of the sailors lay dying of starvation and disease like the soldiers, and those who were still on their feet had barely strength to trim the sails. There were four men at the whipstaff to control the rudder, two on each side. One man alone had not the power left in his arms to move it an inch. Behind us, the remaining ships of our broken fleet straggled, unkempt, their sails sagging untrimmed, their yardarms kilted over at careless angles. Captain Oliver was on the forecastle deck, and I made my way slowly towards him, holding the rail, for I was unsteady on my feet.

'Where are we now?' I asked.

Without answering, he pointed to some jagged rocks thrusting up out of the sea ahead, amidst a churning maelstrom of waves, while the ship, groaning as if her timbers had been wrenched in the tempest, began to turn gradually to starboard.

I shook my head. 'I'm no seaman. What are those?'

'The Scillies,' he said, and his voice creaked as though the lack of water had caused rust to set in. 'Off the tip of Cornwall. Did you not see them on our way out? Nay perhaps not. I remember, the rain was as thick as a heavy mist.'

He coughed, a dry hacking sound.

'The men are too weary to sail as far as Plymouth tonight,' he said, when he could speak again. 'We'll heave to when it gets dark, and reach port in the morning.'

I carried the good news to the soldiers down below, that we were in sight of the tip of England, but they looked at me with lacklustre eyes and made no response. When I found Dr Nuñez in his cabin, he was little better.

'Plymouth?' he said. 'Well, at least let us hope there will be food in Plymouth.'

His face was pinched and grey, and his eyes sunk in dark hollows below his tangled eyebrows. Like all the men, he had neither shaved nor trimmed his beard for weeks. Apart from the young cabin boys, I was the only beardless person aboard. As for all our hair, it was matted and lice-ridden, and lately frosted with salt from the spray. And filthy, as our bodies were filthy. I sank down on a joint stool opposite him, where he sat on his bunk, slumped in despair. I was so tired I could not keep on my feet any longer.

'Though there are few enough of us left to eat it,' he said, picking up his thought again. 'Any food. In Plymouth. And then the reckoning comes.'

'What will happen to the men?'

He shrugged. 'Given a meal and turned ashore, I suppose.'

'Without pay?' I stared at him. 'After all they have suffered?'

'Who has the wherewithal to pay them?' He lifted his eyes to mine. They were full of despair. 'The investors have sunk everything in this expedition, with nothing to show for it. None of the Dom's glorious promises made good. I shall be near ruined myself. The men were to have been paid with the booty seized from the sack of Lisbon.'

'That was a shameful pact,' I said. Exhausted as I was, I still spoke vehemently.

'It was. It should never have been countenanced.'

'There was the gold Drake took at Cascais.' I ventured this suggestion without much hope, for I had a good idea what the answer would be.

'The Queen's gold?' He shrugged. 'Aye, well, she may grant them a little of it, when Drake returns from the Azores. Perhaps he will have increased his bounty there.'

I could not sleep that night for the gnawing hunger in my belly, as the ship yawed to and fro, as if she was uneasy, hove to. To my haunted mind it seemed that the ship herself was starving and dying, here on the last few miles of the sea. The pains in every one of my joints had grown even more acute. The thought that food was only hours away made it all the harder to endure, this final agonising wait. I was dizzy with hunger and thirst. From the gaunt faces I had seen around me in the ship, I could imagine how I myself must look. My doublet and breeches hung on me. They stank of sweat and dirt and sickness. Once I was home I would burn them, for they were so full of rents and tears that even a pauper would scorn them. My stockings gaped with as many holes as a fisherman's net and my shirt barely reached my waist, for all the lower part had been ripped off to make bandages. Even my precious physician's gown had suffered the same fate. The stuff was too thick for bandages, but in the end, no one cared. We used what we could.

I wondered whether Simon would recognise the ragged sunburnt skeleton I had become, but realised bitterly how little it mattered. I was nothing to him but a passing acquaintance, a male companion to share a meal or a visit to the playhouse. Why did I torment myself with foolish thoughts? I found myself longing to break out of my disguise, to become a girl again, Caterina, my father's daughter, dependent, handing myself over to the guardianship of others. It would be nothing but joy to lay aside the burden of my manhood, my responsibilities and cares. I was nineteen years old, and I longed to abandon my travesty of a life.

All through that last night on board, I wrestled with my crowding thoughts, with the flashes of memory that ambushed me. Isabel, laying her cheek briefly against mine. The fires in the citadel of Coruña and the drunken soldiers lying in the streets below. Teresa holding the new babe. The snake and the taste of its venom on my tongue. The men dying and dying and dying on the march. The severed head of Father Hernandez on the walls of Lisbon. The heat. The thirst. The hunger. The wounded soldier dying in my arms on deck. And Isabel, Isabel. I felt such black despair I wanted to howl, and yet even to utter a sound would have cost me too much effort. In the morning we would see England. What did I care? My wits were so dulled that it no longer had any meaning for me. All through that last terrible night, I lay awake.

By first light I had crawled my way up on deck. It was our tenth day – or was it the eleventh? – out from Cascais. The second of July, Captain Oliver said. At least that was what he thought, for like all of us he was confused and weak from hunger and sleeplessness. The sailors were making sail, going about their tasks with maddening slowness, as if they were sleep-walking, yet they must have been as eager as any of us to quit the *Victory* and find themselves on dry land again. As we made our way slowly along the coast of Cornwall to Devon, one of the sailors pointed to a tiny village that seemed to climb vertically up the cliff and hang suspended over the water.

'That's Polperro,' he said. 'That's my village, and I never want to leave it.' Like the captain he gave a dry, rasping cough. 'I'll never set foot in a ship again. Once I get my feet on English soil, you'll never see me step off it.'

'How far to Plymouth?' I asked.

'You see that break in the coast? Ahead, a little further along? That's the mouth of Plymouth Sound. Not far now, God be thanked.'

And I noticed that he crossed himself furtively, as the Catholics do.

Plymouth Sound is a large and complex body of water, all inlets and small islands, and what look like the mouths of many rivers, but which may perhaps be deeper inlets running into the land. As usual it was crowded with huge galleons and smaller ships, which apart from their size all looked much the same as one another, for I do not have an eye for a ship. I could not have named any of them.

230

Dr Nuñez had come on deck to stand beside me, and the soldiers had limped and crawled their way into the light and air, looking anxiously around, as if they feared that England were no more than a mirage, sent to torment them. Even Dom Antonio and Dr Lopez had come on deck, and the Dom had insisted that his standard should be flown, which was unwise of him.

'The harbour is very crowded,' I said, to no one in particular. It seemed we would have difficulty finding anchor room. The *Victory* was too large to be able to berth at most quays, but I realised that we were feeling our way slowly towards the principal quay, where it seemed there was deep water, instead of dropping anchor out in mid harbour, as I had expected. All the sails had been furled but one foresail and the lateen sail on the mizzen. A pinnace with a towline had its oars out, though I do not know how any of the sailors found the strength to wield them. I saw that there was space enough for one large ship, beside another galleon, already trimly moored. We were gliding slowly toward it, without the need for the pinnace.

Suddenly Captain Oliver gave a cry, so agonised that I wondered for a moment if he had run mad in these last hours of our ordeal. He pointed to the other galleon moored at the quay and shouted. It was taken up in fury by the sailors.

'The *Revenge*! It's the *Revenge*! Drake never sailed for the Azores at all! He's here!'

Drake had betrayed us once again. He had taken all the food and drink and sailed straight home to Plymouth, leaving us to starve and die on the high seas behind him.

Our reception in Plymouth was furious and frightening. The families coming to welcome home their husbands and sons had learned the truth of the expedition when Drake arrived the day before us. Instead of men with their pockets full of gold they found men weary and penniless, and news of many deaths. The men on Drake's ships, however, were those in better health. The hopes of the families that their men had survived were kept alive until Norreys's fleet made port. When the poor remains of our army stumbled or were carried ashore from our last ships, deathlike in their gaunt pallor, a terrible cry arose from the women and children crowding round the quays. I hope I shall never hear the like again. Then the despair turned to anger, and the anger to fury. Dom Antonio, trying to make a dignified descent of the gangplank in the tattered remnants of his finery, suddenly caught their attention. They recognised him from our triumphant departure in April.

'Dog!' they screamed. 'Cur! Jewish thief! Liar! Bastard king!' (Which last was true enough, though rarely mentioned.)

They picked up stones from the ground and hurled them at the never-to-be king of Portugal. He escaped unhurt, for their aim was poor, but one caught Dr Nuñez on the left cheek, and it bled a little. Luckily for me, I was no more than some unknown youth of the company, probably a midshipman, or someone else of no account. They did not recognise me as one of the hated Portingalls. As unobtrusively as possible, I made my way ashore with Dr Nuñez. Both of us, without exchanging a word, chose to avoid the company of Ruy Lopez and Dom Antonio.

In Plymouth I stayed at an inn (none of us could endure another moment aboard the *Victory*), where I ate and washed, but I still wore my threadbare clothes, for I had nothing else. I owed my lodging to Dr Nuñez, for I had no more than two Spanish *reals* left in my purse. He urged me to keep them in case I needed money on my journey home, so I changed them at the inn for good English coin, which jingled thinly in my purse with the handful of pennies and groats he had managed to give me.

Someone, somewhere, found a paltry dole for the men. I do not know whether Drake had loosened his grip on the gold, which he proposed to share with the Queen. Perhaps it was the City investors, who had hastened to Plymouth when they learned of Drake's arrival, and who met us with grim faces and their account books under their arms. They would have been unwilling to part with yet more money, but if the troops were not dispersed quickly, there would be trouble.

There was a small amount of booty aboard the ships, the booty taken at Coruña, which was to be auctioned off and used to repay some of the creditors. In the event, the aftermath of the expedition proved to be months of legal wrangling between the investors, the leaders of the expedition, the ships' captains, and the Mayor of Plymouth. Bitter accusations flew between them, but it was nothing to me. I knew my father's thousand pounds would never be repaid.

Nevertheless, someone, somehow, did find that dole for the men. They were given one meal when they stepped ashore at Plymouth, handed five shillings each, and told to disperse to their homes, those who were fit enough to walk. This was their reward at the end of the glorious expedition which they had been promised. Norreys spent an evening writing licences for them to beg their way home. It did not take him long, there were so few men left.

'Five shillings!' I cried to Dr Nuñez, when I heard of it. 'Five shillings for so many months of suffering! How can they be so unjust?'

He shrugged. His eyes were dull and the skin on his face sagged like soft old linen, washed till it has barely any substance.

'It is more than you will have, young Kit.'

'Oh, I have my memories,' I said bitterly. 'That is payment for this venture, and more than enough.'

My work with the expedition was not quite finished. The men who were too sick to be moved were quartered in one of the warehouses which had held the provisions for the fleet before our departure. One of those very warehouses, indeed, which had been broken open and looted by the raw recruits, some of whom now lay here in such a pitiful state. There were plentiful medical supplies to be had in Plymouth, so that Dr Nuñez and I were able to make our patients more comfortable. With careful feeding and further nursing, those who had survived the horrors of the death march and the voyage home would probably recover. Dr Nuñez managed to arrange for two local physicians to take over the work from us, for it was clear from our own physical state that we could not continue much longer.

He chose to remain for a time in Plymouth. As one of the major investors in the expedition, he would have meetings to attend. Certainly, there would be acrimonious discussions about how matters were to be resolved. Already we had heard muttered rumours about seizing certain of the largest ships in lieu of payment of debts. Dr Nuñez would try to see fair play, though I knew he would have preferred to return home to London with me.

'Nay, I shall stay a little longer, Kit,' he told me wearily. 'I have written letters to Beatriz and to the manager of my spice business in London, if you will be kind enough to carry them for me.'

'Of course,' I said. 'Though I still wish I could prevail on you to come with me. I fear you will be able to do little here.'

He shook his head, and would not be persuaded. I do not think he believed he could do much good, but felt it his duty to try his utmost. For myself, I could not cast the dirt of Plymouth from my heels fast enough. Three days after we had landed, I set out to ride back to London. I might, indeed, have travelled in more comfort by ship, for some of the smaller ships were sailing to Chatham for repairs, but I could not stomach a single day more at sea.

The green and lush countryside of southern England looked inexpressibly beautiful after the wasteland of our overland march and the grey wilderness of the Atlantic. The full heat of an English summer seemed no more than balmy to my skin, parched and peeling as it was from the Iberian sun, and even that mild warmth was tempered by soft breezes that lifted my unkempt hair and rippled through my horse's mane. All around me as I rode eastwards the land looked rich and bountiful. The air was filled with birdsong and the sweet scent of new mown hay. The fields of wheat and barley and oats were well grown and the crops plump and healthy. In the meadows half-grown lambs followed their freshly sheared dams. As I rode along lanes and high roads through Devon and Dorset and Hampshire, before heading north, cows gazed at me over hedgerows, placidly chewing the cud. In the villages, women nodded their greetings while small children hid behind their skirts and the bolder lads followed me, firing questions, guessing perhaps from my appearance that I came from the expedition. It seemed that word of our return had travelled ahead of me, reaching even the smallest villages.

Had I hurried, I could probably have covered the distance in three or four days, but in my weakened state I could not ride for long hours, as I had done in the past when on a mission for Sir Francis. He would have to wait for my report. News had already gone ahead of me by fast messenger from Plymouth to London, sent by the leaders of the expedition. How truthful it was, I could not say. And of course Essex's ship *Swiftsure* would have reached London some days ago. There was no need for me to hurry. Each day I stopped before I was too exhausted and spent the night in some modest village inn. I owed my post horses, like my lodging in Plymouth, to Dr Nuñez, but the small purse of coin I carried would not lodge me at any great expense, and I feared it would barely last me all the way to London.

As I neared the end of my journey, I began to hear gossip in the inn parlours about the heroic deeds achieved by the Earl of Essex in Portugal. It seemed that, single-handed, he had captured the city of Peniche and driven out the Spanish garrison there, before personally crowning King Antonio. He had then led a victorious march south to Lisbon, where he had instituted a siege. The Spanish garrison quartered there had been too cowardly to meet him in single combat for the Queen's honour, nor would they emerge from the city to settle the affair in pitched battle, like honest men. Nay, they had cowered behind their defences like silly girls and Essex had only been persuaded to abandon the siege because of the English army's lack of supplies and the failure of the Dom's Portuguese supporters to appear. Reluctantly he had returned to England, but he was ready, at a day's notice, to set out once more and fight the Spanish hand-to-hand.

Had these stories not concealed the tragic truth of the Portuguese affair, I would have laughed. As it was, I came near to weeping.

Soon it began to be whispered that Drake had returned from Portugal with fifteen Spanish galleons, each and all loaded from bilge to deck with gold, silver and precious gems. Even the ballast had been replaced with weighty treasure. Men's eyes gleamed.

It was more than a week after leaving Plymouth that I found the roads more crowded, busy with those on foot or on horseback, carts of produce heading north, empty carts returning, packmen with their laden ponies, and from time to time a gentleman's cavalcade, before which all men must give way.

It was beginning to grow dusk as the crowds on the road drew together and slowed, forced together like a flock of sheep through a gate. A slow, gentle English summer dusk. There ahead of me was the Bridge. The gold of the setting sun flashed off the

Thames, turning it to molten metal. The first lights winked out in houses and taverns, both in Southwark on this side of the river, and in the city itself on the far side. St Paul's tower, which had once been topped by a spire, stood on the rising ground almost opposite me.

London. Home. The Portuguese affair was over.

When I had crossed the Bridge and reached the city, I left my post horse at an inn in Gracechurch Street and walked the rest of the way to Smithfield. London seemed curiously unchanged, as though it had been asleep during the long weeks of our travails, but the cobbles under the worn-out soles of my boots were real and painful enough, and I found myself limping before I reached Duck Lane. I was ravenous with hunger and hoped Joan would have a meal on the fire, for I had eaten little on my way from Plymouth, guarding the handful of silver Dr Nuñez had given me. My father and I would need to live even more frugally in the future, now that all our savings were lost.

As I rounded the corner into the lane, something hurled itself at me, a dark shape exploding from a dark corner so that instinctively I threw up my arms to protect myself. The next minute I was flat on my back in the dirt and a shaggy, smelly creature was half on top of me, alternately whining and licking me.

'Rikki!' I said, trying to sit up. I put my arms around his warm familiar shape. Unaccountably I found myself crying into his shoulder. His rough tongue set to work again.

'Good lad,' I said, managing at last to lift myself part way off the ground.

I ran my hands over his sides and back. His fur was matted and beneath it he was thinner than I remembered. I could feel the knobs of his backbone.

'Rikki! Why are you so thin?'

His only response was to sit on my feet and pant lovingly into my face. He was still wearing his collar, but otherwise, as far as I could judge in the growing dusk, he was in poor shape.

'Has Joan been ill-treating you?' I frowned. Joan had been annoyed when I had brought the dog back from the Low Countries and tried to throw him out into the street, but my father and I had always insisted that she must treat him with kindness.

'Come on, lad.' I managed to heave him off my feet and scramble up. 'We both need a good meal and a wash. And I can see that I'll have to spend hours combing the tangles from your fur.'

He leaned against my leg and pressed a wet nose into my palm. I rubbed my damp face with my ragged sleeve. My heart ached with the joy of seeing him again, the dog who had followed me halfway across the Low Countries from love and loyalty, at a time when I had barely known him. I owed my life to him.

We started up the lane together. Outside our house, a woman I had never seen before was sweeping the front step and scolding a boy of five or six back indoors. She was lit from behind by the light from the doorway, and I could see clearly that it was not Joan. Had my father taken on a new servant? But the woman looked too well dressed to be a servant. I approached her cautiously, for the past months had taught me to be even more distrustful of strangers than I had been before.

'Is Dr Alvarez at home?' I asked her.

The woman stopped her sweeping and stared at me. Then she leaned on her broom and frowned. 'Are you his son? We were told his son had sailed on the Portugal venture.'

'Aye,' I said cautiously. Something was wrong.

'I am his son, Christoval Alvarez.' I frowned at her, suddenly full of mistrust. There was no Inquisition here. Surely my father was safe in London. Why was he not coming out to greet me?

'Where is he?' I demanded harshly. 'Where is Dr Alvarez?'

'You had better come inside,' she said.

.

The Author

Ann Swinfen spent her childhood partly in England and partly on the east coast of America. She was educated at Somerville College, Oxford, where she read Classics and Mathematics and married a fellow undergraduate, the historian David Swinfen. While bringing up their five children and studying for a postgraduate MSc in Mathematics and a BA and PhD in English Literature, she had a variety of jobs, including university lecturer, translator, freelance journalist and software designer. She served for nine years on the governing council of the Open University and for five years worked as a manager and editor in the technical author division of an international computer company, but gave up her full-time job to concentrate on her writing, while continuing part-time university teaching. In 1995 she founded Dundee Book Events, a voluntary organisation promoting books and authors to the general public.

Her first three novels, *The Anniversary*, *The Travellers*, and *A Running Tide*, all with a contemporary setting but also an historical resonance, were published by Random House, with translations into Dutch and German. *The Testament of Mariam* marks something of a departure. Set in the first century, it recounts, from an unusual perspective, one of the most famous and yet ambiguous stories in human history. At the same time it explores life under a foreign occupying force, in lands still torn by conflict to this day. Her second historical novel, *Flood*, is set in the fenlands of East Anglia during the seventeenth century, where the local people fought desperately to save their land from greedy and unscrupulous speculators.

Currently she is working on a late sixteenth century series, featuring a young Marrano physician who is recruited as a code-breaker and spy in Walsingham's secret service. The first book in the series is *The Secret World of Christoval Alvarez*, the second is *The Enterprise of England* and the third is *The Portuguese Affair.*

She now lives in Broughty Ferry, on the northeast coast of Scotland, with her husband, formerly vice-principal of the University of Dundee, a cocker spaniel, and two Maine coon cats.

http://www.annswinfen.com